Mercy

MERCY

Susan Sims Moody

To Polly
God bless,
Susan Sims Moody

iUniverse, Inc.
New York Lincoln Shanghai

Mercy

iUniverse books may be ordered through booksellers or by contacting:

iUniverse
2021 Pine Lake Road, Suite 100
Lincoln, NE 68512
www.iuniverse.com
1-800-Authors (1-800-288-4677)

ISBN-13: 978-0-595-38364-1 (pbk)
ISBN-13: 978-0-595-67615-6 (cloth)
ISBN-13: 978-0-595-82737-4 (ebk)
ISBN-10: 0-595-38364-5 (pbk)
ISBN-10: 0-595-67615-4 (cloth)
ISBN-10: 0-595-82737-3 (ebk)

Printed in the United States of America

For Sarah Evelyn Golden Sims: my mother, my teacher, and my friend.

ACKNOWLEDGEMENTS

Although this is a work of fiction, much of the plot revolves around economic history and scientific fact. I spent a good deal of time researching these aspects of the story. I would like to especially thank Steve Walls, my high school physics teacher and dear friend, for his invaluable help with the periodic table of elements.

Credit goes to Andrea at the Noxubee National Wildlife Refuge and to Terry Schiefer, Curator of the Mississippi Entomological Museum for their help in researching the local wildlife. To Betsy Milward Smith, thank you for watching the kids while I took pictures of your pinecones. Thank you also to Earlene Broussard Echeverria with LSU's Department of French Studies for help with my Cajun. Gratitude goes to the boys of TiderInsider for giving me Bobby Jack's name.

To my cousin, Kenneth Gordon, and to my sister-in-law, Anne Johnson, I offer appreciation for their assistance with the legal aspects of the plot. To Tracey Sims Malone, my sister and personal stylist, thank you for helping me put my best foot forward. To my second, third, and fourth sets of eyes, Daddy, Mama, and Frances McGuffey, bless you, and I love you all. To Michael Wells Glueck, my editor, thanks for the trans-Atlantic communication during the project. I finally got it done.

Special thanks to Jim Fraiser, Lucas Boyd, Warren St. John, and Carolyn Haines for their candid, refreshing, and professional demeanors while taking precious time from their own pursuits to consult with a fledgling in their field.

And most importantly, to my husband, Tom, I express heartfelt gratitude for loving and encouraging me, and for feigning lucidity during the countless times I bounced ideas off him in the wee hours of the night. All of these people were instrumental in the construction of Mercy. If the facts are wrong, it's only because I blew it.

May God bless you abundantly,
Susan

ONE

Although the backbone of winter was decidedly broken, the Ides of March in Bedford, Mississippi, still meant a black sky when Davis Sanford began the day. Coupled with the monsoons that had plagued the area for more than a week, the sky was even darker than usual.

When his alarm clock had sounded at a quarter past five, Davis had begrudgingly dragged himself from the flannel sheets between his down comforter and feather bed and made his way to the shower for an extra-long eye-opener.

He had spent the day before pulling wires for a security system in an eight thousand square-foot home under construction in Clarksdale. The drive there and back had added insult to injury. Hot water pounded his shoulders, turning his skin pink. The bathroom was dark—he had not bothered to turn on a light. And his itinerary today was more of the same: finishing the work that he had started. He would have a welcome sense of satisfaction when the job was done. This was his first *real* customer—one who actually owned enough belongings to warrant a security system. It would mean a good reference, finally.

He fumbled for soap, razor, and shampoo mentally rehearsing what he had to accomplish that day. As he rinsed the final suds from his thinning hair, the ringing phone in the next room surprised him. *Somebody's dead,* he thought, as he snapped the towel down from the shower curtain rod and quickly wrapped it around his waist.

A white glow illuminated the eastern window, but the sun was still far from peeking over the horizon. He tripped over the blue jeans that lay where they had fallen the night before and stumbled to the bedside table, grabbing the phone.

"Hello?" he said, as he plopped down on the edge of the bed.

"Davis?"

"Jennifer?" he asked, concerned.

"Annie," the reply came.

"*Annie*," he said, trying to place the name. The fog lifted. "*Annie*. Who's dead, Annie?"

"Nobody. At least not yet, but it won't be long. It's Pawpaw."

"Where is he?" Davis asked, drying his ears on the corner of the sheet.

"Lanier General. I'm watching him on my shift, but there's not much left to do. They're talking hospice. Maybe today, maybe tomorrow, before they let him go home."

"Okay," Davis said. He began re-arranging the next few days in his mind. There was silence between them.

Annie broke it. "Davis?"

"Yeah?"

"You coming?"

"I'll be there. How's my father taking it?"

"Fine, I guess. He's been lurking at the house a lot. Taking inventory I suppose."

"Well, Mom ain't dead."

"No, but might as well be once Pawpaw's gone."

"Yeah."

Silence.

"You figure he was gonna call me?" Davis asked.

"Nah. But *I* did."

Silence.

"Well," Annie said. "I have to go. I'm pulling into the parking lot now."

"Okay."

"Call me on this number when you get on the road."

"Okay. Is it all right if I stay with you and Marcus?"

"Well, you can stay with me. Don't think Marcus'll be here. Been gone three days. Don't think he's coming back this time. I filed papers yesterday."

Davis paused and then said, "You okay with that?"

"Can't help but be okay with it. I'll be fine."

"All right. Well, I figure I can get out of here by four. I'd come sooner, but…"

"I'll keep him alive till you get here. Just come as soon as you can."

"Okay. I'll be there by six-thirty, seven at the latest."

"I'll see you," Annie said. "Love you."

"You, too," he said and hung up.

Davis sat there for a moment, staring at the phone on its cradle, and subconsciously noted the ever-increasing daylight. He twisted his pinky in his ear, trying to get the last of the water out. The alarm clock beamed a red 5:45.

Annie would be clocking in at the hospital within the next fifteen minutes to begin a twelve-hour nursing shift in the cardiac intensive care unit at Lanier General. Davis had six hours of work to do and three hours of driving time to the job site and back before he could leave on the almost three-hour drive to Mercy, Mississippi, his hometown.

He removed the loops of sterling silver from his ears and placed them carefully in a pile on his nightstand. He did the same with the brow ring that he'd been wearing steadily for more than a year. He heaved himself up from the bed to dress and get moving. He would call Jennifer on the way to Clarksdale.

TWO

Francis Carrothers Sanford—Frank to the citizens of Mercy, and Pawpaw to Annie and Davis, would be only sixty-five years old on the first day of April, too young for a dying man. He'd begun his professional career at the age of twenty-one, when he first hung a shingle on the diminutive Main Street of Mercy, as a Certified Public Accountant. When he'd graduated from the University of Alabama, the only things he could call his own were his wife of two years, his one-year old son, another baby on the way, and a large student loan.

Before long, he had completed the taxes of a sufficient number of his neighbors to learn that the real rate of return on Loblolly pine trees ranged from ten to twelve percent. Short of southern pine beetles or root rot, those returns simply overwhelmed any thoughts of bonds or T-bills as investment vehicles.

Trees were big business in Lanier County. Weyerhaeuser owned forty percent of the real estate there, and since the Fifties, the giant wood products and paper company had methodically decimated the hardwood forest and regenerated the land with Loblolly seedlings planted in neat rows not less than eight feet apart. Pine products—pulpwood, chip-n-saw, and sawlogs—were the second-leading, legal agricultural crop in Davis's old stomping ground, falling just behind the poultry industry.

With a little over half of the county in timber, private, non-industrial foresters, the likes of Davis's grandparents, owned the rest of the woodlands. The remaining forty thousand acres of trees were divided among one hundred fifty landholders, most in twenty- or thirty-acre tracts. Frank Sanford's share of the woods was mammoth in comparison. He and Cora had put every dime they'd earned into property ranging from fifty to three hundred dollars an acre, thereby amassing a pine and oak plantation of five thousand acres—nearly eight square miles. Income from any federal conservation reserve plans or hunting leases notwithstanding, the gross annual return per acre from Mississippi pines was roughly one hundred thirty dollars before expenses, forty-five dollars after. The big payout came only once every thirty-five years, when they harvested the sawlogs.

Frank and Cora had made out like bandits in 1979 when the price per thousand board feet of saw timber skyrocketed to one hundred seventy dollars. They had clear cut the pines, leaving forty acres of virgin oak forest as their homestead, erecting in its center a six-thousand square foot log cabin in homage to the trees. After seventeen years of public service, Frank summarily retired the accountancy shingle.

A federal assistance program had helped with reforesting the land. Then, in 1995 they hired a certified wildlife manager, high-fenced a thousand acres, and brought in whitetail genetics from Minnesota. Day hunters paid them anywhere from three thousand to twelve thousand dollars apiece to harvest deer of freakish proportions for the area. Each of eighty other leaseholders paid seven hundred fifty dollars *per annum* for deer and turkey hunting rights on the other four thousand acres. And, after twenty-five years of forest stewardship, the Sanfords were just a decade shy of cashing in once more on a rising lumber market, in which the current price of sawlogs was approaching four hundred twenty dollars per thousand board feet. For Mercy, Mississippi, they were rich, to the filthiest degree.

Cora ignored the carnal pursuits of the men in her life by spending her autumn days out-of-doors, wearing a wide-brimmed straw hat and wielding a hand spade. The knees of her pedal pushers stayed a murky, charcoal gray, and the toes of her lightweight canvas sneakers bore the same stains.

In the early years of their retirement, Frank left her alone with her cultivation, opting instead for the deer stand in section eighteen. When the walls of their home grew crowded with the taxidermied trophies of his victories, he moved to an old cabin in section twenty-six where he could sit on the porch and reflect. This was an especially good spot for the man whose health continued to deteriorate. There was no doubt as to where Frank would post himself, twice per season, on those raucous days when Marcus Broussard, the young man hired to oversee the hunting club, ran the dogs.

Both Annie and Davis had spent time on that front porch with Pawpaw, learning how to sit still and say nothing. Buck fever never really afflicted Davis, but Annie contracted a full-blown case of it, and when Pawpaw was not propped on the porch with his Carolina Precision custom rifle, Annie was there, face paint artistically applied, lying in wait for her Boone and Crockett specimen. That's why her pairing with Marcus had seemed so natural.

Ten years her senior, Marcus was a graduate of Louisiana State University's School of Renewable Natural Resources. He held a Bachelor of Science degree in Fisheries and Wildlife Management, with a minor in forestry. He was accurate to four hundred yards with just about any rifle, and he was equally proficient with a single-cam bow.

He'd watched Annie grow from a thirteen-year-old girl into a nineteen-year-old, raven-haired beauty. Two weeks before her twentieth birthday, he stole her from her father and grandfather, marrying her in the living room of his employer. Four years and several separations later, Marcus had finally pushed Annie to her limit, or so it seemed.

Davis was glad to hear that she had finally decided to divorce Marcus. Between hunting seasons, Marcus had been spending most of his time at the County Line Club, drinking draft beer and picking up women. Sometimes he would disappear for a week or more, hanging out with hunting buddies in town. He was quick to anger, especially when drunk. Annie had called Davis more than once when she had suffered broken bones at the hand of her husband. On many occasions, she had threatened to leave him. Davis hoped that she really meant it this time.

After dressing, he activated the security alarm on the house that doubled as his office, closed and dead-bolted the front door, and headed for the little, baby blue Nissan pick-up truck that housed all of his portable equipment. He would finish the house in Clarksdale by two-thirty if he worked through lunch. He hoped to find Jennifer before then and coax her into making a three-day trip with him. He knew that the newspaper had just come out, and that on Fridays the activity in the pressroom slowed. Hopefully, Charlotte and Devon would let her off for the weekend.

From his cell phone he dialed the offices of *The Bedford Sentinel.* Charlotte would be in. He didn't know if Jennifer would.

"*Sentinel,*" Charlotte said, short and crisp.

"Charlotte. It's Davis."

"Yep. Whaddya need?"

"Is Jennifer in?"

"Not yet. Probably won't be 'til eight, though she's *supposed* to be here at 7:30."

"Y'all still got people standing in line at the front door waiting for you when you get there?" Davis smirked.

"Shut your smart mouth," Charlotte said. Davis could hear her slurping coffee. Without being there, he knew that she was drinking from the ivory mug with indelible coffee stains, the mug that read, "Be still and know that I am God."

"Can you tell her I called?"

"Can you call her at the apartment?"

Davis said in a deadpan monotone, "Sure, Charlotte. Thanks for your help. Have a great day." He pressed "end" before she could respond.

Davis hated to call Jennifer at her apartment. He surmised from the early hour that she would be generally unsociable or that she might not answer the phone at all. The other possibility was that, as she had done on more than one occasion, she might answer it, conduct a totally lucid conversation, hang up, and remember none of it afterward. It was ill-advised to interrupt Ms. Martin's sleep patterns. But, he did so anyway. The clock on the dashboard of his pickup said 6:30.

Three rings, and "Hello?" His girlfriend of seven months answered.

"Hey," Davis said. "You up?"

"Yeah, I was fixin' to get in the shower. Who's dead?"

THREE

With Charlotte and Devon apprised of Davis's familial situation, they granted Jennifer leave through Monday, with an option to call in "bereaved" on Tuesday, if necessary. She took a company laptop with her to work on ad design and page layout, leaving her employers to cover her beat while she was away.

The single greatest accomplishment Jennifer had achieved during her short time at the *Sentinel* was putting some modern technology to use. She had converted the mom-and-pop operation to desktop publishing and digital photography, saving herself hours of time in the pressroom and darkroom. She could essentially put the paper to bed while sitting in her own.

Jennifer liked it that way. Especially after she had spent twelve weeks on crutches from a gunshot wound suffered the previous summer, telecommuting was about the only commuting that she had done for a while. Even after eight months, with a surgically implanted steel rod supporting her femur, she still walked with a cane, and the doctors advised that she would do so for the next six months at minimum.

Davis arrived at the pressroom at two minutes of four o'clock. It was starting to drizzle again as he hurried from the truck to the building. Anticipating a possible funeral, Jennifer had already packed for the weekend, and she was awaiting the ringing of the cow bell that would announce Davis's presence.

"You ready?" he called out from the lobby.

"I'm coming. Be a gentleman and get my luggage, would you?" she responded, shouldering her purse and PC bag onto her petite frame.

"Whaddya, handicapped?" he asked, as he loped into the pressroom.

"Yep, and you'd better watch it, or I'll beat you with my cane," was her reply. She looked up and saw him for the first time that day, sans the usual jewelry that she'd learned to overlook. She raised an eyebrow but said nothing.

Charlotte watched their shenanigans through the plate glass window of her office. Jennifer yelled a goodbye and gave a wave. Davis chose not to acknowledge his girlfriend's boss, gathering Jennifer's duffel bag, cosmetics case, and a shoebox from her now unused paste-up table and headed for the parking lot.

They would leave his truck there and take Jennifer's vehicle instead. It would be a much more pleasant ride because of it. The summer prior, she'd gotten a steal of a deal at a police auction on a slightly-used, black Mercedes S430V. The first bid on the car, which had been seized in the Marascalco drug bust, was her offer of two hundred fifty dollars. Much to the dismay of several used-car dealers in Bedford, the auctioneer was partial to that bid, and quickly closed the auction without acknowledging other contenders. Jennifer had written the check, praying that it wouldn't bounce, and she had taken ownership of the car on the spot.

Davis loaded her bags into the massive trunk space and then transferred his own bag and Sunday shoes from the truck. She assumed the position of pilot, and he took the role of navigator.

"All right. Highway 82 to Starkville. Hang a right just past the vet med school. Wake me when we hit gravel," Davis said.

"Wrong again," Jennifer said. "You have to keep me awake. I didn't get much sleep last night. Rain equals pain," she said, rubbing her palm on her thigh.

"Oh, I'm only kidding. Stop at the Velvet Cream. I got to eat before we blow town." He reached into his back pocket and pulled out his wallet.

Jennifer pointed the nose of the luxury sedan out of the *Sentinel* parking lot, goosed the gas, and leapt across the highway to the hamburger and ice cream stand that she and Davis frequented. She put the car in park, and Davis bolted through the rain to the walk-up window to place their orders. She tuned the radio while she waited to dine on a burger, all the way, fries, and a shake.

Minutes passed, with Davis huddled under the red awning that offered little shelter. Finally, the order was up, he paid, and returned to the car. Jennifer threw the engine in reverse, backing directly onto the highway. Once around the old town square and they were pointed east, toward Mercy.

Davis doctored her hamburger by carefully unwrapping and then re-wrapping the wax paper around it to keep the proliferation of condiments contained. He passed it over to her as she drove.

She took the burger, thanked him, and said, "So, tell me about where we're going. I don't know much at all about this side of your family." She maintained silence about his earrings.

"What's to tell? They're all crazy. Been living in the woods too long, huffin' pine rosin or something."

Jennifer nodded. She didn't think it was unusual to have to admit to crazy relatives. "Okay. So who am I gonna meet tonight?"

"Depends on who's still livin'," he said through a mouthful of fries. "Mom, that's my grandmother, and Pawpaw, my grandfather," he continued. "They own the place.

"Annie and Marcus—my cousin and her shiftless husband who I'd like to beat to death, except he's half a foot taller'n me. He's a worthless piece of human flesh." He talked and chewed at the same time.

"And then Uncle Danny Robert and my father." His tone dismissed the last two as though they were afterthoughts.

Jennifer drove with her left hand, holding her burger with her right. She motioned at Davis with it. "So, what are they like?"

"Oh, hell, I don't know. Haven't been there in years. My father hasn't talked to me since I got out of rehab the second time. I'm sure they're both still the same. Danny Robert'll be making waffles when we get there, to give to his pack of dogs. Come hell or high water, the dogs get waffles. Who knows? If the weather keeps up, we may get both of 'em tonight.

"And my father'll be into his third drink, unless he started early."

"So they all live together?" she quizzed.

"Might as well. Mom and Pawpaw have a place, and Danny Robert lives with them. My father has a house, but not that far off. And Annie, too. They all live within a par five of each other, on family property. They all eat dinner together, three, four nights a week."

"Stifling. How'd you escape?" she asked, only half joking.

"My mom. She left my father when I was in the third grade and brought me and Daniel to Bedford. This is *her* hometown. Then she met James, got married, got a real life, and fourteen, fifteen years later, here we are." He wadded up the wrapper from his first burger and tossed it in the bag. He dug for another.

"Oh, I'm supposed to call Annie," Davis remembered. He pulled his cell phone from his waistband and dialed her number.

"Hey, it's me," Davis said into the flip phone.

Jennifer listened to the one-sided conversation.

"Just now leavin'. We'll be there 'bout 6:45."

He paused as she spoke.

"Me and Jennifer. Yeah, y'all can meet when we get there."

Jennifer strained to hear what was being said on the other end, but had no luck over the ever-increasing rain and road noise.

"Okay, so we'll go straight to the house, then. Bridge ain't out, is it?" He paused again for her reply. "Okay, then. See you as soon as we can get there. Might be comin' on the ark, but we'll be there." He closed the phone and sighed.

"What?" Jennifer asked, handing her neatly-folded hamburger wrapper to him.

He stuffed it into the white paper sack. "They took him to the house at three. Some home-health people are there now to set up the bed and oxygen and stuff and get the DNR orders signed."

"DNR?" Jennifer asked.

"Do not resuscitate."

FOUR

Blackjack Road became Oktoc Road, and Oktoc Road ran south, curving this way and that, until it became Bluff Lake Road, in the heart of the Noxubee National Wildlife Refuge. Bluff Lake Road ran past its namesake as well as Loakfoma Lake, and finally wound into Lanier County. By this point in the journey, Jennifer was bleary-eyed from the darkening sky, pouring rain, and narrowing thoroughfares.

"Okay!" she exclaimed to Davis when the chip-tar pavement gave way to a rub-board gravel road. "I don't care how much farther it is. You have to drive!"

"All right, city girl," Davis said. "It's not but another eight or nine miles, but swap with me." He opened his door, jumped from the passenger's side, and dashed around the back of the car while Jennifer climbed from the driver's seat to the passenger's side without leaving the shelter of the car.

"Woo! That's some cold rain," Davis exclaimed, slicking his hair back with his hands and wiping the water onto Jennifer's cheek.

"Hey!" she protested dramatically, pushing him away. He flashed a toothy and perfect smile, put the car into drive, and slowly made his way toward home.

State Highway 490 ran north from Mashulaville and dead-ended into the Sanfords' place. That was the civilized path to Pawpaw's. However,

- 13 -

Mashulaville was well out of the way, taking 82 to 25 to Louisville, and then east across 14. But by going straight to Starkville and then south through the Refuge, Davis cut forty-five minutes off the trip, even if the roads were in some disrepair. It was the way he had always come, and he surmised the faster route to be the better one, in light of the situation.

Mercy proper was east of his grandparents', less than two miles through the timber, as the buzzard flies. It was twelve miles by county road. The hospital was there along with what was left of a town that had been never been much more than a train station thirty years back.

The old people still referred to it as Mercy's Station, although the town had officially shortened its name to Mercy in 1975. There was no station any longer—not even a relic for tourists to visit. And when the blue jeans manufacturer that had employed three hundred of the town's inhabitants had pulled out for Mexico, the citizens believed that not much else would be stopping by anyway.

The last five miles of the trip were almost unbearable, with the rain hammering down and wind gusts coming out of the southwest. Davis kept the car moving at twenty miles per hour, regardless of how little he could see, and Jennifer kept her eyes closed for those last fifteen minutes.

When they got to the firebreak that marked the beginning of Sanford property, Davis loosened his grip on the steering wheel, and his knuckles regained their normal color. "Piece of cake," he said to Jennifer. "You can relax now."

She opened her eyes and saw nothing but Loblollies on either side of the narrow strip of roadway. They continued driving through pines for more than a mile, the foliage partially buffering them from the wind and rain. The cover of trees broke, giving way to another firebreak ten yards deep, which was followed by another stand of timber, this time oaks, gated and fenced. Above the gate there hung a wooden sign that read "Sanford's Mossy Horn Sanctuary," and below that hung a massive European mount whitetail, eighteen non-typical points of glory. This was the gate to what Davis had known as a second home for most of his life. An electric fence skirted the perimeter.

"What's *Mossy Horn* mean?" Jennifer asked, her green eyes taking in the skull-and-antlers trophy.

"That's redneck for *big-ass deer*," Davis said, looking over at her and winking.

The gate was already open, and they eased through, taking it slowly along a winding drive. It was dark—ten minutes past seven o'clock, and all they could see in the beam of the headlights was rain. Then, in the distance, a porch light shimmered, and barking began. Within half a minute, baying dogs surrounded the car. Jennifer's head swiveled as she counted. Davis slowed the vehicle to a crawl as the dogs continued to circle.

When they got within shouting distance of the porch, Jennifer looked up to see a two-story log castle of a house looming in the dark. A figure stood on the veranda. Davis lowered the window enough to shout, "Call 'em off, Danny Robert!"

Danny Robert squinted at the car, took a drag from his cigarette, and then flicked it into the flowerbed. He gave one shrill, short whistle, and the dogs turned heel and rallied at the bottom of the front porch steps, none daring to ascend.

"Good grief, there's more than there used to be," Davis said, putting the car into park and slumping down with exhaustion. "We'll have to get the hose out before we'll be allowed in the house; we won't be able to keep 'em off us." The rain continued.

Ignoring the rain, Danny Robert descended the steps and approached. "Didn't recognize the car, Davis. Sorry 'bout that." His blue-plaid flannel shirt hung unbuttoned on his tall, lank frame, revealing a printed tee shirt and drooping, unbelted Levis that dragged on the wet St. Augustine grass beneath his bare feet.

"No problem," Davis said through the two-inch crack in the window.

"Pull around back. We got a carport back there now that you can park her under."

Davis smiled an affirmation, gladly doing as he was told, while Jennifer gathered food wrappers and drink cups into a bag. She could not believe that Davis had kept this place a secret for so long.

"What did his shirt say?" she asked as she flipped down the sun visor to look at herself in the mirror. She inspected her teeth for food particles and then tucked her straight, brown hair behind her ears, all the while attempting to appear nonchalant.

"Didn't see it," Davis replied. "I was too busy playing dodge-dog. But knowing Danny Robert, I'm sure that it was something offensive."

As he eased into the carport, Jennifer noted Davis's uncle, kenneling the dogs in a low building that she estimated twenty feet square, fashioned of board and baton cypress, covered by a green metal roof. She could see several cyclone-fenced runs projecting from the rear of the structure. The "Dog Pound," as it was aptly dubbed, formed an L shape with the main house, a covered walk joining the two. The canines continued to file into their house, and as soon as Danny Robert gave the "all-clear," the pair exited the car to greet him properly.

Their host wiped his hand on the back of his pants and extended it to Davis. "Long time, no see, fella. How you been?" Danny Robert pulled Davis toward himself and patted him on the back. His long, unkempt black hair was wet from the rain and he self-consciously slicked it back with his hand. He looked exceptionally unwashed.

"Good, Uncle Danny Robert. Hate to come back the way things are, but it's good to be back."

"Where'd you get the ride?" he asked, motioning to Jennifer's car. "Quit usin' and start dealin'?"

Davis refused to let the insult bother him. "It's hers," he said, motioning to Jennifer, as she came around the end of the vehicle. The license plate read *Jenn G.*

"Jennifer Martin, I'd like to introduce you to my uncle, Danny Robert Sanford."

"Howdy," Danny Robert said, leaning forward and extending his hand. Jennifer could see the family resemblance.

She reciprocated, still trying to read the wording on the front of his shirt. "Nice to meet you," she said. She might have thrown in an "I've heard a lot about you," but she hadn't; so, she stayed mum.

"Pleasure's mine, young lady. What's the *G* for?" he asked, pointing to the back of the car.

"Gimpy," she replied and raised her cane.

Danny Robert shrugged sheepishly, and then motioned to a screened door off the back porch. "Come on inside. When it rains, the skeeters like it under here 'bout as much as the dogs do." He turned and led the way up two steps and onto a screened deck off the back of the house.

"Nice place," Jennifer said over her shoulder to Davis as they went inside. She added, *sotto voce,* "I see why he never moved out."

"You haven't seen the half of it," Davis said.

Coming in the back way, the homestead's grandeur took longer to sink in. Davis and Jennifer wiped their feet on a sisal welcome mat in a small kitchen. Off to the right stood a heavy Italianate table with a marble slab for a top, complemented by four unmatched chairs, each heavy and masculine. The floor appeared to be natural stone tile, and the walls in this portion of the house were sheetrock, painted a dark bark brown. Jennifer observed a paper plate atop the kitchen counter, stacked high with waffles, just as Davis had predicted. The room smelled of sausage grease and fried bread.

"Come on through," Danny Robert urged. They continued down a hallway lit by wall sconces made of marbled glass adorned with oil-rubbed bronze pinecones. A bedroom flanked either side of the passageway before it opened into a two-and-a-half-story trophy room built of hand-hewn pine logs. The vaulted ceiling was braced three times along its forty-foot span with trusses that fanned out like spokes on a wheel. The only denizens of the room were the trophies: from Africa, South America, and Canada, from Alaska, New Mexico, Colorado, and central Mississippi, taxidermy covered the walls from the tongue-and-groove, heart-of-pine floor to the highest point of the bead board ceiling. Jennifer was spellbound.

"There's a few new ones," Davis remarked.

"Yeah, Dad and Bobby Jack went to Alaska a couple years back. That's where the Kodiak come from," and he motioned to the far-left corner where a nine-foot brown bear mount stood on hind legs.

"Dang," Davis exclaimed. "Wouldn't want to forget that's there on a midnight kitchen run."

"Yep," Danny Robert replied. "And, the zebra and warthog are still over at Larry's. Been waitin' on them almost a year. That was from the Namibia trip."

"Zebra?" Jennifer asked.

"Yeah. Dad's havin' it made into a rug. 'Cept, I don't reckon it'll ever see the floor. Mom'll hang it on the wall to keep if from gettin' stepped on."

Jennifer continued to gaze at the stuffed menagerie. "It's like," she paused a moment, "like a treasure room of animals," she said to Davis.

"Or something like that," Davis mumbled.

"A museum," she offered, in awe. She finally took a moment to look at the remainder of the room—not just its trophies—and was soothed by the doubly-worn leather sofa and chairs and distressed cherry-wood tables.

Davis rubbed his chin and held his jaw in his hand for a moment, looking about at the silence. "Where's everybody?" he queried.

"Mom and Dad are in their room. Honestly, we weren't expecting you until about half an hour ago, when Annie told us you was coming."

"And where's my father?" Davis asked, looking up, for no reason in particular, at the antler chandelier.

"Oh, he left about fifteen minutes ago. Had midterms to grade, he said." Danny Robert knew Davis felt awkward. "Annie's at her house. Said she'd be over. Should be here any minute. And Mom'll be out in a few. Just got finished signing some papers, and she's pretty shook up."

Davis sat down on the edge of the sofa and patted the space next to him as a cue to Jennifer, who quietly obliged. He sighed, and she reached for his hand to give it a reassuring squeeze.

"Well, Miss Jennifer Gee. I thought you could take Annie's old room, across from mine." He motioned toward the direction from which they had just come. "And, Davis, you can take the couch in the loft—"

"I was planning on staying with Annie," he said. "But Jennifer should stay here, if that's okay." She looked at him quizzically, as though it were not.

"Got to keep up appearances, I suppose," Danny Robert joked. "That's no problem. She'll just have to make friends with Lovey before you go," he said.

"Who's Lovey?" Jennifer asked, hesitantly.

"She's my *inside* dog," Danny Robert said.

"Oh, really?" she said.

"Yeah, a little Schipperke. She's old and set in her ways. Just like me. I bought her for Annie's fourteenth birthday. She stayed with me, though, 'cause her husband don't believe in dogs as pets. Anyway, she thinks Annie's room is hers now."

"Oh, I love dogs," Jennifer said.

As if on cue, the three of them heard the *tick-tick-tick* of toenails on tile, and a small, square, squat of a black dog waddled into the room. She had obviously just awakened, since she stopped to stretch and gap, and then trotted up to Danny Robert and reared up onto his knee for a scratch between the ears.

Her owner took her small, fox-like face in both of his hands and gently tussled her back and forth. Her coarse, black fur formed a sort of mane about her gray countenance. She growled playfully, and wagged the quarter-inch nub of a tail that is characteristic of the breed.

"It's a walking ottoman," Jennifer said, smiling.

"Never heard her described that way before," Danny Robert said, "but I'll give you that. She *is* a might square. The vet keeps insisting that she's a little short for her weight, but Lovey disagrees."

Danny Robert paused for a moment and then said, "Well, I'm gonna get out of these wet clothes. If Mom ain't out by the time I'm back, I'll run get her." He stood and shed his flannel shirt to reveal the words that Jennifer had been trying to decipher:

NO MA'AM
National
Organization of
Men
Against
~~All~~
Most Women*
See back for exceptions

Jennifer half-stood so that she could read the back of the shirt as he retreated to his room. And it said

EXCEPTIONS
Bimbos
Sluts
Women Who Obey
And
Our Mamas

She sat back down and looked at Davis. "That's a joke, isn't it?" Lovey had moved from her perch beside Danny Robert's chair over to Davis's seat.

He looked up, dazed.

"Tell me that's a joke," Jennifer said.

"What?"

"That shirt."

Davis turned to catch a glimpse of Danny Robert's back, just as he turned into his room. He knew it by heart as soon as he saw it. "The 'No Ma'am' shirt?" He reached down to scratch the dog's head.

"Yeah."

"Yeah. It's a joke. Sort of."

FIVE

Danny Robert Sanford was Annie's father and Frank and Cora's first-born. He'd attended Mississippi State University on a Future Farmers of America scholarship, majoring in animal husbandry. He had only finished his freshman year when he'd become smitten with a young girl named Dee, a Zeta Tau Alpha there. One too many drunken miscalculations and he'd gotten her pregnant. They had wed at the justice of the peace in downtown Starkville.

No one from either family had even known about it until the baby was born, her mother left town, and Danny Robert came back to Mercy to live and raise their daughter. He had christened her *Annie*, as *Danny*, take away *Dee*, equaled her name. Several years later, he received a certified letter containing divorce papers. Since there was no request for custody, he quietly signed and expeditiously returned them to the attorney in Mobile, Alabama.

"He has another shirt that's a little better," Davis said.

"Oh, boy," Jennifer replied.

"It says something like, 'The more I get to know women, the more I like my dogs.' Or something like that."

"A real ladies' man," Jennifer replied, slumping back onto the couch. "And you're leaving me here with him?"

"Trust me. He's our best option." Davis appeared distracted and stopped petting the dog. Lovey reminded him of his duty by sitting on his foot and looking up at him, whining.

Danny Robert cared for the dogs at the club—twenty-seven of them—and appeared oblivious to everything else going on around him. He had hounds to run deer, and he had hounds to track deer. And then he had hounds that were just there because Danny Robert loved dogs. He kept a strange menagerie of breeds that he did not bother to keep separate; therefore, he fought a constant battle of trying to find homes for mongrels: Schipperke-Blue Tick mixes, Beagle-and-Springer combinations. The ones that he couldn't dole out, he kept, so that over the years the pack continued to grow into the motley crew that ran roughshod over the forty acres of hardwood forest.

At night the dogs would congregate under the back carport of the Sanford estate to await the waffles that Danny Robert would prepare as their treats. Sometimes the wait became tiresome, and in-fighting would begin. More than once blood spilled over the sausage-flavored waffle bites, or the paucity thereof.

Before Jennifer could further protest the sleeping arrangements, the pair heard the rattle of keys in the front door. Davis stood and crossed the room to greet the new arrival. Lovey seemed agitated that she was being ignored.

Annie appeared in the doorway, still dressed in scrubs. Even after a twelve-hour shift, still wearing her hospital attire, she was gorgeous. Shining black hair framed her heart-shaped face, accentuated by the widow's peak inherited from her father. The high cheekbones and flashing eyes proved that she and Davis were closely related.

Her olive complexion required no makeup, though she chose to highlight her gray-blue eyes with a heavy-handed black eye pencil and mascara application. The only thing that kept her from a career as a professional model was her height, a mere five feet, two inches—that and her place of residency. Just about the only thing that got discovered in Mercy was the shortest route out of town.

"Annie," Davis said, both hands extended.

She responded by dropping her purse and keys where she stood and half-running to him. He bear-hugged her, lifting her off the ground and swinging her around full circle. Her feet flew outward from the centrifugal force, and she smiled and hugged him back. As he twirled his cousin around, Davis felt something unusual that caused him to quickly set her down on her feet.

"What's this?" he asked, and smoothed the smock she was wearing so that the girth of her stomach was revealed.

Annie instinctively pulled away, but then stopped herself. She made light of it, saying, "It's a baby, you big doof. Ain't you ever seen a pregnant woman?"

"Oh, gosh, Annie," was all he could say.

"Oh, be happy for me," she said, rallying with an upbeat tone. She bent down to pick up her purse and keys. "I've always wanted to have a family. You know that. And now I'll have one."

Davis looked as though he would cry. He was fourteen hours into a day that had started off poorly and then deteriorated. Unable to think of something positive to say, he turned to Jennifer for help in changing the subject.

"Annie, this is Jennifer. The girl I told you about."

"So glad to meet you," Annie said, crossing the room to shake hands with her visitor. "Davis deserves somebody good, and I hear you're about the best thing going."

"Well, that's nice to hear," Jennifer said, smiling. "I'm sure I can store that for later use."

"Now, don't go using anything I say against him," Annie continued. "Davis is my knight in shining armor." She sighed. "And my pioneer husband. And my truck-driving partner."

Jennifer looked confused.

"See, there's not much to do in Mercy when you're a kid," Davis said, "which does wonders for your imagination."

"Yep. Davis and I used to play 'tend like' up in the woods between here and his dad's place. Everything from beauty pageants to fighting pretend forest fires. You name it; we pretended it."

Davis smiled, and then clarified, "I was always the beauty pageant *judge*," he said.

"And, amazingly, I always won," Annie replied, tossing her head and flipping her hair with the back of her hand.

"She was always Miss Washington, D.C.," he added.

"And, Miss America, after the pageant was over."

"Of course," Davis said.

"Y'all come on back. I got to get some tea. I'm 'bout parched." She made her way to the darkened kitchen off the back of the living room. "Drink and pee. Drink and pee. You know, all you do when you get pregnant is drink and pee." The two visitors followed Annie to the main kitchen, and Lovey brought up the rear. As the foursome arrived at the darkened doorway, Annie reached to her left and flipped a switch to illuminate a kitchen that would make a gourmet's heart palpitate.

The room was an enormous four hundred square feet. Black granite with flecks of copper adorned the tops of the cabinets. A farmhouse sink, fashioned of hand-hammered copper, large enough to bathe several of Danny Robert's dogs at once, punctuated one side of the expanse. The island was large as well, housing an icemaker and a wine cooler. A second, smaller copper sink nestled within it as a vegetable prep area. Stainless steel and over-sized appliances rounded out the room, weighting each corner heavily.

Annie reached into the door-within-the-door of the refrigerator, stepping over a set of bathroom scales that blocked ready-access to the food inside. She pulled out a gallon pitcher of tea and placed it on the countertop.

"Y'all want some?" Annie asked, reaching to the cabinet just right of the refrigerator for a glass.

"I'm good," Davis said. "Can't do caffeine."

"I'll take some," Jennifer replied. She perched on a barstool next to the island.

"It's sweet, now," Annie said. "'Round here we like a little tea with our sugar." She retrieved a second glass and then moved to the icemaker.

Jennifer nodded her affirmation that sweet was acceptable. "Pour on," she encouraged.

Ice cubes clinked in the glasses, and then several clattered onto the floor, where Lovey quickly trotted over to enjoy them. "Good thing she thinks ice cubes are a treat, or she'd be fatter than she already is," Annie said.

As she was pouring, Danny Robert appeared in the doorway. "Hey, hon. Did you shut the gate?"

"No, sir. I was just coming to get Davis, and then headin' straight back to the house."

"All right. Well, I didn't want to keep the dogs locked up all night. So, don't forget to shut it on your way out."

"Oh, Daddy, those dogs ain't coming out of that house unless you force 'em. It's comin' a frog-strangler out there. You can't see your hand in front of your face."

"Make me a glass," he instructed, and she complied.

"So, I talked to Herschel this afternoon," he said, changing the subject, as Annie reached for another glass. Herschel Peters was the Lanier County supervisor for District Three. "He said for us to get the family cemetery approved, we just need to get Henry Jacobs to sign this standard agreement saying that he don't mind it being here." He pulled a rumpled piece of paper, folded lengthwise, from his back pocket, and smoothed it out on the countertop.

"And who's gonna cross that bridge?" Annie said before taking a long drink.

"Ain't gonna be me," her father replied. "I'd soon shoot the sum-bitch as look at him. He's crazy as a loon. Besides, once Daddy's dead, he won't care where he's buried. I think we just tell him we got it cleared. It'll give him some peace of mind, and he'll quit worrying me about it."

Jennifer watched the banter as though she were at a tennis match.

"Jesus will forgive you," Annie concurred.

Jennifer looked to Davis for explanation.

"I can go talk to him, if you want me to," Davis said. "I can get a signature out of him. Just give me that." He reached for the document, but Danny Robert pulled it away.

"You ain't going over there. I don't think anybody goes up there anymore except the UPS guy. He says it's gotten down-right abnormal up there."

"Oh, it can't be that bad." Davis walked to the cabinet where the glasses were stored and got one down. He filled it at the sink.

Jennifer sipped her tea and looked from side to side, trying to appear uninterested in the conversation by studying the details of the décor. Her curiosity grew, however.

"He's got a 7-Up Jesus in his front window now."

"A what?" Jennifer asked. She could not stay silent any longer.

"That's what everybody calls it: a 7-Up Jesus. He's got this window he made out of the sawed-off bottoms of green 7-Up bottles. I hear he arranged them in a two-by-four frame with a chicken-wire screen, then poured concrete around them and let it set up. From a distance, they say it looks like a picture of Jesus. Least ways, that's how it's told."

"Who is this guy?" She could no longer contain her questions.

"Oh, an old Korea veteran, Hank Jacobs." Jennifer liked the way Danny Robert put the emphasis on the *Ko* in *Korea*. "Lives not too far from here. Only neighbor we got."

Davis added, "The only neighbor who didn't sell to the Sanfords."

"Got twenty-five acres, dang near smack in the middle of Pawpaw's land," Annie said.

"He's certifiable," Danny Robert continued. "Got a sort of *Apocalypse Now* feel going with his yard art."

"Good grief," Jennifer said.

"Oh, he's not dangerous," Davis said. "Jennifer and I can run by there tomorrow morning and get him to sign. We'll take the four-wheeler over."

"I don't know about that, Davis. He's been known to wave a gun at folks."

"Well, long as he doesn't shoot, I suppose we'll be all right, don't you think?"

"You're as hard-headed as your Daddy. Go on, if you want to," he said, and shoved the paperwork from the county across the counter toward him. "The bridge between here and there is out. You'll have to go through town. Take the old railroad bed in. Use the big Polaris. It's at the cleaning shed. Load 'er up in the back of Marcus's truck."

"*My* truck," Annie injected.

Davis grimaced, taking the one-page document and scanning it. Jennifer leaned over to read it as well. Davis looked up, digesting everything his uncle had said.

"I prefer to think that I'm as hard-headed as my mama," he countered.

"That's fair," Danny Robert said with a note of finality. He stood for a minute, palms pressed on the cool granite. He stretched up onto the balls of his feet and then rocked back. "Well, I reckon I'll go get Mom. Annie, you want to come back here and check all these wires?"

She set her glass down on the counter and wiped the back of her hand across her lips. "Yep. Got to pee first."

"You know, honey, you don't have to announce it ever' time you got to go."

"I don't announce it *every* time. If I did, it'd be all I ever talked about," she replied flatly. "I'll be there in just a minute."

Jennifer watched Danny Robert as he left the kitchen and shuffled down a darkened hallway to the presumed master suite. Davis looked up from his paperwork and smiled at Annie. Jennifer took the paper from him to read more carefully.

"So, what's the scoop?" he asked her.

"Which one?" Annie asked. "There's so much horse puckey flying 'round here, we all need a scoop," she said, playing charades at shoveling manure.

"You're a mess," he said. "Start with what the doctors are sayin'."

She launched into a medical monologue that Davis and Jennifer attempted to decipher. "Well, we're dealing with congestive heart failure, end-stage renal disease, an inflamed gall bladder, pancreatitis, eruptive xanthomatosis, poor circulation to his feet."

She continued, "Y'all, his feet look like a dang war zone; he's already had three toes amputated. Needs another one cut off, but he can't feel it, so we figure, why bother, at this point?"

Jennifer nodded her head, wondering what *eruptive xanthomatosis* entailed.

"Basically, he's an out-of-control diabetic," Annie said, shaking her head and looking at the floor. "He's known he was diabetic since before I was born. He's essentially killed hisself, smoking and drinking and eating wrong for the last twenty-five years.

"He won't quit neither. I'll go back there in a minute, and he'll say, 'Annie, go fix me some sausage biscuit and strawberry preserves.' And then he'll eat five of 'em. He weighs near four hundred pounds now. He can barely haul it around."

She sighed heavily and pressed on her diaphragm. "Dang heartburn."

"So, what are they doing for him?" Davis asked.

"Well, the last three weeks he's been on nothing but IV fluids, his pancreas is so bad. That's been hard on ever'body. We've had nothing but ranting and raving out of the man. Had to take his pocket change for fear he'd go to the vending machines at the hospital."

Davis grinned.

"You laugh, but we were close to having to tie him down." She shook her head. "Then the fluid build-up got crazy, and we were dosing him triple his normal amount of Lasix, trying to keep *that* in check. I don't know. You get to a point where you just want to quit giving them nine hundred different kinds of drugs to prop 'em up. I guess that's where we're at now."

"Yeah."

"We've been dosing him here at the house for five years for his skin problems, ever since I got my RN. I give him cortisone shots for that. We used to drive him to Memphis to see a dermatologist up there. But, at that price, we just get the steroids from the vet in Louisville and do it here. It's faster, easier, and cheaper that way."

"The vet?" Davis asked.

"Oh, it's the same stuff—exact same stuff. He gets his pancreas medicine from the vet, too." Annie looked around the room and saw a bag on the counter top. "See?" she said, opening the bag and producing a bottle of pills.

The prescription bottle was clearly marked for veterinary use, yet it had Frank Sanford's name on the label. Davis took the bottle and read. Jennifer picked up the bag where a receipt was stapled.

"Please have Frank Sanford wormed regularly?" she read aloud from the computerized receipt.

"Yeah, that's a hoot, ain't it?"

Danny Robert's voice emanated from the back of the house, calling to Annie.

"Coming!" she bellowed back. She turned to address Davis. "You want to come?" she asked.

"Did they even know we were coming?"

"Mom knew."

Davis looked at Jennifer, who first caught his eye, then ignored him by taking a long drink of her tea and intentionally looking away. She wasn't willing to go back there, and he knew it.

"Well, I'll just wait for Mom out here, then. Y'all can let him know we've come, and then we'll see."

"Chicken," Annie taunted.

"You better believe it."

Annie emptied what was left of her ice cubes into the sink, and leaving the glass on the counter, she took a deep breath, squared her shoulders, and dove into the abyss. "If I'm not back in five minutes, send help," she called over her shoulder.

Davis and Jennifer looked at each other. He smiled, looked away, and then wiped both his hands over his face. A half-laugh, half-sigh escaped him, and he leaned back against the kitchen counter and crossed his arms over his chest. "Boy, this sucks," he said.

Lovey waddled toward him, sat down on his left foot, and scratched behind her ear. "Dang footstool," he said, and gently removed his foot from underneath the thirty-pound canine.

"I'm sorry," he continued his disjointed monologue.

"For what?" Jennifer asked.

Davis currently felt sorry for a lot of things, but said, "For bringing you."

"Don't be."

"This is not going to be a fun trip."

"Well, I didn't figure it was gonna be a joy ride," Jennifer said, walking to the sink to dispose of her ice.

"We'll see how it plays out tonight. Tomorrow we can go into town, eat at Mercy Station Market and then hop the tracks to Hank Jacobs's place. Does that sound okay to you?"

"I'm game. Wouldn't want to miss an exclusive chance to see a 7-Up Jesus," Jennifer said, searching under the kitchen sink for dishwashing liquid.

"Don't do that," he said, as she pulled out a bottle of soap. "The cleaning lady will take care of that in the morning."

"You got to be kidding?" Jennifer said.

"Who do you think cleans this monstrosity? The 65-year-old diabetic heart-patient? Or the 65-year-old arthritic, osteoporosified *grande dame?*"

"*Osteoporosified?*" Jennifer said, laughing.

"Shut up."

"To tell the truth, I really hadn't thought about it," she said, putting the soap back under the sink.

"Yeah, well, you come from a family where people actually work for a living."

"I thought you did, too."

"I try to fake it," he said, moving toward her and encircling her in a bear hug. He buried his face in her shoulder.

She tried to comfort him but sensed it was pointless. She ran her hand over his hair and then patted him on the back. "All right, buck up," she said. "We didn't drive through all that weather tonight for you to hide in the kitchen. If you didn't want to talk to him, we could have just waited it out in Bedford. You obviously have something to say to the man."

"I guess so. Problem is, I don't know what it is."

"How 'bout, 'Boy, sucks to be you'?" Jennifer tried some levity.

"Yeah, no kidding."

Annie reappeared in the doorway to the kitchen. Her eyes were wilder than normal. "Davis, call your daddy and then get back here. This is it."

SIX

She walked across the front lawn, carrying something small, dried, and brown, cradled in two cupped hands. She focused intently on her prize, all but staggering across the uneven terrain of yard. Making her way to the eastern edge of the grass, she scrambled up the stonewall that retained a two-foot-high day lily bed, using her elbows to pull herself up, not willing to relinquish the gift, even for a moment.

She stepped through the split rail fence and seemingly wandered through the oak forest until she came to a firebreak where the piney woods arose before her. She looked about, searching for a place to set down the trophy, but, finding none suitable, she carefully nestled it in the pocket of her sundress. She then turned to a rotting stump in close proximity to the border fence where she had left a hand rake wrapped in yellowed, brittle newsprint.

Slowly, she unwrapped the garden tool with the rotting wooden handle and rusting tines. She laid the paper on the ground and picked up a sandstone rock that she had deliberately left nearby to keep the wind from blowing the wrapper away.

She surveyed her garden plot, consisting of a triangle of three daffodil plants, now withered and dried from the summer heat, planted in the four feet between the stump and the fence. Determined to augment the plantings with her current treasure, she reached deep into the pocket of her dress and pulled it out. It was the size of a fig, with dried skin not unlike an onion. Taking her rake, she cleared a spot in the loamy soil and lovingly placed the daffodil bulb into its bed.

Covering it back over with dirt, she stopped for a moment, thinking she heard a rustle in the underbrush. Pausing, she heard only silence, so she carried on, rising and using the toe of her white canvas sneakers to tamp down the ground.

Again she paused, again hearing a rustling noise, this time clearer and closer. It was too loud to be a snake, not loud enough to be a deer. Surely it was Davis. Not wanting to see him, not wanting to give away the location of her secret flora, she quickly wrapped the rake back in the newspaper, propped it up against the easterly side of the stump, and began to trudge determinedly back to the house by a circuitous route.

The crashing in the woods continued. It was, indeed, Davis, eight years old, and full of himself. His eyes betrayed him as his father's son, and his cheekbones revealed him to be a Sanford, high and strong. He spotted and hailed her.

"Hey!" he shouted. "What are you doing?"

"Just walking," she replied.

"Can I come, too?"

"Sure. They'll be ringing the dinner bell soon."

"Yeah, Mama told me not to get dirty before dinner, so I'm keeping my hands in my pockets."

"Good plan. Your daddy home?"

"No, but supposed to be for dinner."

"I reckon we oughtten hold our breath."

"Reckon," Davis said, shrugging. "I can hardly wait to go to camp tomorrow."

"You think I can go and stay with you?" she said, looking at him for the first time, still doggedly making her way to the house.

"That'd be funny," Davis said.

"Yeah, I reckon."

"You could, but I don't think church camp would approve of that!"

"Probably not," she agreed.

"What's wrong?" Davis asked.

"Nothing. Just going back to the house." She sniffed and wiped her nose on the back of her hand.

"Wish I could spend the night at your house," Davis said.

"What's wrong with yours?"

"Dad. He stays mad. Him and Mama yell a lot."

"Not much better at our house."

"Yeah, but Pawpaw's there."

"Yeah."

The dinner bell pealed in the distance. "We better get a move on, else Pawpaw will keep all the cornbread to himself if we're late," the young boy said.

"He always leaves at least one piece," she offered.

"Yeah, but eatin' the last piece will make you go bald, won't it?" he asked, wide-eyed.

"That's what Pawpaw says."

Davis pulled his hands from his trouser pockets and smiled. "Well, I ain't goin' bald!" he called over his shoulder as he sprinted away. "Last one to the house is a rotten egg!"

SEVEN

"What's the number?" Jennifer asked, moving to the phone.

"4832," Davis said, looking around for a place to set his glass.

"483-2 what?" Jennifer asked.

"Just 4832," Annie said. Don't have to dial the first three digits around here."

Davis was fumbling around in the middle of the kitchen. Jennifer went to him, took his glass, and pointed him toward Annie, giving him a shove. "Go. I'm calling."

Davis nodded and walked, trance-like, toward Pawpaw's bedroom. Annie grabbed his hand and pulled him down the darkened hall. "Snap out of it, Davy. I already got one patient and a couple of basket cases back here. Don't need another," she said.

When they got to the master suite, Davis could see in the lamp-lit room the empty bed, tussled sheets, and a bright light in the adjacent bathroom. Annie continued to drag him toward the lavatory. They could hear a commotion within.

"Good God!" Frank Sanford did his best to bellow, but could manage only a hoarse whisper. He had been unceremoniously positioned on the toilet, his pastel blue cotton pajama trousers wrapped around his elephantine ankles. Danny Robert held him steady by kneeling on the floor, one hand at his father's elbow, the other on his knee. Cora stood beside the pair, hands clenched together at her mouth.

"Get this God-forsaken tube out of my nose," Frank ordered. All four individuals made motions to assist, but Annie was the one who stepped up and pulled the oxygen supply from his red and bulbous nose, unfastened the ear straps, and pulled it over his head. She began to roll up the clear tubing from her thumb to elbow, thumb to elbow, working her way back toward the oxygen tank on wheels.

"Don't go lighting no cigarettes, none of ya," she said, turning off the supply.

"I've a mind to light two of 'em," Frank replied.

"Stop it, Pawpaw," she said sternly. "Can we try to make this as pleasant an experience as possible?"

"It's my death, I'll do it like I see fit," he replied.

"Have it your way. Always have," she said, wheeling the tank out of the bath and into the bedroom. She propped it in a dark corner and returned.

There was silence. Davis leaned on the doorjamb to the bathroom, saying nothing, but watching the melee unfold.

"It ain't right that it should happen this way," Frank continued his hoarse, whisper of a rant. "I'm supposed to die peaceful—in my sleep."

"Oh, Frank," Cora said, and she kneeled beside him. A fecal odor began to permeate the room. "You can't leave yet. You got to stay with me a little while longer."

Frank's face softened as he looked into the eyes of his wife. "Baby," he said, "I can't stay much longer. This old body of mine's give out."

"No, you have to stay a little while longer," Cora said. "Our anniversary is coming up. Stay for that, won't you?"

Frank looked away, as though he heard something. He stared intently at the wall. Mumbling something indiscernible, he finally said aloud, "Just a second. I need more time." He returned his gaze to Cora and gave her a weak smile.

Davis watched from the doorway, arms crossed, lips pursed into a hard line across his tanned face. His eyes welled up as he realized that Annie was right.

Frank reached to stroke Cora's short, white locks. "You used to have the prettiest red hair, Cora. Too bad the boys got my hair instead of yours."

"Don't go, Frank," Cora implored. "I still need you here. Who's gonna take care of me?"

"Danny Robert will take care of the dogs. Annie can cook." He clutched her hand with one of his, and pressed the other against the wall. His face turned more ashen than before, and he looked around frantically.

"You need a trash can, Pawpaw?" Annie asked. She produced one from beside the clothes hamper, helped Mom up with one hand, and positioned it in front of his legs with the other. "Help him, Daddy," she instructed Danny Robert, and pulled Cora away, back into the bedroom. Davis retreated as Annie dragged Mom through the doorway, past where he had been standing.

The three of them stood in the bedroom and listened to Frank vomiting in the next room, Danny Robert offering indistinct, muffled words.

"Mom," Annie said, taking Cora's shoulders in her hands. "Look at me. You got to tell him it's okay to go."

"But it *ain't*," Cora pleaded with Annie. "It *ain't* okay."

"Look at him, Mom. He is doing what you're telling him, and it's all he can do. Tell him that it's okay and give the man his peace."

"But, I'm not ready for him to go yet," Cora said. She looked over at Davis and gave the first sign of recognition. She begged him, "Tell her, Davy. Tell her he can't go yet."

Davis put a hand on her shoulder, forming a triangle of the three. "Mom, Annie's right. He's in there, waiting for you to tell him that it's all right. Let him go. It's his time."

The retching had quieted, and Danny Robert's low whisper could be heard in the otherwise pervasive silence. He finally called out. "Mom, Daddy needs you."

All three returned to the bathroom, and Danny Robert, still on his knees for fear of upsetting the behemoth that was his father, deftly set the garbage can in Annie's path. She picked it up and carried it into the bedroom to empty later.

Cora hesitated, reluctant to come closer. Annie returned, took a wash-cloth from a stack on the vanity, wet it in the sink, and came to mop the patriarch's face. Frank nodded appreciation and looked up at the specta-tors. He saw Davis for the first time.

"Glad you could make it for the show," he whispered. His sarcasm was not lost on his grandson.

"Didn't know you were bad off 'til this morning," Davis said, moving closer, arms still crossed.

"Damn way to go, ain't it?" His grandfather's trembling hands were black and blue from the IV's that had been removed just hours previously. He stared again at a spot on the wall, muttering, "I'm not ready. Just a few more minutes."

At that, Davis knelt beside him, taking Danny Robert's place. "How about a courtesy flush?" Pawpaw said in Davis's ear. Davis did as his grandfather instructed.

"I hear you got religion, boy," Frank said.

"Yeah, I suppose you could call it that. Who told ya?"

"Oh, you hear things, you know." Frank looked disoriented and lost. "He's calling me, Davy. He's calling me home."

"Well, what say you?" Davis said, patting his grandfather's sore-ridden knee.

"What about Mom?" Frank asked.

Cora cried outwardly now, clutching a tired, old tissue in her fist. Bent at the waist and knees, she gasped for air between sobs.

"Now, Pawpaw, she's gonna be fine."

"She's not ready for me to go yet. Tell her," even his whisper was begin-ning to fail. "Tell her I got her some stuff to look at in the gun room. It's in the vault, in a manila envelope with her name on it: a gift, a letter."

"Okay, Pawpaw, she's right here; she heard you. And she's ready." Davis maneuvered in his crouch in order to extend a hand to his grand-mother. "Mom, come here," he commanded.

She obeyed and shakily moved toward the pair, kneeling beside them.

"Okay Pawpaw, now Mom's got something she wants to tell you," Davis said and nodded toward her, giving her a firm look.

Without anyone noticing, Bobby Jack appeared in the doorway of the bathroom, with Jennifer lingering behind.

Cora snubbed and gurgled a bit, wiping her nose, her tears wetting her wrinkled face.

"Frank?" she said, hesitantly.

Frank was not looking at her, but again stared at a spot on the wall. He muttered under his breath. His wheezing became more pronounced.

"Frank," she said again, more decidedly. "Annie and Davis tell me I got to tell you this. I don't want to, but they say I got to."

Frank looked up at her again; his dark eyes were failing, staring into a dimension unseen by the rest.

"Frank. It's okay," she said, unconvincingly. "It's okay for you to go now. I will be all right. You hear?" No one in the room was sure he could.

"Frank? I say it is okay for you to go," she said a little louder. "I will be all right without you for a little while."

Frank's eyes focused on the face of his bride, and there was clarity for an instant. "Thank you, baby," he said. "I'll see you soon." And with that, Frank Sanford slumped over and was gone.

The wind-up Regulator clock in their bedroom struck eight o'clock.

EIGHT

Bobby Jack Sanford was the second child of Frank and Cora Sanford. Named for Bobby Jackson, the Crimson Tide's leading rusher in 1958, he preferred as an adult to be called *Bob*. His mother and father had flatly refused. He tolerated the situation, as three ex-wives had called him far worse names during the course of his life.

Bobby Jack was tall, muscular, and attractive. He had married Davis's mom during their second year of college. She had already borne one child, a boy, and they very quickly conceived Davis. Their marriage had lasted almost nine years before she could no longer tolerate the late nights and lewd women that Bobby Jack had a habit of keeping. The summer that Davis turned eight, she'd packed up her two boys and their belongings and moved back home to the Delta.

Davis came back for two months each summer, as well as for Thanksgiving and Christmas. Summers meant work, but during the winter holidays it was a high time at Sanfords' Mossy Horn Sanctuary. The running of the dogs was scheduled for the first available day of each season: Thanksgiving Day and Christmas Eve.

Davis would arrive, throw on his camouflage, and ask to be dropped off at Section Twenty-six where he would walk the half-mile to the cabin. Annie and Pawpaw would be waiting for him there. By the time he would settle himself in his straight-backed chair, he could already hear the dogs baying by the house. Within ten minutes, anything that was going to move in those piney woods would be careening down the creek bed, directly toward Section Twenty-six.

Davis spent the summer months working under the tutelage of Marcus, repairing ladder stands, filling automatic feeders, and mending fences. Until he turned sixteen, that had been his routine.

However, the summer of Davis's sixteenth year had been spent at Parkwood Hospital in Olive Branch, drying out from alcohol. The next summer, he was back, learning how to live without cocaine. Bobby Jack had rescinded his standing invitation after that.

Essentially, Bobby Jack didn't have time for a good teenaged boy or a bad one. By the time Davis was a senior at Pillow Academy in Greenwood, Bobby Jack was contemplating divorce number three, as that union was starting to run short on marital bliss. His own addiction to Booker's, uncut and unfiltered Kentucky whiskey, made him even more uncomfortable around Davis, especially the cleaned-up version.

Bobby Jack's current unwed state was one that he had vowed to keep. Although Mississippi law provided for equitable division of assets based on marital contribution, the "standard of living" clause had burned him three times on alimony payments.

Besides, his tenure at Mississippi State in the School of Accounting gave him license to survey the coed population, with a new batch to choose from every August. The freshman accounting students called him "Dr. Bob" behind his back, as his reputation preceded him. Interested female students made themselves known, and there were more than enough to keep him busy. It had worked well for him these last five years, until Mary had arrived on campus, straight from Ho Chi Min City. Mary Nguyen, a nineteen-year-old freshman accounting major, was his latest addiction.

Bobby Jack had arrived just in time to witness the passing of Frank Sanford, and his broad shoulders and overall brawn were put to use in moving the man-mountain from the throne room to the bed. Davis's father had used his cell phone to call the coroner, who was both his cousin and the local funeral director, during the two-minute drive from his home to the big house. While Annie and Danny Robert took charge of cleaning and dressing the corpse, Davis and Jennifer attended to Mom in the great room. Bobby Jack stood on the front porch and smoked.

Jennifer shoved a pillow down beside Cora in the over-sized leather chair and pushed the ottoman closer. Cora said nothing, but clenched a soggy tissue in her fist, and stared into space. "He had his faults, but he was a good husband," she finally said. Davis appeared from the kitchen, holding a glass of tea. He handed it to Jennifer, who, after prying the tissue from Cora's hands, replaced it with the beverage. The ice clinked against the glass as Cora's hands shook.

Davis sat on the footstool and steadied her hands with his. "It's going to be okay, Mom. We're all going to get through this."

"We haven't even gotten permission to bury him yet," she said, finally noticing the glass in her hand and taking a small sip.

"Jennifer and I are going to take care of that first thing in the morning. We're riding over to Hank Jacobs's house and getting him to sign the paperwork. Don't worry about that."

Cora pursed her lips and settled into the chair, relaxing a little.

"Can I get you anything, Mrs. Sanford?" Jennifer asked. She felt odd with nothing to do, not knowing anyone but Davis.

"No, honey, I'm fine," she said. "You sit down and rest. I'm fine."

Jennifer sat, as she was instructed, and Lovey hopped up on the couch next to her and lay her head down in Jennifer's lap. She instinctively began to scratch the dog between the ears.

"Davis," Mom began. "Frank said something about the vault."

"Yes, ma'am. I suppose he put some paperwork together for you in there. Said there was an envelope with your name on it."

"I want to look at it."

"Now?" Davis asked.

"Yes, now."

"Mom, Cletus will be here in a few minutes. Why don't we wait until we get all that taken care of before we go down there?"

She looked antsy, but settled down at the mention of the coroner's name. Annie and Danny Robert came in, and Cora placed her glass on the end table and smoothed her hair. Danny Robert slumped down on the opposite end of the couch from Jennifer. Lovey arose and moved to sit with her master.

The front door opened, and Bobby Jack returned to the room as well. He stood in the doorway, hands shoved deep in the pockets of his khakis.

"Still raining?" Danny Robert asked.

"Yep, but it's startin' to slack off some."

"Good, I didn't want to have to go get the damn cows out of the low pasture tonight."

"You don't want to do anything for those cows. How come you don't just slaughter 'em? Sell 'em. Do something with 'em, other than complain about 'em."

"A man's got to work for a living," Danny Robert said, propping his feet on the coffee table and crossing them at the ankles.

"Not any more," Bobby Jack said, feeling in his designer shirt pocket for another smoke.

"What the hell's that supposed to mean?" Danny Robert bristled.

"What's it mean? It means you're a grown man, with a grown daughter, and she's moved out and you haven't yet."

"Hell, Bobby Jack, you just can't admit that you'd be livin' here too if Mom would let your little girlfriends sleep over."

"Least I didn't let one woman make a eunuch out of me twenty-five years ago."

"Well, now that's one thing that you, me, and the entire freshman class can agree on," Danny Robert said.

Bobby Jack continued, undaunted. "With Dad gone, you can quit trying to fake the rest of us off, and go ahead and take the rest of your inheritance now. You've been spending it your whole life, anyway."

Danny Robert half rose and virtually shouted, "Spending it? How about earning it? Where have you been for all the doctor visits? The cooking, the cleaning, the wiping, the catering?" He itemized the list on his fingers. "Who the hell was propping him up the last five minutes?" He paused for a split second, then continued, "Five minutes?" he asked himself incredulously. "More like the last five years!"

Jennifer arose and ducked into the kitchen to search again for the dish-washing liquid or anything else to avoid the display. Davis stood up and held out both hands like a traffic cop, stop signals to each of the brothers. Before he could speak, Cora intervened.

"Boys, he ain't even cold yet. Show some decency, would you? And if you don't have any, then just pretend like it for awhile," she said. The room fell silent. Danny Robert sank further into the couch and sulked. He then reached for the remote and turned on the television. Professional bull riding was on. He watched it intently.

No one spoke for a moment, so Davis sat back down at the feet of his grandmother. She looked over her shoulder to Bobby Jack, who still stood in the doorway. "Where's that nice Japanese girl, Bobby Jack?"

"Vietnamese, Mom."

"Right. Vietnamese. I knew she was some kind of—*nese*. Where is she?"

"At the house. I didn't figure I should bring her over, you know, con-sidering."

"You know, your Daddy never was goin' to approve of her. Said it was no better than dating a colored girl. But, I suppose she is nice enough." Cora trailed off for a moment and then said, "Is she a Communist, Bobby Jack?"

Davis looked first to Mom, then to his father. His eyes questioned, but he said nothing. Bobby Jack noted the query but ignored it, digging in his pocket for a lighter. "I'm gonna go smoke," he said, opening the front door to return to the porch. The rain had slowed to a drizzle, but the pop-ping and splattering in the downspouts continued. Bobby Jack held the screen door open as he lit his cigarette. "Cletus's here," he said, the Salem flopping between his lips. He took a drag and let the door slam with a creak of the hinges and a bang in the doorjamb behind him.

NINE

"Where's your mom and Daniel?" Pawpaw called out as he tied up the rope to the dinner bell that adorned the top of a four-by-four post in the center of the flagstone patio.

Davis replied, out of breath, "They sent me on without 'em. Daniel's got to get a shower and unpack, Mama said."

Frank Sanford nodded at the explanation. "Well, come on in and go wash your hands. If you're late to the table, there won't be any cornbread left for you."

Davis never checked his speed as he hurtled through the atrium doorway and made for the bathroom to wash.

"So, the day is almost here, ain't it?" Pawpaw said to Davis when he reemerged, wiping his hands on the back of his jeans.

"Yes, sir," he replied, his eagerness beaming. "I get to go to Oxford for a whole week!"

"Well, now, you won't really go into Oxford. But camp is nearby there. You know, that's where I met Mom, many, many moons ago." Frank knew that Davis was familiar with the story. He knew it was one of his favorites.

"Tell me about it again, Pawpaw," Davis said.

"Here, you peel this tomato," Pawpaw instructed, handing him a paring knife. "And I'll slice these onions. And when Mom and Annie and Danny Robert get here, we'll eat."

"Tell me the story, Pawpaw, please?" Davis entreated his grandfather.

"Well, it was springtime, and well, it had been a rough semester for me."
Pawpaw began the story that Davis had almost memorized, word for word.

"All my fraternity brothers were going to Florida on spring break, but I couldn't afford to go. That was back in the day when it didn't cost an arm and a leg to be in a fraternity. Back in the day when it really meant something to be a Sigma Chi. I had some doctor's bills to pay, and there wasn't enough money to go around."

Davis quietly peeled the tomato he'd been presented, and bobbed his head back and forth to the rhythm of the familiar words.

"I'd been to church at home, here in Mercy, a couple of weeks back, and they'd mentioned there was an opening for a Christian singles retreat to Lake Stephens. A fella had planned on going, had even paid for his room and board, but then had to up and go off and join the Army."

Davis smiled and mouthed the words along with his grandfather, "Dang, Kennedy." Never mind that Kennedy would not for another five years make the famous speech to which Frank alluded. Davis did not know it, and Frank took every opportunity he could find to show his disdain for both Catholics and Democrats.

"So, I got to take that poor sucker's place."

They could hear a commotion in the back of the house. "Sounds like your grandmother's here," he said, rinsing the peeled onion under running water.

"Hurry, Pawpaw, tell the rest before she comes in."

Frank Sanford smiled, and sliced the onion like an apple, laying it on a platter beside a half-dozen deviled eggs that he had already prepared.

"Well, long story made short, the first night we were there, there were the women on one side of the camp, and the men on the other. And back in those days, they didn't have the bathrooms inside the camp house. You had to go out of your bunkhouse to go to a central shower and toilet area.

"Well, it was late, 'round 11:30 at night, and we were all supposed to be asleep. And, I tell you the truth, the men were asleep. But those women, they'd been up, playing Rook, and your grandmother had been drinking so much Wink that she had to go to the pot in the middle of the night.

"And well, you know, I didn't know it at the time, but I was already startin' to get diabetic, and couldn't hold my pee for nothin'. Didn't know why I couldn't; just thought I had a small bladder or something. So there I am, out in the middle of the night, thinking nobody else is gonna be at the latrine, when I run smack into your grandmother, coming out of the bath house, wearing nothing but her baby doll pajamas."

Davis started to laugh, as he always did.

"And you know the law of the hills?" Pawpaw queried.

And the two said in unison, "Once you seen 'em nekkid, you got to marry 'em."

"That's right, boy," he said, tussling the child's hair.

They continued to laugh, and then, looking up, they saw Davis's mother standing in the kitchen.

"Frank, don't go filling my boy's head full of stories like that, all right?"

"And a fine howdy-do to you, too, Brenda," Frank replied.

"I mean it. I've had just about enough coarse humor as any one woman should have to tolerate in a lifetime. Davy, wash your hands and go get in the car."

"Aw, Mama!" Davis interjected.

"I said it, and I meant it, Davis Carrothers Sanford. Go get in the car."

Davis put the round, slick tomato on the crudités plate and placed the paring knife beside it before he wiped his hands on his trousers.

"Brenda, there's no harm in telling a story like that, and you're plum crazier than I thought you were if you think different."

"Well, maybe not, Dad, but between the drinking and carousing he's learning from his daddy, I'd hope that maybe you could refrain from teaching him about nekkid women until he's at least the age of consent." Brenda patted Davis's head as he turned the corner in the kitchen and headed to the back door. He lingered there and listened.

"Well, that nekkid woman was his grandmother, and it was at a church retreat, and honestly, I don't see a reason to justify my morality to a woman working on her second divorce. I tell you one thing, if you're half as loony as Bobby Jack says you are, I'd try not to say too much as to call attention to *myself for fear of being locked up where they can keep you from hurtin' yourself."*

"Is that supposed to be some kind of a threat, Frank? 'Cause if it is, it doesn't scare me. You and Bobby Jack are two of kind, aren't you? Anybody who questions your authority in this little sex empire is automatically dubbed 'crazy.'"

"And what the hell is that supposed to mean?" Frank asked, eyebrows raised and temples throbbing.

"Exactly what it sounds like, Frank. Exactly what it sounds like. You, me, and this whole God-forsaken town know what it means." Brenda reached into her purse and pulled out a legal-sized document, folded lengthwise.

"And speaking of working on divorces, I'm about through working on this one." She handed the papers to Frank. "And if your son would ever come home from whatever bar he's taken up residence in this month, I'd give him these myself. But since he won't, I figure it'll give you great pleasure to hand 'em off to him."

Frank took the papers as she turned to go. "You'll be back, you crazy wench. You can't deprive your children of this kind of lifestyle."

Brenda paused in the doorway. A slightly hysterical laugh escaped her. "Oh, yes I can, Frank. Just watch me." She didn't turn her head as she spoke to him. "I just thank God every night that he never gave me a baby girl, Frank." And although Davis was much too old for it, his mother picked him up and carried him over the threshold to the car that was still idling in the driveway. The screen door closed, with a creak of the hinges and a bang in the doorjamb.

TEN

The rain had completely stopped by half-past midnight, when Cletus finally closed the back door of the hearse and pulled away from the Sanford house. Bobby Jack and Davis did not speak to each other before the father figure made his retreat. Cora still sat in the same spot in which Jennifer had placed her four hours earlier.

Danny Robert sat down on the couch and sighed. "You stayin'?" he asked Annie.

"I reckon," she said. She looked beaten. She had to be at work again in less than six hours. "I can shower here and change clothes at the house on the way out."

"All right. Take my bed. I'll sleep here," he said, swinging his feet onto the couch and pulling an afghan down from the back.

"Davis, where you sleepin'?" Annie asked.

"Uh," Davis looked around. "The loft, I reckon."

"Okay, and Jennifer gets my room?" Annie asked.

"Yep, her stuff is there already." Jennifer nodded an acknowledgment.

"Okay, Mom, let's go to bed. We have a lot to do tomorrow," Annie said, taking Cora's elbow in hand.

"I can't sleep in that bed, Annie," Cora said.

Annie stopped and thought. "Okay. You take Daddy's bed. Dad, you take Mom's bed, and I'll take the couch."

"I ain't sleepin' in that bed neither," Danny Robert said, rearranging the throw pillows under his head. "I'm fine right here."

Annie thought again, frozen in her half-bent stance over Mom's chair.

"Isn't there another extra bed in this monstrosity?" Jennifer asked. As soon as the words escaped her mouth, she wished she could take them back.

Danny Robert mumbled with his eyes half-shut, "It ain't that there's more rooms, just bigger ones. You got to have it that way when you weigh four hundred pounds and have a fancy for dead animal art." He rolled over and faced the back of the couch.

Jennifer looked at Davis for help. He directed. "Mom, you take Danny Robert's bed. Annie, you take your own bed. Jennifer, you can sleep on the couch in the basement. I'll sleep on the couch in the loft."

"Danny Robert's bed is too soft," Cora announced, sitting up in her chair, the first indication that she might stand.

"Okay, you take Annie's bed then. Annie, take your daddy's. Is that all right?"

"I suppose," Mom said, in somewhat of a huff, and she shoved herself up out of the chair.

Annie began to protest. "But, Jennifer is a guest. She shouldn't sleep on the couch."

"And neither should a pregnant woman," Jennifer said. "I'll be fine. Trust me. I'll just get my stuff out of your room, and y'all can show me where to go."

Cora was already making her stiff, arthritic way toward Annie's childhood room. "Annie, can you get my nightgown out of my nightstand drawer? The powder-blue one," she called over her shoulder.

Annie screwed up her face and muttered for the benefit of Davis and Jennifer. "Yes, ma'am," she called, doing as she was commanded.

Jennifer came up behind Cora just as she flipped on the light switch in Annie's room. "Lovey!" Cora pronounced harshly. "What are you doing?"

Lovey looked up from her amusement and panted a dog smile at her admirers. Jennifer's purse had been turned over and rummaged through by the canine. She had found her cosmetic bag and was making short work of its contents. Her black nose was smeared tan with full-coverage foundation. Her teeth and tongue were blackened from the waterproof mascara that she had smeared across the bedclothes.

"That will never wash out!" Cora exclaimed, snatching up the remnants of the feast, first with one hand and then with the other. Lovey descended from the bed with a thud, not showing the least remorse.

Jennifer's mouth was agape at the sight, but she stood quietly and said nothing. Davis approached from behind, looking over Jennifer's shoulder at the fracas. "She's been a giant pile of steaming turds ever since they got her," he whispered into her ear.

"Your grandmother or the dog?"

Davis stifled a laugh and whispered, "We'll get you more tomorrow when we go into town." He then announced his presence to Mom by breezing in and saying, "Here, let me help you with that," taking the makeup from Cora's clenched fists. "I think Windex will get that out just fine, Mom. Honey will deal with it in the morning."

"This is a custom-made Schumacher duvet cover, you know. It's not the dime-store variety."

"It *is* nice," Davis agreed, as he dropped the cosmetics into the wastebasket by the doorway, smoothed the bed linens down where the dog had been lounging, and then turned down the covers. Jennifer maintained her silence, shouldered her purse, and gathered what was left of her belongings to wait in the hall while Davis tried to settle his grandmother.

Annie came in, dropped off the nightgown, swept up the make-up-stained dog, which bared her teeth at her former owner, then circled out of the room with a sheepish "Sorry" to Jennifer. Annie popped Lovey atop the snout when she continued to growl in defiance. Long ago, Lovey had decided to show her disdain for Annie. When Annie was forced to choose between the dog and Marcus, Lovey never forgave the choice.

Jennifer could hear the conversation between Cora and Davis, although she tried to mind her own affairs. Cora began, "You know Davis, your grandfather and I knew he wasn't going to make it much longer."

"Yes, ma'am," Davis nodded, turning on the table lamp by the bed.

"We didn't plan for it to end this way. It wasn't six months ago, and we'd decided we were going to just plan to have an accident. You know, we both knew in our hearts that one of us couldn't live without the other."

"Now Mom, that's just crazy talk. You are going to be fine," Davis said.

"Well, I reckon." She thought for a moment. "We were gonna do like what Edith Wharton wrote about in *Ethan Frome.*"

"Well, you remember how well that turned out for them," Davis said, remembering eleventh grade American literature. "It's better this way, Mom. Come on now, he's in a better place. You'll come to see that soon. Let's get some rest and start over tomorrow." He walked toward the door.

She nodded and took her nightgown in her hands, staring down at it.

"Love you, Mom," Davis said, as he turned off the overhead light, pulled the door shut, and smiled at Jennifer.

"Come on. I'll take you downstairs." He picked up her laptop and duffel bag and led the way to the basement.

To the left of the front door was another doorway that led down to the basement. The runners of the steps were pine; the risers were oak, fifteen in all, leading to the lower floor that was covered in natural oak planks, six inches wide. They walked through a darkened lounge area furnished with a wet bar and a bubbling Wurlitzer, and entered a great room furnished with more oversized davenports and a ball-and-claw billiard table. There were no windows in the finished area, making it exceedingly cave-like, in Jennifer's estimation.

"Best couch in the house," Davis said, setting her belongings on the coffee table in front of an extra-long, extra-deep Drexel Heritage sofa.

"Thanks," she replied, her energy waning quickly.

"And, it's dark as a freakin' tomb in here, so you'll get to sleep until you wake up."

"Don't say *tomb.*"

"Don't be a ninny," he said, kissing her forehead. "I'll see you when you wake up, okay?"

"And not a minute sooner."

Davis turned to go, but added, "There's a bathroom through that door-way on the left." He continued toward the stairs. "I'm all the way upstairs, if you need anything."

"Thanks," she said, looking after him, putting on the best smile she could.

Davis left, and she sat down, relieved to have some solitude. She thought about changing clothes, but opted to stay dressed instead. She laid her walking stick on the barrel-front French-provincial coffee table, within an arm's reach of her place of repose, and tried to calm her thoughts. She breathed in deeply and reveled in the comfort of the couch. "This ain't the dime-store variety, either," she murmured, and drifted off to dream.

ELEVEN

It was later, but how much so, she could not be sure. It was also very dark, as Davis had predicted, and Jennifer could not see the face of the wind-up wristwatch that she had inherited from her grandmother. She stretched and started to roll over, when she saw a line of light under the doorway to the right of where she lay. She stopped, mid-turn, and stifled a gasp.

Jennifer listened and at first heard nothing. She sat up, rubbed at her eyes with her knuckles and tried to blink some moisture into her contacts that felt more like potato chips. Now, more awake, she did hear something. Someone was in the basement with her, and she felt sure that they did not intend for her to know about it.

She groped for her cane, found it, and navigated through the dark, past the jukebox, and up the two-toned wooden staircase to the main floor. It was still dark outside; so, Jennifer knew that she couldn't have slept very long. She began looking for a staircase to the second floor, serenaded by Danny Robert's snores that were emanating from the couch. A light was on in the back wing.

The Regulator from the master bedroom struck once. *One-thirty? Two-thirty? Three-thirty?* Jennifer thought to look at her watch. Her eyes were still trying to recover from falling asleep in her contacts. She blinked and refocused, and then gave up, continuing to look for the stairs.

Locating them, she silently ascended to the loft both in search of Davis and in hopes of discovering what Sanford was hiding in the basement. It was not as dark upstairs, since the outside lights filtered through the windows of the colossus, and Jennifer's eyes continued to adjust to the darkness.

At the top of the stairs, Jennifer was greeted by a full-mount taxidermied American alligator, five-feet long and charging. She squelched a scream and struck at it only once with her cane before regaining her composure. Muttering some expletives she'd not used since her beer-drinking days at Madison, she gasped for air until her autonomic system calmed and she was able to spot Davis, asleep in an awkward heap on the couch. In front of him a 65-inch plasma television, tuned to the weather channel, classical music barely audible, cast dark and morphing shadows across his face with the flickering of its blue-white light.

"Davis," she whispered intently, as she crossed the room, keeping watch for any nearby taxidermy. He did not budge. She moved closer and leaned forward toward him. "*Davis!*" Her whisper was imploring. Still nothing came from the heap of man that lay under a tartan plaid woven throw, one bare and tanned arm draped over his forehead, in a sleep-deprived stupor.

She sat down on the coffee table and touched his side, patting him, and whispering, "Davis, wake up. Davis," she continued. She finally resorted to shaking him, and groggily he began to stir, grunting and wiping drool from the corner of his mouth. He sat upright on the couch and his covers dropped to the side, revealing the fact that he was wearing only his Levi's. His sparse hair was in disarray. "I'm up; I'm up. What's wrong?" he spouted, before he truly knew to whom he spoke.

"Hey," Jennifer whispered.

"Hey, what's wrong?" he mimicked her whisper, giving her the first look of recognition, wiping down his hair. He wiped his mouth again with the back of his hand.

"Somebody's in the basement," Jennifer said.

"Who?" Davis was still befuddled by sleep.

"I don't know," she whispered. He stood up, and the afghan fell to the floor. He looked around for his shirt. Bending over to retrieve it from the floor, Jennifer caught sight of a large tattoo in the middle of his back, something prior to which she'd not been privy. The slow-motion disco light of the 600-mile Doppler radar map revealed a Celtic cross in navy and gold, spreading from shoulder blade to shoulder blade.

"When did you get *that*?" she asked him, pointing to his back.

Davis looked over his shoulder as if he could see what she was referring to. "Oh," he said, as he shrugged his shirt over his head and down over his back. "Long time ago."

He clearly did not want to discuss it, and Jennifer did not press. He picked up the throw from around his feet and placed it back on the couch. "Do you want to stay here?"

"Are you kidding?" she asked. "The alligator just about gave me a heart attack. I'm sticking with you in case any of these critters decides it wants its spleen back and gets a little testy."

"Yeah, forgot to tell you 'bout the gator." Davis walked toward the stairs and Jennifer followed closely. "He's a doozy."

The two descended the stairs to the main floor, circled around past the slumbering Danny Robert, and descended again into the basement. Past the bubbling neon tubes, Davis and Jennifer crept. The light was still on, creating a thin, white line of illumination at the bottom of the door. Davis felt the wall until he found a light switch to the main room. With a flip of the switch, the room was illuminated, and any indication that there was another person lurking there was gone. Where the line of light once beckoned, a bookshelf, lined with books, now stood.

Davis looked at Jennifer and smiled. She was thoroughly confused, and he got a good laugh out of it. "Watch," he said softly, and flipped the lights off again. The room darkened and the light under the door reappeared. On again, and the evidence was gone.

"What the—?" was all Jennifer could manage.

Davis eyeballed it again, flipping the light off and then on. He then made a purposeful and straight line to the spot he'd marked in his mind, straight for the center bookshelf unit. He moved a large Masonic Bible that sat alone at doorknob height, pulled a latch that had been hidden by the tome, and watched the shelf unit pop out on springs to roll freely to the right over the other stationary units. "Scooby-doobie-dooo," he whispered gleefully, his eyes glinting at the humor he found in Jennifer's shock. Behind the shelves was a steel door that opened inward, a deadbolt where a doorknob might have been.

He motioned to Jennifer, who came forward in total disbelief. When she got close enough to him, he put his forehead to hers and said quietly, "This is what stupid rich people do with their money."

"I'm not going in there, Dave," she said, and started to back toward the couch.

"You're probably right. It's my father, no doubt, trying to see what's been left him in the will. You go back upstairs and wait for us."

"No, I'll wait here," she said, posting herself on the edge of the couch. "In case you need me."

"Right," Davis said, winking his eye and clicking his tongue. "I'll be right back." And he pushed open the door whose deadbolt had been left unturned.

The room inside was lined with glass cases that housed Frank Sanford's gun collection. A total of one hundred eighty-three long guns encircled the 15-foot square room, each one mounted and displayed behind locked, bulletproof glass. The only taxidermy here consisted of antler mounts of whitetails, none smaller than a Boone and Crockett 110, twenty all together, spaced evenly about the room along the fir downs. Another doorway to the right opened up into the vault where Pawpaw had arranged his personal office. A heavy oaken desktop set on two three-foot tall pine log pedestals was the focal point of the room. Richly appointed bookshelves were built into the walls, displaying waterfowl taxidermy and remarkable photographs of men on safari. Davis crossed the display area determinedly, ready to have words with his father for the first time in years.

The door was slightly ajar, and the banker's lamp was on at the desk where she sat. Cora Sanford was slumped down in the chair, holding tightly to her left arm with her right. Davis ran to her and knelt beside her. A manila envelope lay on the desktop, torn open.

"Mom!" he shouted. She looked up at him in a daze.

"Why do I have to hurt, Davis? When will I stop hurting?" was all she could say. Her gaze drifted from his eyes to her arm, where he saw a large blister and ulceration starting to form. There were multiple needle marks showing.

"What in God's name have you done to yourself, Mom?" Davis's voice was at a feverish pitch. "Mom!" he shouted, "What in the hell have you done?" He saw a rubber tourniquet lying in the floor and an emptied needle and syringe on the desk. He scrambled around, looking for what might have been in the needle.

Jennifer's silhouette darkened the doorway. "Go upstairs. Call 911. Get an ambulance. Wake up Danny Robert! She's trying to kill herself!" he shouted one order after another. Jennifer turned on her heels and hurried upstairs to awaken the house.

On the floor beside the chair he found a vial: *melarsomine dihydrochloride* was typed on the label over a veterinary seal. "What is this?" he asked her, holding the vial up for her to see. Cora did not respond; she looked down at the floor and did not move. Davis pulled her up in the chair. "Can you hear me, Mom? Can you hear me?" He shook her, and she did not respond.

Davis heaved his grandmother up out of the leather office chair and rolled it away with his foot. He laid her down on the floor and put his head to her chest to listen for a heartbeat. As he placed his ear to her limp body, he looked underneath the kneehole of the desk, and his heart commandeered his throat. He saw four more empty vials, lying topsy-turvy in the floor.

Davis tried to assess the situation. "What do you do? What do you do?" He thought aloud. "What do I do?" He began to try CPR, but thought that would be pointless. He made a false start at mouth-to-mouth resuscitation, but then sat back on his heels.

"What do you do?" he asked no one in particular, and reached underneath the desk to scoop up the vials. He brought them in handfuls up to his chest. "What do I do?" he asked again, backing, crawfishing, away from what was doubtless by now only his grandmother's corpse. He leaned against the cherry shadow-box paneled wall in a befuddled mound, holding the vials up to read them. *Melarsomine dihydrochloride,* they all read.

Danny Robert appeared in the doorway, wild-eyed and frantic. "Where is she?" he said to Davis. Davis motioned behind the desk where Danny Robert had not looked. He virtually leaped across the room to try to assist. With one glance at his mother in the powder-blue nightgown, he knew that it was too late, and he turned to Davis, who was reduced to tears and could not speak.

Jennifer had made it back to the door. She watched as Danny Robert took one of the vials from Davis and read it. "Oh, shit," was all he could say, and he dropped his hands in resignation.

Jennifer hobbled across the room in a half-crouch, all but kneeling toward Davis before she reached him. He curled in a fetal position as she glanced toward the body and then turned back toward him. She wrenched a vial out of his hand and looked at it.

"What do you do?" he asked her, tears pouring freely now.

She pulled him up into a sitting position. He dropped the vials, and they rolled away on the green Berber carpeting. He collapsed onto her, wrapping his arms around her, clutching at the back of her shirt. "What do you do?" he said, almost unintelligibly. Jennifer looked over to Danny Robert for help. He was slumped in his father's chair, head in hands, fingers laced through his hair.

"What *do* we do?" Jennifer asked him.

"Go upstairs and wait for the ambulance. And the sheriff, too, I suppose."

Jennifer and Danny Robert arose, and after helping Davis to his feet, the three of them somberly filed to the main floor to await the arrival of the authorities.

TWELVE

It was already a blazing eighty-four degrees at seven o'clock, when the bedroom door swung open in condemnation of her deceit. The squeak of the hinges and the banging of the doorknob against the log wall awakened her from her morning stupor. She opened first one eye and then the other to see Mom standing in the doorway, a wad of newspaper in her right hand and a rusted hand-held garden rake in her left.

"What, pray tell, do you have to say about this, Annie Mae Sanford?"

Annie rose up on her elbows and squinted at her grandmother. She stared for a moment at what Mom held in her hands, and then cast her eyes down and away from Cora Sanford's iron stare.

"Your no-account daddy and my no-account husband have left us here for the last two weeks with those blasted, fool dogs. Well, Hank Jacobs calls me this morning at ten past five and says he's got ten of 'em up at his place. Lord only knows where the othern's are."

Annie was relieved that Mom had begun a tirade. As long as she vented about the dogs, Annie did not have to explain the hand rake.

"So, I go get them this morning in your daddy's truck, and then I get the pleasure of walking forty acres of fence line, trying to find the break."

Annie sat up fully and swung her feet over the edge of the bed. She wore a tee shirt and a pair of knit shorts as her pajamas. She reached for her house robe, tears already beginning to well up in her eyes.

"And so, I'm walking along, and before I ever get to the downed tree, what do I find?" Annie did not attempt to answer the rhetorical question her grandmother posed. She just sat to await the wrath.

"This!" Cora said, emphasizing her point by thrusting the hand rake skyward. "This," she reiterated, "and what looks like two dozen or more of my prize daffodil bulbs, planted out in the woods, dang well labeled and everything. Too bad for you it ain't farther along into the summer, or you might've gotten away with it for God knows how long."

Annie held her face in her hands, but said nothing.

"Child, you'll be thirteen years old tomorrow. And I'm sure your daddy and granddaddy are planning on bringing you some fine present when they get back. You better come up with something good to tell me about this, or I've got half a mind to just cancel your birthday out-right. You know the rules: don't pick 'em and don't touch 'em. The daffodils are mine, no ifs, ands, or buts." She paused to catch her breath, but then continued, "Ain't you got something to say for yourself?" For the first time in her diatribe, she gave Annie the opportunity to speak.

"Pawpaw give 'em to me," was all Annie could muster, and that was in a whisper.

"What?" Mom asked. "Speak up, young missy."

"Pawpaw give 'em to me," Annie repeated, this time, holding her head up just enough to be heard.

"Pawpaw give 'em to you?" Mom sneered. "Pawpaw give 'em to me. I get a new one every year on our anniversary. These bulbs ain't the dime store variety, you know."

Annie defended herself as well as she could. "He did. He give 'em to me, he said, for being his special little girl. Told me not to tell you, or I would've, honest."

"And you expect me to believe that? These flowers are special for me and Pawpaw only. They're what I carried at our wedding. They are special to us because we've been married for so long. He wouldn't have just give 'em to a little girl. Don't you understand, Annie? I earned the right to these flowers for the sacrifices I've made; for being his wife, for—" Cora stopped short of finishing *her sentence when she saw Annie's tears. She placed the hand rake on the end of her bed and sat down next to her.*

"He give 'em to me, Mom, I promise it to you; I promise it. *He made me promise not to tell anyone. Said they were my presents for being his special little girl. Honest, Mom, I wouldn't lie to you. He said if I told, he would tell Daddy and you that I've been a bad girl and that I'd get into a lot of trouble."*

The sternness melted from Cora's face. She wrapped her arms around the pitiful child. "It's okay, honey," she began, rocking her back and forth. "They are just flowers, after all." Cora stared expressionlessly into the center of the child's room and continued to rock her as the girl sobbed. She couldn't think of anything else to say, so she simply asked, "How long?"

"H-how long?" Annie choked out between her tears.

"How long has he been giving you my flowers?" she stroked Annie's crumpled hair and tucked it behind her ears. She dried Annie's face with the back of her hand.

"Since the summer that Davy went away."

Cora nodded her head and exhaled heavily through her nose, her lips pursed. She continued her vice-like grip around the weeping child, rocking, rocking, on the edge of her bed. "It's okay, baby. It's okay. Mom's going to do something to make it better. I don't know what just yet, but let me think on it. I'm gonna try to do something."

Annie nodded, her head hanging to her chest, and gripped her grandmother more tightly. Cora enlaced her gnarled, arthritic fingers with Annie's, and the two women wept.

THIRTEEN

At a quarter past eight, Jennifer smelled coffee and slowly began to recall the last few hours before she'd closed her eyes. Not wanting to open them just yet, she inhaled deeply, reveling in the aroma of leather sofa and java. The sheriff had left around five, after the coroner had been gone just a few minutes. Annie left directly after that for her second twelve-hour shift of the week. Jennifer had collapsed in the trophy room on the first available horizontal space.

There was really no crime to investigate. The cause of death was obviously self-inflicted. Danny Robert related to everyone that melarsomine dihydrochloride was an anti-parasitic drug used in dogs to treat heartworms. An arsenic-based therapy, when given in high-doses, a lethal toxicity level would be easily achieved. He'd used it on more than one occasion with stray dogs that he'd incorporated into his pack.

Keys rattled in the front door, and Jennifer was obligated to rouse herself when she saw that it was Annie returning. "Did you get some sense and decide to come home?" Jennifer asked her as Annie dropped her purse and keys right inside the door.

"The nursing director made me," Annie said.

"Well, somebody's got some sense, then."

Annie put her hand on the small of her back and stretched. "Where's Davis? Cletus is coming out here at ten to talk about plots at the old Cumberland Presbyterian churchyard. I called him on the way back home."

"I don't know; I just woke up," Jennifer admitted. "What about that 7-Up Jesus guy? Aren't we supposed to go talk to him?"

"Well, that's what I'm wondering, if Davis wants to bother."

"Yes, I want to 'bother,'" Davis called from the loft. He leaned over the railing, revealing his location. He bounded down the stairs, putting on the best face he had.

"Well, that's strictly up to you. We can get two free spots at the church. Just got to pick which ones."

"I think Jacobs will give us permission, don't you?"

"I don't know, Davis; he's a weirdo, and he and Pawpaw didn't get along for a really long time. Why would he?"

"A dying man's wish?"

"I repeat, 'Why would he?'"

"It's worth a shot, and besides, who could turn down a chance to see a real, live 7-Up Jesus?"

"Me?" Jennifer interjected.

"Hush up, woman. Come in here and get you some coffee. I got to go load up the Polaris and we're goin' into town."

Jennifer harrumphed as best she could, but she would not seriously attempt to dissuade him. She stood and walked to the kitchen, only to catch Davis on his way out the back door. A woman with dark brown skin and eyes was mopping the kitchen floor. She appeared to be in her early forties, maybe younger. Her hair was pulled back in a ponytail at the nape of her neck, braided and fastened with a red-coated rubber band. Jennifer had not heard her arrive, but she smiled an acknowledgment at the good morning nod she received.

There was a thick, oversized coffee mug next to the pot, as well as a sugar bowl and a cream pitcher filled to the top. Jennifer smiled and filled her cup, doctoring it appropriately. She then padded in her bare feet across the floor and out the door to the patio. She sat down on a green wicker settee and watched across the yard as Davis placed a ramp onto the back of a white Ford pickup. The back window was tinted dark, and emblazoned across it were the words *Ain't Skeert.* He crawled underneath the tailgate—performing safety checks, she assumed—and then mounted a large, green, four-wheel all-terrain vehicle and started the engine.

Jennifer watched as he backed it out of the skinning shed and drove it into the bed of the pickup. Finding it somewhat nerve-wracking to watch, she rose, clutching her coffee cup and digging her toes into the patio. He finished, unscathed, and swung off the machine, hopping down from the back of the truck. Davis unlatched the ramp, folded it in half, and slid it underneath the four-wheeler for the planned dismount in town.

He came bounding down the hillside and up onto the patio, leaping over a day-lily bed that was just starting to sprout green shoots. "Get your purse, and let's go," he said.

"You sure do have some energy this morning," Jennifer said to him, and then took a slurping sip from her cup.

"Yeah, I think I got my second wind."

"I think you're sleep-deprived and hyper-alert."

"Probably. Let's go. I want to go get some steak and eggs at Mercy Station Market."

Jennifer pondered the thought of food. Her feet were starting to get cold on the blue and gray flagstone. She held first one foot up to her shin, and then the other, trying to warm them. Davis stared at her, awaiting her response. Finally she said, "Well, I need to go change clothes first. I suppose if I'm going to be found shot dead at the psychopath's house, I'd like to have on clean underwear before I go."

"Okay," he relented. "But, there's no need to shower, because by the time we ride up there and back, you'll be needing another one."

Jennifer shuddered from the cool damp air. "I have to get in the house!" she exclaimed, hurrying back to the door, walking stick in one hand and coffee cup in the other as she picked her way across the uneven terrain.

Once they were inside, the cleaning lady greeted the two again. "Morning, Master Davis," Honey called.

"Morning, Miss Honey," Davis replied.

"You all stayin' on for breakfast?" she inquired. Her eyes stayed lowered, even as Davis tried to make eye contact.

"No, ma'am. We are goin' into town. Can we bring you anything back?"

"Naw, suh, I done et already this mornin'."

"All right then," he said. "Has anyone introduced the two of you?" he asked, looking between the two women.

"Naw, suh," she said, again, not looking up from her business of wiping down the kitchen counter top.

"Well, I'd like to introduce to you my friend, Jennifer Martin."

"Dey calls me Honey," she said. Her voice was a melodic mixture of singsong Gullah with a faint South Carolina low country drawl. "Anything you need, doll baby, Honey git it for you."

"Miss Honey," Jennifer said, nodding. She started for the sink to deposit her cup.

"I take care of that, Miss Jennifer," she said, taking the cup with both of her dark, gnarled hands. "You and Davy go on and take care yo' b'ness in town."

"Thank you," she said, relinquishing the cup.

"And I'll be doin' the wash here in a little bit; so, if you have anything, just let me know," Honey advised.

Jennifer was dumfounded, but she smiled and nodded before making her way downstairs to change clothes. She turned the corner and hobbled past the Wurlitzer and the pool table. She could hear it before she could see it.

Lovey was growling. Interspersed between growls, Jennifer could hear ripping and tearing. She approached the couch from behind and peered over to find Lovey, standing on the coffee table, a pair of Jennifer's underwear, shredded and hanging from her jaws.

"Hey!" she shouted, and Lovey ducked her head in a playful stance. She held the underwear between her front paws and gave them another rip. Jennifer reached out to take them from her, and the growling commenced again, nub tail wagging. "What are you doing, you little fiend?" Jennifer made another advance for her clothing, and Lovey backed up this time, one step too far, and fell off the back of the coffee table.

Undaunted, the corpulent canine bolted around the back of the couch, booty in tow. Jennifer could hear the toenails as they clicked their way up the stairs.

"Davis!" she shouted in sheer frustration. She looked on the floor to discover three other pairs of underwear in equally disheartening disarray. She didn't have to look in her bag to see if there were more. She knew she'd only packed four. She sat on the couch in disbelief. Thirty seconds passed before Davis rounded the corner, all smiles.

"Nice," he said, holding up the mangled pair of pink lace panties. "I never knew," he said.

"Davis, that dog is the anti-Christ."

"Well, technically, I think the anti-Christ is supposed to come in the form of a man."

"I'm gonna knock you out," Jennifer said.

"Oh, why?" he continued to prod her. "Look, I think these are still okay. I mean, they don't have a crotch, but you can still wear them, don't you think?"

She looked up at his twinkling eyes and cracked a smile.

"You better go find that dog and hold it down. 'Cause if you don't let me beat the fool out of it, I'm gonna take it out on you." And she threatened him with her cane.

"Woman, you oughta have a license for that thing," and he grabbed it from her and hugged her tightly. "We'll add them to our list of things to get in town."

"Those were my nice ones," Jennifer said into his shoulder.

"I noticed. So, what'll it be? Status quo or commando?"

FOURTEEN

Cora had spent the first years of her marriage to Frank as a private baker. She'd been studying American literature at Mississippi College for Women, or just *the W*, as it was called, prior to her betrothal to Frank, but she gave that up after their marriage. A petite five feet high, she was a red-headed firecracker of a lady. Her masterpieces were multi-tiered wedding cakes, proliferated with butter cream frosting roses. Every young woman from Lanier County who aspired to the Junior League coveted a Sanford Sweets wedding cake. Cora had personally crafted no fewer than three for her son Bobby Jack.

But, after they'd cut the trees, she abandoned the mixing bowls to begin a second avocation in gardening. Her penchant for flowers soon gave her the epithet of "The Daffodil Lady" among the townsfolk, especially the members of the garden club. Her first project had started small, with a plot no more than ten feet square, planted in common, old-fashioned varieties. But, as the years passed, the bulbs doubled and tripled in number. Being deer-resistant, the flora thrived.

Her expertise increased, and Cora added exotic selections to the mix. And, as Davis and Annie grew, the houseplace flourished with the yellow and white harbingers of spring: Ice Follies, Tête-à-Tête, King Alfred, and Scarlet Gem varieties swept across the gentle swells and dips of the gray, sand-clay soil. Mount Hood, Peeping Tom, Barrett Browning, and Spellbinder specimens flanked the western hedgerow of forsythias. Carlton, Unsurpassable, Viking, and Cheerfulness decorated the ground beside an easterly sandstone wall that marked the edge of the official lawn.

As Davis and Jennifer loaded into Annie's truck and pulled onto the gravel drive in front of the Sanford family home, Jennifer caught her first glimpse of how Davis and Annie's grandmother earned her nickname. The yard was awash in gold, intermixed with pink and peach and white varieties of daffodils, buttercups, and narcissus. Most of the flowers' heads were bowed low with the remnants of the night's storms, but their beauty could not be denied. A strip of green grass ran along either side of the driveway that cut diagonally across the front lawn. Jennifer had never before seen anything like it. Davis rolled down the windows to the truck and hung his arm out to acknowledge Annie. She was standing on the front porch steps.

"Cletus'll be here before y'all get back. I'll talk with him and pick us out something," Annie said to them through the open window. "That way we're okay, however it turns out."

Davis agreed, and waved as he pulled away and down the drive. "Shut the gate on your way out!" she called, and began walking back to the Dog Pound to let the dogs out for the day.

Jennifer held a half-liter Dr Pepper as they bounced down the drive. Davis stopped outside the perimeter fence just long enough to shut the gate, and then they continued the short drive into town. She might have applied some lipstick or powder, but she had none; so, she just stared out the window at the beauty of the pine forest.

"Nice to have rain," Davis said. "Otherwise, by this time of year, everything is covered in pollen."

"Helps to keep the sinuses in check," Jennifer agreed.

"Well, unless you're allergic to mold," Davis said.

Trees were budding out everywhere, and their yellow-green hue against the cloudless blue sky of March was breathtaking to behold.

"I think they're ahead of us here," Jennifer said, noticing the naturalized daffodils along the roadbed.

"Maybe, by a week or so," he agreed. "Don't rush us along too far, though, 'cause I can do without the heat for a few more weeks."

"Hear, hear," Jennifer said and raised her bottle in salute to the idea.

Inside the city limits of Mercy there was one main intersection. Over the years it had been a four-way stop, a two-way stop, a four-way yield, and a traffic light. As Davis approached with Jennifer, he cruised through the flashing yellow light and up the hill toward Main Street.

Main held the business district of Mercy. A bank stood on the northwest corner, and a barbershop was on the southeast end. In between dilapidated storefronts languished, some in use, and others vacant. The truck eased down the main drag that provided parking spaces along the middle, and Davis waved the one-finger wave so often seen in the country, as he allowed the elderly and those with children to cross in front.

Two men in overalls stood in front of a parked pickup truck, going over a schematic that they had spread on the hood of the vehicle. One spat and looked on while the other one pointed and gesticulated at the drawings. It was Friday morning, spring break, and teens in tight tee shirts and workout pants stood outside a recently renovated fitness center. Three young girls, too tan and too thin, strolled out of the tanning parlor in their tank tops, short-shorts and flip-flops, making their way toward the males of the species a few storefronts down.

Jennifer remembered the days of "almost summer" when she and Davis were fourteen: too young to be in love, but she didn't know it at the time. It was the last "almost summer" that she had lived in Bedford—before her parents moved them to the country. Heady Saturdays were spent in town, circling the square with friends who could drive, eating soft-serve from the Velvet Cream, and feeling invincible.

"This place has all the makings of a John Cougar song," Jennifer remarked as they continued their slow roll to the end of the strip.

"Wynonna song, honey," Davis said, pulling into a parking spot and putting the truck in park. "And here we are: Mercy Station Market."

A ramshackle building stood alone at the end of the strip, right next to where the railroad tracks had crossed the road. In fact, the steel beams were still imbedded in the asphalt, but on either side, nothing more than a bed of white rocks and Bermuda grass extended outward.

Above the disheveled front porch was a white Coca-Cola sign with the words "Mercy Station Market—Mercy's only self-proclaimed four-star restaurant" stenciled in red. There were antique, rusted Texaco gas pumps in front and slightly to the right of the building, encircled by Johnson grass and thistle. One side of the edifice had been recently veneered with fence-grade cedar planking, while the other side was sheathed in pressed tin ceiling tiles, painted white many years ago.

"We're gonna eat here?" Jennifer asked.

"Well, I am. You don't have to. But I bet you can't help yourself." He let himself out of the truck and circled to assist her from the jacked-up four-by-four.

They entered the dining hall and took in the Americana. Locals occupied four or five of the tables. On the right side of the room ran a long counter top, and behind it stood hardware store shelving with wooden drawers, not unlike an ancient card catalog. At one end of the counter perched a three-foot tall cash register dating from the 1920's. Push the buttons, crank the handle, and return to the days of the old-time candy store. It wasn't restored; it didn't shine, but it did appear that it was still functioning, as a young man rang up a ticket for a customer on his way out the door.

At the far end of the room stood a refrigerated meat display case. Different cuts of beef were in neat stacks, butcher paper in between each piece, and small plastic flags proclaimed each steak *USDA Choice.*

Jennifer looked around at the red-checked tablecloths on the square tables that studded the room. Two large, square posts held up a twenty-foot ceiling that was adorned with pressed tin tiles. And then there was the taxidermy: elk, bobcat, rabbit, fox, raccoon, opossum, and a plethora of deer—all old, and all miserably in need of retirement.

Davis walked over to a cooler, pulled out an orange cream soda, and held it up for Jennifer to inspect. "You want one?" he asked.

"Sure," she replied, and he reached in for another.

He popped off the bottle caps with an old Coca-Cola bottle opener that was screwed onto one of the two support posts in the room, and then seated himself at a nearby table. Jennifer did the same, still gazing at the ambiance.

"Y'all know what you want?" a waitress called from behind the counter across the room.

Davis responded: "New York strip, medium rare, two eggs over light, and toast."

"White or wheat?"

"White."

And the lady?

"Can I just get a biscuit?" Jennifer asked hesitantly, and then she saw the pie rack. "No, can I get a piece of chocolate pie?"

"You want regular or fried?"

Jennifer had not heard of fried chocolate pie before; so she looked to Davis for instruction. He shook his head negatively. "Regular," he said to the server.

"All right. Be up in a little bit," she replied. And then she bellowed down the countertop, "Billy! Warm me up a Big Apple and pass two eggs over the coals."

"Fried chocolate pie?" Jennifer asked, taking a pull from the cold brown bottle.

"Yeah, you'd think it'd be good. Fried pie, chocolate pie—but it just doesn't work very well. Turns out kinda, I don't know, gummy and—wet."

"I'll take your word for it," she said, screwing up her face at the idea.

Davis drank from his bottle, leaning on his left forearm and his right elbow. He swung the bottle as a pendulum, back and forth between his thumb and middle finger. He stared at the graffiti carved in the post. Jennifer fingered the dusty silk daisy that adorned the RC Cola bottle centerpiece.

"Man, what a night," Davis finally said.

Jennifer inhaled and exhaled and studied the silk flower some more. "Yeah, it wasn't what I was expecting."

"Who was?" he said, and drank again. "I'm sorry if I came off like a blithering idiot," he began.

"Honey, give me a break! You just witnessed the deaths of two family members in less than six hours."

"I know, but," and he trailed off. "You just imagine that you can handle yourself a little bit better in situations like that."

"Davis, anybody who imagines situations like *that* needs to be medicated."

The waitress brought out Jennifer's pie. "You want whipped cream?" she asked. She wielded a can of Reddi-Wip.

Jennifer passed with a wave.

"Yours'll be out in a minute," she called over her shoulder to Davis, who smiled and nodded in reply.

They were silent for a moment, and then Davis confessed, "She told me she was going to do it, Jen."

"What?"

"Mom. She all but told me she was going to do it. I thought she was just talking out of her head, spouting off about books like she always does—*Ethan Frome*."

"I heard her say that last night, but didn't know what it meant."

"You don't know *Ethan Frome*?" he said, looking up. "You mean to tell me I've read a book that the illustrious Jennifer Martin has *not*?" Davis said, drolly.

"I hate to admit it, but perhaps you have," she said with a smirk. "Give me the Cliff's Notes version."

"Let's see. Old coot marries his cousin out of guilt, but falls in love with another cousin later. Or was she his cousin? I can't remember exactly how it goes."

"Whatever, okay. Jerry Lee gets married, and then what happens?"

"Um, marries a hypochondriac, but falls in love with the nursemaid. They decide to kill themselves in a horrible sledding accident or something like that. But they don't; they just both get maimed, and then the old biddy wife has to take care of the both of them for the rest of their lives."

"Nice! And your grandmother was planning to do this?"

"I think her mind was starting to slip when it came to small details."

They sat there, saying nothing, staring at the pie.

"Eat that, before I do," Davis said.

"But your food—"

"Will be out in a minute."

Jennifer conceded and took a bite. They had warmed it just enough. "Hmmmmm," she said, inhaling as she chewed.

"But, I reckon she wasn't slipping so much that she couldn't overdose herself on parasite medication," Davis said.

"Who in the world keeps that much heartworm treatment around the house?"

"Who in the world keeps twenty-seven dogs and has a veterinarian on retainer?" he countered.

"Right." Jennifer thought as she chewed her pie. "For the dogs and yourself?" she said through a bite, hand held to her mouth.

"Right," Davis agreed, then continued, "Who in the world, as their dying wish, tells his wife to go kill herself?" Davis said.

"I was thinking it, but I wasn't saying it." She cut another bite of pie and offered it to him across the table.

The conversation was interrupted as the waitress presented a plate of meat and eggs, topped with four slices of white toast. "Steak sauce?" she asked. Davis quickly took the bite of pie and then answered.

"I'm good," he replied. He attacked the plate ravenously, not bothering with fork-and-knife-swapping etiquette. He slashed three times across the top of the eggs, making a sort of soup run across the plate.

They said nothing as Davis made short work of the sop-and-mop special he'd ordered. He finished off his drink, looked at Jennifer, smiled, and belched. He hit his chest with his fist. "Ugh," he said.

"Nice."

"You're welcome," he said, scraping his chair back across the wooden floor. "Let's get this 'come to Jesus' meeting over with."

He sidled up to the counter and pulled out his wallet. He dug out a hundred dollar bill to pay. Pulling a toothpick from the dispenser by the cash register, he caught a sideways glimpse of Jennifer's stare.

"Danny Robert," he said. "Said it was combat pay."

"Combat that you've seen? Or that you've yet to experience?"

He shrugged his shoulders while the cashier counted out his change. "Probably both," and he rolled the toothpick back and forth between his teeth.

Davis held the door for Jennifer and then followed her. They sauntered across the street to Annie's truck. He worked on getting the four-wheeler ready, while Jennifer attempted to remain calm as he backed the machine down the ramp at nearly a 45-degree angle. Once it was safely on the street, Davis helped Jennifer get on board, and then he, too, climbed on.

"Hold on tight," he said, and revved the engine.

"Go slow," she implored, arms around his waist, cane clutched in her right hand.

"I will." And he eased across the street and headed down the railroad bed to Hank Jacobs's.

FIFTEEN

About two hundred yards down the old railroad bed, Davis turned south off the tracks and cut up through an old logging road. Pines towered above them on both sides. The ground was carpeted in rusted pine needles as far as Jennifer could see. The road was rutted, but appeared to be still in use. The four-wheeler mired down in the water-saturated earth, spewing black smoke from the exhaust.

"This is doing worlds of good for my sinuses," Jennifer announced in his ear.

"Oh, you will be amazed at what you blow out of your nose tonight, young lady," he said over the roar of the engine. He shifted into four-wheel low and pulled out of the quagmire.

They continued up the hill, veering southeast as they went. Then the first of them appeared. Staked into the ground, crude and rustic, it was not much more than two tomato stakes nailed together in the shape of a cross. It had been painted white, and scrawled on it in black were the words "Hell is HOT, HOT, HOT."

"We're getting warmer," Davis said with a singsong lilt.

The road narrowed as they drove. "Is this the way the UPS guy gets in here?" Jennifer questioned, holding on more tightly as the all-terrain vehicle made short work of the steep hill.

"I reckon," replied Davis, and then pointed ahead to what appeared to be a parking area. A crude sign read: *All Vehicles Must Stop Here.* In close proximity stood another sign emblazoned with the words *Stop, Drop, and Roll Will Not Work in Hell.*

"This is new," he said, and pulled the four-wheeler over. "We can walk the—" he broke off his sentence, and restarted the engine.

"What am I thinking? Go ahead. Beat me with the cane," and he backed the vehicle out again.

"It says to leave the four-wheeler here."

"Yeah, well, you can't walk up there, so he'll understand."

"Charles Manson, I mean, Hank Jacobs will understand?"

"Trust me."

The farther they went along Jacobs's drive, the more prolific the crosses became. Some were white, some were unpainted wood, but most of them had an inscription of some kind scrawled in crude and shaky block letters. One cross, fashioned from two pieces of plywood, read: *You Will Die! Hell Is Hot! Jesus Is The Answer!*

"Davis," Jennifer said over the buzz of the engine, "This man is not right."

And the crosses grew thicker and taller. There were crosses that held up crosses. Metal crosses, crosses nailed to the trunks of the ever-present pine trees, crosses stuck in the ground, lying on the ground, hanging from fence posts. Twenty-foot tall crosses made from two Loblolly trunks lashed together.

They reached the top of the hill and found the crowning glory of the display: a singlewide house trailer with a screened-in deck on the front perched atop the ridge. A carport of sorts had been constructed over the trailer itself, and it ran the length of the abode. A picket fence in sore need of paint surrounded the estate. Dripping with crosses, it added the finishing touch to the ramshackle appearance.

"Who needs clean underwear before seeing this?" Davis asked Jennifer as he killed the engine. A six-by-six whitewashed sheet of plywood stood in front of the trailer, nailed to two four-by-four posts. The words upon it read, *For Sale by Owner—$10 Million—The Lord Set the Asking Price.*

"Huh!" Davis remarked after reading the sign. "It was only five hundred thousand when Pawpaw tried to buy it off him."

"You know, it's not too late for us to go back," Jennifer said, hoping he would change his mind. A squeak and a bang announced that someone had opened a screened door from the trailer to the darkened screened porch. Jennifer and Davis both looked up.

"Who's out there?" Hank Jacobs called. He chambered a shell in his shotgun, and Davis and Jennifer both bristled.

"Davis Sanford!" Davis called. "It's me, Hank, little Davy Sanford!"

Jennifer smirked at the moniker by which Davis announced himself. Davis elbowed her in reply.

There was silence, and then the two interlopers could see a figure move inside the porch. His silhouette came to the outer door, and he swung it open to see out.

"Dave?" he said, squinting, shading his eyes with one hand and holding the shotgun with the other.

"None other, Mr. Jacobs. None other."

"Well, I didn't know who that was comin' up here on that dang four-wheeler." He exited the house, and Jennifer got her first glimpse of him, standing there in cut-off Mossy Oak pants and nothing more. He was barefoot, bare-chested, and hairy all over, almost all of it white with age.

Davis walked toward the porch, hand extended. "Haven't seen you in a while," he began. "You've gone off and gotten a little gray."

Jacobs extended his hand and smiled. "It can turn gray as long as it don't turn loose, I reckon. Who you got with you? Annie?" He squinted.

Davis self-consciously smoothed back his thinning locks. "No sir. This is Jennifer. Mr. Jacobs, I'd like to introduce to you my friend, Jennifer."

"How'do," Hank Jacobs said, nodding and already walking back toward the porch. "Come on in, y'all. Mosquitoes are bad," and he ducked back into the shelter. Jennifer looked around for the 7-Up Jesus, but saw nothing.

"What brings you home, youngin'?" he called out before Davis and Jennifer could enter. He was already sitting down on an old, overstuffed, upholstered sofa, the shotgun draped across his lap. Two other straight-back chairs flanked the doorway to the trailer. The floor was covered in green indoor-outdoor carpeting that was riddled with cigarette burns beside each of the chairs.

"Well, it was Pawpaw."

"I heard from that niggra UPS boy the other day that he wasn't too well off."

"Well, it's true. He passed last night."

"Couldn'ta happened to a finer individual," Jacobs mused.

"Is it Biblical to speak ill of the dead?" Davis questioned.

Jacobs was quiet for a moment, and then said, "I reckon not, but it's Biblical to speak the truth. What got him? Pride or envy?"

Jennifer said nothing but looked around at the hovel, old and rickety, but clean and neat, nonetheless. She was still keeping an eye peeled for the portrait of Jesus.

"A number of things, they tell me. His heart I suppose or maybe his kidneys. He was diabetic you know, and he had a bad heart. I think his kidneys were shutting down. Anyway, they sent him home yesterday from the hospital. Said they couldn't do more for him. And he passed last night around eight o'clock."

The three shared a moment of silence, and Jacobs said quietly, "The government."

There was more silence, and then Davis asked, "The government?"

"Sure, the government. They're gonna eventually get all the draft dodgers, you know."

"What do you mean, Hank?"

"Your Pawpaw, as you and Annie liked to call him. You was too young to tell you then, but might as well let the cat out of the bag, now."

"Pawpaw didn't dodge the draft. He couldn't serve. He had bleeding stomach ulcers, and he ruptured his spleen playing football his freshman year at Alabama. And, he was diagnosed as diabetic in college."

"Hell, Davis, he was 'bout as 4-F then as I am now."

Jennifer raised her eyebrows, but said nothing. Hank continued. "He bought that 4-F status off of Chuggie Wadsworth."

"Who?"

"A cousin of your grandfather, an old country doctor—from Chunky. He wasn't but about a hundred miles from Tuscaloosa. A lot of the fellas done it. He just diagnosed them into never having to serve a minute of compulsory military duty. That's where that diabetes crap come from."

"I see," Davis said. "You learn something new all the time, I reckon." He tried not to sound too patronizing, but his disbelief was hard to mask.

"You wanna blow one?" Jacobs asked. He reached across the shotgun to the army footlocker that was doubling as a cocktail table. On top of the locker was an oriental box, inlaid with metal and enamel filigree. As he opened it, Jennifer noticed that Jacobs was missing all but a portion of his pinky and his thumb from his right hand. He pulled out a plastic bag and a book of cigarette papers.

"I'm trying to cut back," Davis said, holding up his hand and shaking his head.

"I've been thinking about it," he said, and he hovered there a moment with the two visitors watching. "I reckon today's as good a day as any," he mused, and dropped the paraphernalia back into the box.

"That's a pretty box," Jennifer commented.

"Thanks," Hank said, leaning back in his seat again. "Korea, 1959. Bought it off a hooker for my mama while I was on duty there."

"Really?" Jennifer said. "Well, it *is* beautiful." She decided not to try any more conversation.

"Davis, I hope your granny hasn't ended up as collateral damage in all this."

Davis and Jennifer looked at each other and then at him. Jacobs saw the exchange and queried, "Has she been showing signs of it, too?"

"Signs of what?"

"Poisoning. That's how the government's gettin' 'em all."

"Well, no, she's been in fine health up until now," Davis said.

"That's a relief," Hank continued. "I guess she's been drinking bottled water, and ol' Frank was drinking from the well. You know, I quit drinking well water in 1993, the first year they discovered the arsenic."

Jennifer refused to look at Davis at this point. "N-now, when was this?" Davis asked.

"Oh, you remember. In 1993, they sent in crews of people to dig wells, and they tapped into some ground water with arsenic in it, and it's been killing the babies and the unborn, and the weak and the frail for years now. That's why I drink bottled water now."

"Where was this?" Davis asked, trying to get Jacobs to reconcile with reality.

"Bangladesh," Jennifer said, quietly. "UNICEF. A big scandal about it in 1993."

"Well, I don't know nothin' about Bangladesh," Hank said, "but it's been goin' on right here in Lanier County here for a decade or more."

He continued, "And it don't just kill you outright. It's a slow and painful death. First your kidneys start to fail, and then you get psoriasis of the liver, and then you get cancer—cancer of the worst kinds: prostate cancer, melanoma, brain cancer, stomach cancer. And then you get the leprosy, you know, lesions all over your body, on your palms and your feet."

Hank touched each part of his body as he mentioned the maladies. "And then the gangrene sets in, and they have to cut off your legs and arms. And then your blood pressure goes sky high, and you get hardening of the arteries.

"And eventually you get so sick you can't do nothing but puke and shit, and then you die."

Jennifer had never been good at hiding what she was thinking; so, she stood up and turned to look out upon the garden of crosses in Hank Jacobs's yard. She could not let her host see her face, especially since the shotgun still had a shell in the barrel. Davis sat forward in his straight-back chair, his elbows on his knees, hands clasped together.

"Wow," he said softly. He nodded his head and rocked back and forth for a few seconds. He let there be silence for a moment, and then he reached into his back pocket and pulled out the paperwork from the county.

He cleared his throat. "Well, um, Herschel Peters gave us this paperwork, and I came by to talk to you about it," Davis said.

"Peters, eh? What's he, mayor now?"

"I reckon he wants to be, but he's still a supervisor."

"I ain't got my glasses on. What's it say?" Jacobs asked, leaning over to inquire.

Davis moved to sit next to Hank on the couch and offered to take the shotgun. Jacobs relinquished it, and Davis propped it in a far corner before sitting down beside the old man.

"Well, in Lanier County, you have to have approval of any private land-owners whose property touches your land if you want to establish a family cemetery."

"Family cemetery, eh?"

"Yes sir."

"I see."

"Yes sir, and, well, Hank, I haven't told you all of it yet," Davis said, and he pulled the paper back toward himself and sat up to look at the old veteran.

"What is it, Dave?" Hank asked him. He examined the young man's face and said, "There's a heavy sadness, a burden that you're carrying, son. What is it?"

Jennifer turned to watch the exchange.

"Well, it's Mom."

"Wait, your mom, or Mom-mom?"

"Mom. Uh, Cora, Mom."

"Okay. I thought you just said she hadn't been affected by the poisoning. Is it something else?"

"Well, Hank, Mom took her own life last night shortly after Pawpaw passed."

"Oh, that poor, dear woman." Hank was noticeably grieved. "Should we say a prayer?"

"I've been prayin' most of the day, Hank." But Hank's head was bowed, and his lips moving, speaking indiscernibly. Jennifer and Davis bowed their heads as well until he finished.

"So, tell me, Dave. Tell me about the family cemetery."

"Well, it just says here," and he pushed the paperwork back out onto the footlocker, "that if you'll sign here, acknowledging that it's okay for us to bury them in the yard over by the house, then the county'll let us do it."

"And are you gonna be buried there?" Hank asked.

"Well, I hope not any time soon."

"Well, now, that's not what I meant."

"Right, well, I hadn't thought much on that."

"And, what about your girl here? I reckon y'all'll get married. I can sense these things, you know." Davis smiled at Hank's suggestion. Jennifer turned to face the front yard again.

"Now, is she gonna want to be planted out in the woods where Weyerhaeuser's gonna be stompin' as soon as Bobby Jack can sell out?"

Davis cut his eyes toward Hank and said lowly, out of the corner of his mouth, "Well, we really hadn't gotten that far along in the negotiations, there, Hank."

"Oh, yeah, I gotcha," Hank said, and he made a zipper motion across his lips. "Well, I don't see why not. I just got to sign here?" he asked, pointing to the line with the stub of his pinky.

"Well, we got to sign it in front of a notary down in town. Is that all right with you? I can take you right now."

"In town?"

"Yeah, just down at the Rexall, right there on the corner, I figured. Mr. Bowdrie's a notary."

"I don't know about that, Dave. Not today. I ain't' showered." Jacobs scratched his hairy chest thoughtfully.

"Well, how can we do this then? Could I bring somebody up here to you this afternoon? Or tomorrow?"

"I reckon, but not before Monday, cause I don't do no work on the Sabbath."

"So, um, is that Saturday or Sunday?" Davis asked, not wanting to rock the boat.

"Well, since we can't technically be sure, I just make sure I don't do no work, except the Lord's work, on Saturday *or* Sunday. But Monday will be fine. I can sign my name then."

"And not this afternoon?"

"No, I don't think so. I ain't showered," the old man said again, staring out at the yard.

Davis was reluctant to give in, but said, "All right, then. I'll be back Monday if that's okay, and we'll get this done." He stood and extended his right hand to shake Hank Jacobs's. He reciprocated, standing, saying, "Well, Davy. You've grown into a fine young man. I don't care what your daddy says about you."

"Thanks," Davis said, and reached out to pat the old man on the shoulder. "We'll be seeing you Monday."

"Bring that pretty thing with you," he said, nodding to Jennifer. She ducked an awkward curtsey and smiled. The two descended the steps and picked their way across the muddy, dirt yard to the four-wheeler. Davis helped her on board, and he, too, began to mount, when Hank called out.

"Wait!" He opened the screened door and descended the steps toward them. He had the shotgun tucked under his right arm the oriental box in his left hand. He was looking straight at Jennifer.

"You liked this. And my mama was dead when I got back from Korea. You can have it." And he thrust it toward her. Jennifer looked up in amazement. She couldn't find any words to say.

"Don't say nothing," he said. "It's not that big of a deal. Just been sitting around here gathering dust." He turned to walk away, but then came back to open the lid. "I forgot about this. I wanna keep it." And he took his baggie and papers and walked back to the house, his bare feet making muddy indentations in the yard.

Jennifer looked down at the beautiful box she held and ran her finger along the design. Once Hank was out of earshot, Davis said under his breath, "Unless something's changed that I don't know about, his mama's still living in Tupelo with his brother, Harvey." He started the four-wheeler, eased off the clutch, and pointed the vehicle down the hill and back toward town.

SIXTEEN

Down the hill, along the naked railroad bed, and back into town, the pair negotiated the path they'd taken into the Jacobs estate. Jennifer put Hank Jacobs's box on the front seat of the truck, while Davis loaded the ATV. After wiping his hands on the seat of his pants, he extended one to Jennifer. "Let's go buy you some drawers and face paint, woman."

"Where?" Jennifer asked. She hadn't seen any place that appeared to sell those wares: a florist, a funeral home, and a gift shop, yes, but not a Wal-Mart.

"Over to the Rexall Drugs," and he pointed to the orange and blue sign, circa 1945. She agreed, and they crossed the street to do some shopping.

There were three steps up from the street, thin, high, and ill-suited for the handicapped. Davis helped Jennifer up. The sidewalk that led to the door was cracked and uneven before it gave way to black-and-white tile mosaic flooring within the entryway to the pharmacy. The door was flanked on either side by plate glass display windows at a forty-five-degree angle from the door, forming an alcove beneath which a patron could stand and adjust a rain bonnet if the subtropical clime had brought on an afternoon thundershower.

The Rexall had a black, fourteen-foot high wooden door featuring small, individual-paned windows in a grid pattern. It was heavy and thick. The hardware attached to it had been painted over multiple times, and it no longer functioned properly. Davis yanked it open, and the tinkling of a brass bell at the top of the door announced their arrival.

"Can you think of anything else you have that Lovey might want to chew up?" Davis asked. "We can get that now, too."

"Smartass," Jennifer declared.

"Toothbrush?"

"Stop it."

"Panty hose?"

"It'll take more than a funeral to get me in panty hose," Jennifer said.

"Got any embarrassing prescriptions she might want to eat? We can go ahead and call in a refill." Davis walked to the cosmetics aisle and began looking for the most atrocious color he could find. "This is you, honey," he said, holding up a bottle of yellow glitter nail polish.

Jennifer ignored him and started searching for her brand and shade of foundation. She quickly gathered up lipstick and eye shadow, liner and mascara.

"Can I get you a basket, ma'am?" the pharmacist called from behind the counter.

Jennifer looked around for the person who was speaking to her.

"Yoo-hoo, up here," he called. He was an older gentleman, perhaps in his late sixties, balding, with black plastic framed glasses. He wore a white jacket with *pharmacist* embroidered on the chest.

"Mr. Bowdrie," Davis called out and waved.

Mr. Bowdrie peered over his glasses at the man hailing him. Davis knew he would not recognize him.

"Davis Sanford," he called out and came down from behind his post. A couple of patrons who had been busily shopping for baby formula two aisles over looked up to catch a glimpse of the prodigal Sanford.

"Davis Sanford? I haven't seen you, in, well, ages!" Mr. Bowdrie replied. He came down and around to the front of the prescription counter, walked toward the couple, and said as he approached, "The Lord made only a few perfect heads, you know. The rest, he had to put hair on." He extended his hand, adding, "How in the world are you, son?"

Davis smiled and chuckled, shaking the man's hand. "Good, good," he replied, "considering."

"Yes, son, I am so sorry to hear about the passing of your grandparents," the pharmacist said more soberly. "What a pity. Such fine individuals they were."

Davis nodded his head as Mr. Bowdrie continued to shake his hand.

"I guess Miss Cora just had a broken heart," the family pharmacist said.

Davis nodded again, and then turned to Jennifer. "Mr. Bowdrie, this is my friend, Jennifer Martin. She came with me from Bedford when we heard the news."

"Well, it's fine to meet you Miss Martin. Sorry about the circumstances, but a pleasure, nonetheless."

Jennifer smiled and nodded. "Nice to meet you," she said, attempting to shake his hand, but finding hers full of cosmetics.

"Oh, let me get you a basket for those. Are you still shopping?"

"Yes," Davis replied. "Danny Robert's dog got into her luggage last night and made short work of most of her personal stuff."

"Oh dear," Mr. Bowdrie said. "Well, I'll hold these things up here, and y'all get what you need, and I'll ring you up."

Jennifer located the rest of what she required and rejoined the men at the counter. As she approached, she heard Mr. Bowdrie say, "Well, it is a shame that it had to happen that way. And I'll tell you, Davy, the whole town is in a stir about it."

"I'd kind of hoped for a little time before the word got out," Davis confided.

Mr. Bowdrie said, "Well, when Cletus makes two trips to your house in one day, and Sheriff Artiss makes one, there's not much secrecy gonna be found in a town this size. How does the saying go? The only way for two people to keep a secret is for one of 'em to die?"

"Something like that."

Mr. Bowdrie began to ring up the wares. He totaled them, pulled the cash register tape from the machine, and turned to a small card file at the left of the window. He flipped toward the back of the file, pulled out a card, and stapled the receipt to the ticket. "Danny Robert'll cover it when he comes in," he said, and smiled down at the couple.

The two agreed, and turned to go. When they were halfway out of the store, Mr. Bowdrie called out. "And how's Miss Annie?" Again, the other patrons keyed in on the conversation that was now projecting across the room.

"She's good," Davis said, hoping to avoid much more public discussion.

"And Marcus?" Mr. Bowdrie asked. "Is he home?"

Davis walked back toward the counter, to try to keep the conversation a little more confidential. "Uh, he hasn't been there in a couple of days," he admitted.

"What a shame," Mr. Bowdrie said, shaking his head. "A fool shame, I tell you, with that baby on the way, and a little girl at that! How can a father deny a baby girl?" Mr. Bowdrie shook his head. "I've got three, you know."

"So it's a girl?" Davis asked.

"That's what Annie told me last week when she came in to get her pre-natal refill," Mr. Bowdrie said. "I suppose she felt she needed to confide in someone."

"True," Davis said.

"You know, I try to be more than just a pharmacist to these young folks. Offer my advice where I can; an ear, a shoulder."

"Mmm-hmm," Davis said. "Well, we've got to hurry back to the house. Cletus is coming over to talk about the arrangements."

"Oh, sure. Now y'all run along, and, try to keep those things up from the dog, you hear?" he called out, as they retreated again.

SEVENTEEN

Twenty-seven canines greeted Davis and Jennifer upon their return to the Sanford home. The baying and barking destroyed any chance that Annie might be sleeping. After parking Annie's truck in front of the house, they found their way inside, and Davis hung the keys on the rack by the front door. Honey was dusting the ledges of picture frames when they came in, and she said, "Miss Annie's in the kitchen, making flower arrangements."

"Thanks," Jennifer said, as they headed that way.

In the kitchen, Annie stood at the island sink, filling a vase with water. Jennifer and Davis entered and saw her there, surrounded by a sea of gold. The island was covered in cut daffodils. There were three basketsful sitting on the side counter as well.

"Howdy," she called, looking up from the vase. She turned off the water and set the vase on the counter, then reached for a dishtowel and dried her hands. "So, how'd it go?"

"Oh, he wouldn't come into town to sign in front of the notary; so, we have to go back up there Monday with one. But, he promised he would."

"Monday?"

"Yep," Davis said, stepping over the bathroom scales to reach into the refrigerator.

"Hand me those," Annie said, and he complied. "Nobody here wants to know what they weigh anymore. Especially not me." And she took the scales to the utility room. Coming back in, she said, "I was talking to Cletus, and he said we could do the service Sunday at two. We won't have enough time to wait."

"You think? Do we have to have the county's approval to dig the holes?" Davis opened the refrigerator, and a pink plastic pig that sat on the top shelf oinked at him until he closed the door after inventorying of its contents.

"I don't know." Annie wiped her face with the palm of her hand, smoothing back her ebony bangs. She leaned back on the countertop and sighed.

"Where's your daddy?" Davis asked.

"Out at the skinnin' shed, working on some equipment. Something Marcus broke, he said."

"Well, he should be talking about this, too. And my father, too, for that matter."

"Daddy told me to pick out everything with Cletus; so, I did the best I could. Your daddy and his girlfriend were supposed to be goin' to Gulf Shores this week, it bein' spring break, but I reckon they're just holed up at his place instead. You know—considering." She started sorting through a basket of daffodils, picking out a half dozen before she looked up.

Davis reached for a glass from the cabinet and filled it at the sink. "What's up with the girlfriend?" he asked. He stared out across the breakfast room and through the plate glass window. He could see Danny Robert moving around outside.

"Oh, let's see," Annie said, as she arranged the flowers. "Nineteen, Vietnamese. Um, tri-lingual. A real hotty. Catholic—that's a downer."

"Guys and dolls," Jennifer interrupted. "I hate to leave the party, but when it's past noon and I haven't showered, it starts to become a problem."

"Okay, sweetheart," Davis said, distractedly. "Use Annie's bathroom."

"Okay, and after that, I've got to get online and work. I'm sure I've got stuff from Charlotte that I need to get done."

"Okay, I'll set your stuff up in the office while you shower." He walked to where she stood, kissed her on the forehead, and walked back to stare out the window as she departed. He started to drink from his glass, thought better of it, walked back to the sink and poured it down the drain.

"Is there any Sprite around here?"

"In the cooler out yonder," Annie said, motioning to where Danny Robert was working.

Davis set his glass on the counter and headed out the back door. He crossed the sloping yard and was immediately surrounded by dogs as he mounted the hill where the skinning shed stood.

"Annie says there's some Sprite in here?" he called out.

Danny Robert jumped when he heard Davis's voice. "Son! I wasn't expecting to hear anybody out here," he proclaimed, shaking his head, and wielding a torque wrench.

"What're you working on?" Davis asked, reaching for the door to the walk-in freezer.

"That's the freezer. Yonder's the cooler," Danny Robert pointed an elbow in the general vicinity that Davis should look. "Oh, it's a meat grinder. Supposed to be able to process twenty pounds a minute, when it's workin'."

Davis stopped short of the freezer door and changed directions as instructed. "And you're working on it with a torque wrench?"

"Well, naw. I've never been too mechanically inclined, you know. I was just about to beat it with this." He looked at what he held. "This is a torque wrench, huh?"

Davis laughed. "Can't it wait?" Davis asked, walking into the cooler and searching for a drink. He found cases of sodas stacked in one corner and broke open a pack to retrieve just one. A liver-and-white, shorthaired pointer that had followed him into the cooler methodically licked the floor.

The dog was slick and fat from the waffles and the years. Her whole head was white, and her nose was pink, except for an asymmetrical liver-colored spot. Her eyes were rimmed in pink as well. Davis caught her by the scruff of the neck and dragged her out as he came.

"Heel, Pinky," Danny Robert commanded offhandedly, and the dog obeyed. The remainder of the pack had their noses down to the skinning shed's floor. "Shut that, or they'll all be in there," Danny Robert advised.

Davis closed the cooler door, and Danny Robert continued, "Well, see, that's the thing. It's been sitting here broke for almost a week, and it ain't even been cleaned. Oh, hell, Davis," he said, throwing up his hands. "I'm just mostly lookin' for something to do with myself. Turkey season started yesterday, and Dad's gone, Marcus's not here, and I've got people all over this place trying to hunt and nobody corralling them. I already had to call and cancel one trophy hunt that was scheduled for yesterday. Got nobody to put 'em on a bird."

"Well, you don't need a meat grinder for turkey season; so, just put that aside and think about what else you can do."

"I reckon," he said, staring around at the place. "I reckon."

"Call the university. See if there's somebody at the extension center who can help you." He popped open the can.

"I thought about that, but it's spring break, so nobody's there."

"Well, next week, then. I'm sure there's somebody who'd be willing to get paid to come out here and help. Besides," Davis added, "there's no guarantee that Marcus won't show up again, once he hears the news."

"Sum-bitch better not," Danny Robert said, and he took a swing at the meat grinder with the torque wrench. He made contact, knocking the two-foot tall stainless steel box to the edge of the worktable. It teetered before Davis leapt forward to stop it from crashing to the concrete floor, sloshing soda onto the work surface. Danny Robert dropped his weapon with a clatter and stalked back into the house. "He better not," he reiterated in a mumble.

Davis awkwardly set the drink he was still clutching on the tabletop, and placing his shoulder against the brushed, silver casing, shoved the grinder back onto the work surface. Davis was *not* mechanically disinclined, and he looked at the contraption for a moment. There were no outside moving parts on it. He would have to open it in order to see what was wrong. And, it was indeed quite dirty; whoever had used it last had not even given it a cursory rinsing. Pinky reared up onto the table and began licking the remains from the last butchering.

"Go on," Davis said. He shoved her white and pink paws off the edge of the table, and she did not protest. Davis picked up his drink, wiped it dry on the tail of his shirt, and then took a sip from the can. He looked over the outside of the grinder once more and noted what tools he'd need to get inside it before he returned to the house. He wanted to set up Jennifer's computer before she got out of the shower. The pack followed him to the back door, waited for him to go inside, and then scattered for canine interests.

Annie was placing a vase of daffodils on the kitchen table. "Those look nice," he commented.

"Thanks, I figured why not? Mom only used them for Junior League and church. But she's dead, so I reckon I'm makin' the floral decisions around here now. Besides, the whole town'll be here soon enough, droppin' off casseroles made out of God-knows what. The house should look nice."

"Hey, speakin' of that. What are we doin' with Honey?"

Annie stepped back and eyed the arrangement. She leaned forward and moved the vase a quarter inch to the right. "Keepin' her on, I suppose."

"To do what?"

"Well, she's beatin' the bear skin rugs out front right now."

"Well, she can't beat 'em every day, or their hair'll all fall out."

Annie stopped fixating on the flowers long enough to make eye contact. "I know, but I can't *fire* her," Annie said softly, looking from side to side as though she might be overheard.

"Well, we don't need her here every day, either."

"She can polish silver when she finishes that," she suggested.

"Annie, it's a wake, not a baby shower."

"I guess so." The two looked at each other.

"Don't let your daddy do it," Annie said.

"Let him?" Davis scoffed at the notion. "I haven't even talked to him since I got here, 'cept to say, 'Put that dead body here.' I imagine I don't have much say over what he decides to do or not to do."

He started for the basement and called over his shoulder, "Hold that thought. Let me go set up Jennifer's stuff."

Davis descended the steps and gathered Jennifer's laptop bag on his way into the hidden office. He wasn't sure how she'd feel about working there, but he didn't know of another place where there was an extra phone line.

He pushed aside the papers on the top of the desk and placed the bag on the clean surface. He unzipped it, flipped out the laptop and power cord, and then re-zipped the bag, propping it on the floor against one of the tree-trunk pedestals. He felt around behind the desktop tower that stood on the desk, found the phone cord, and moved it from Pawpaw's PC to Jennifer's. He plugged in the power supply to the back of the laptop, and before crouching underneath the desk to plug the other end of the cord into the surge protector, he sat down in the oxblood leather executive chair and powered up the machine. He leaned back and closed his eyes, listening to the hard drive whir.

The PC chimed as the operating system booted up. Davis opened his eyes and looked down at the desk, noticing a manila envelope, torn haphazardly on the diagonal. His grandfather's palsied handwriting ran across the top: *Cora*, it read. He sat up straight, remembering his grandfather's words: "a gift, a letter."

He picked up the envelope. Its creased and rumpled exterior revealed that Frank had squirreled away the vials of his grandmother's destruction, indentations showing where they had sat for some time, perhaps in a drawer covered by other items for concealment. It was empty now; the vials and hypodermic were in evidence at the sheriff's office.

Davis sifted through the few pieces of paper on the desktop. He found an invoice for twenty gallons of deck sealant from Minor Brothers' Hardware, as well as a letter from the church detailing quarterly tithes and offerings, but he did not find the letter that his grandfather had mentioned.

He reached under the desk and picked up the garbage can. There was nothing in it either, save the cellophane top from a package of cigarettes, clinging only by static electricity to the plastic liner of the can. As though he might find something underneath it, he picked up the rectangle of plastic by the gold peel-away tab. After finding nothing of value, Davis dropped the wrapper back in can. He gazed around the room, hoping it might offer a clue. The waterfowl seemed to stare back at him. He shook off a shudder and went back upstairs.

Jennifer was out of the shower, wearing her favorite cut off blue jean shorts and a *Bedford Sentinel* tee shirt. She'd formulated their new slogan herself, and her boss had latched onto it. *All the news that's fit to print— and then some.* She'd coined it as a joke, thinking especially of the gossip reports that were published each week from the outlying communities. But Charlotte liked it; it stuck, and it actually had caused some upheaval in Bedford regarding what it might imply. Anything to sell papers, Charlotte always said.

She sat at the dining room table, reading a day-old copy of the *Lanier Times-Progress.* She looked up from her diversion when Davis entered.

"You clean up good," he said to her.

Her straight brown hair was still slightly damp, and it hung in sections down the back of her neck.

"Thanks," she said. She had donned her new cosmetics and looked substantially more presentable than she had in town. "I suppose I should shower more often."

"Once a week, whether you need it or not, I always say." He sat down across from her and leaned across the table, elbows out, fingers laced together.

"What?" Jennifer said.

"Nothing. Just admiring the view."

Jennifer waved her hand at him in dismissal. She looked back down at the death notices she had been scanning.

"Who's gonna write the obituaries?"

"I don't know. The paper?"

"No, the paper will run whatever we send to them, I'm sure."

"Oh, I didn't know that," Davis said, and he sat up straight in his chair.

"Well, you can do it. You're good at that sort of thing."

"Nuh-uh," Jennifer said, shaking her head.

"You're the writer. Write us something good."

"I didn't know either one of them."

"What's to know?" he asked, and then added, "What do you want to know? I'll tell you."

"I want to know where my computer is, so I can pull email," Jennifer said, trying to avoid the scenario all together.

"I set you up in the office downstairs."

"In the Scooby-Doo vault?"

"Yeah, it's the only place where the extra line is."

Jennifer groaned audibly. "Please don't throw me in that briar patch!" she bemoaned in her best faux southern accent. "Boil me in oil! Skin me alive!"

"I can't help it. I don't know where else to put you."

Jennifer sat for a moment, then began folding and refolding the *Times-Progress*, delaying her descent. "Do I have to?"

"Sorry," Davis said, wincing outwardly. "Don't hate me."

She arose dramatically and hobbled from the room in a mock huff.

"It's amazing how that limp of yours gets worse whenever you don't want to do something," he called after her.

She turned and squinted at him. She shook her fist in a counterfeit threat and then continued her mission. "I'll have you know, I love hanging out in secret dungeons where people have recently offed themselves," she called over her shoulder as she turned the corner for the stairs.

Annie entered the dining room and looked at Davis. "Okay," she said. "I just talked to Herschel. We have to have that signature before Cletus can dig anything on this property. We're gonna have to go with the churchyard." She paused, waiting for some input. There was none.

"It's almost two o'clock. I am going to have to call Cletus and tell him when we want visitation and services. People are gonna start calling and wanting to know."

"Okay," Davis said, palms down on the table. He picked them up and watched the moist outline of his handprints evaporate from the waxy tabletop. He pressed them down again and repeated the process.

Annie waited impatiently for more of a response. "Okay, what?" she said.

"What, okay what?" Davis countered.

"Stop it," Annie said, truly exasperated. She leaned on the broomstick she carried. "We have to make the decisions, Dave. Nobody else is going to."

"Why are you sweeping? Where's Honey?"

"I told her to go home and come back tomorrow."

"You know, Honey might be good to help out when the baby comes," Davis suggested, looking down at Annie's stomach.

Annie looked shocked, and then smiled. "You know, that had not even occurred to me. Good idea."

"See, I can make *some* decisions."

"Yeah. Well, that's a long way off. Let's talk about right now."

Davis grunted and pushed his chair back from the table. "I just don't know—"

Before he could finish the sentence, Jennifer's bellowing from the basement interrupted the thought. He left the chair askew on his way to the top of the stairs.

On his descent, Davis met Lovey, running up, sporting an impish dog-grin, tongue flailing as she came. "Who knew lard could move that fast?" he said, watching her go.

Jennifer met him by the jukebox, holding one end of her frayed power cord. "I don't suppose Mr. Bowdrie stocks these," she said.

EIGHTEEN

The battery on Jennifer's laptop lasted two hours—long enough for her to pull down email, sort it, and determine what she needed to accomplish before morning. It was then settled upon that they would have to make the forty-minute drive into Starkville in order to find a replacement power supply. The timing of such would place their arrival in the metropolis just around the cocktail hour.

The Radio Shack on Highway Twelve did not have what they sought, and in a foolhardy effort, they even tried the Wal-Mart. The next logical place to look would have been Columbus, or perhaps Tupelo, each more drive time away than there were shopping hours remaining. It was approaching six o'clock when Davis gave up the quest and suggested dinner.

A small brick building on Maxwell Street housed The Cotton District Grill, aptly located in the heart of Starkville's old Cotton District. Large Boston ferns hung from chains, running the length of the porch. A patio courtyard in the back was open and empty, and the rest of the establishment was sparsely occupied.

Davis pulled Jennifer's car into the first parking spot in the otherwise empty lot. He assisted her to the door and opened it for her. They waited for a moment inside the doorway, looking for wait staff.

"Just anywhere," the bartender called out. He was drying a glass before putting it away. Two men, one with curly, auburn and thinning hair, and the other, with a long beard, graying hair, and a Mississippi State baseball cap sat at the bar. The ZZ Top look-alike turned for a moment to see who had entered, tipped his cap to the lady, and returned to his draft. The heels of his biker boots were dug into the rungs of the barstool, and he continued his conversation with his companion. Jennifer overheard a snippet about *mega pixels* and the *naked eye* before they passed the pair of regulars and headed for the patio.

They chose the table in the far corner, next to an elevated flowerbed filled with pansies and mondo grass. In the summer it would be somewhat shaded by an ornamental, weeping cherry tree. That day, white blossoms were just starting to appear on the otherwise barren branches.

A waiter came out to greet them, cardboard coasters in hand. "What'll it be?" he asked. He wore a Sigma Chi tee shirt, blue jeans, and a folded black apron tied around his waist. He looked perturbed to be in town during spring break.

"Water," Davis said, not looking up. "And jalapeno cheese logs," he added.

"Davis?" the waiter looked more closely at his patron.

Davis looked up and searched his face. "Chip?" he asked.

"Davis Sanford, how the hell are you?" he asked, extending a hand to shake and patting him on the shoulder with the other.

"Good, man. How are you doin?" he said, half-rising from his seat.

"Hell, earnin' a livin'," he said. "College starts to get expensive in the sixth year."

"Yeah?" Davis said, "Yeah? Well, good to see you, man."

"Yeah, good to see you, too." They stood there, nodding and bobbing for a moment, and then Davis sat down again.

"Jennifer," he said, "This is my friend, Chip Johnson."

"Nice to meet you," Chip offered up.

"Nice to meet you," Jennifer said, in unison with him.

"Me and Davis were pledges together at State, his freshman year, my sophomore year."

Davis would not make eye contact with Jennifer.

"Yeah?" Jennifer asked.

"Yeah, well, I've been in a lot of pledge classes," Chip confessed. "Took me three years to make the grades. I'm still pluggin' away. Next semester I'll have my grades up enough to get re-admission to the PGM program."

"Cool," Jennifer said, not knowing what *PGM* stood for.

"That turfgrass class has been kickin' my ass the last two semesters."

"I hear that one's tough," she said.

"So, how'd you meet ol' Davis, here?"

"She's from Bedford," Davis said, trying to regain control of the conversation.

"Yeah? You're from there, ain't you?"

"Yeah. How's the golf game?"

"Shootin' scratch, man. Shootin' scratch."

"Rock on."

"Yeah, the game wasn't ever the problem. It's that 3.0 thing they've got."

"Grades'll get you every time."

"Yeah, like they think you should have to *study* or something," Chip said, and he laughed. "I'm kiddin', you know."

"Yeah," Davis said.

"So, what've you been up to man?"

"Same old stuff," Davis muttered, vaguely.

"Hey," Chip said. "When is it you're gonna get me that invite to the wild hog barbeque at your daddy's?"

"Man, I don't know."

"You know, you promised me your freshman year you'd get me in there."

Feral hogs were both a nuisance and a blessing at the Sanfords'. While they caused quite a stir in the pea patch, they also were cause for great celebration around the Fourth of July. Each year Bobby Jack's rifle would site in on two, two-hundred-pound boars, and a pit would be dug for the roasting.

Receiving an invitation to the Sanford's annual pig cookout meant one thing: the opportunity to join the hunt club for the next season. The cookout was for members, their guests, and potential members only. The folks of Mercy and hunters throughout the southeast looked forward to receiving an engraved invitation in June that would afford them the opportunity to hobnob with the Sanfords in July.

Great preparation went into the annual festivities. It seemed as though each year's event had to be significantly more hedonistic than the last. And as the deer herd grew, the management of the place called for more hunters to the membership. Frank was adamant that the maximum number of guns the acreage would support be allowed to join, because filling those membership slots allowed for the financing of superior whitetail genetics and high-fencing without ever touching any Sanford money.

However, as it related to what was essentially the summer Rush party, Frank would spare no expense, and he often dug deep into his own pocket for the gala event. "You have to spend money to make money," he bellowed each year.

A screened-in deck—a necessity in the mosquito-ridden forest—had been added to the back of house the first year of the invitational barbeque. A swimming pool was added the following year, as the heat was nearly unbearable. Years three and four of the annual event spawned the "Deck America" tour, as Davis's mother dubbed it. For, she pointed out, if one could not grow grass in the shade, then one should build decking over the mud so as to provide a nice place to walk.

Every year, besides the large capital improvements, the festivities themselves became more grandiose, almost to the point of obscenity. Prominent recording artists soon replaced a three-piece local band. And although the entrée was always wild hog, the side dishes changed from beans and coleslaw carried around on paper plates to vegetable ragout and honey walnut bread served on Royal Hunt china at white linen-bedecked tables.

Then there was the matter of the beverages. Bottled imports had replaced the kegs of domestic beer early on, only to be upstaged by an open bar. Top-shelf well drinks soon followed. In its eighth year, a social murmur began to swell across the state in regard to the regalia at Sanford's.

By the time Davis enrolled at Mississippi State, the Sanford name had preceded him. Frank veritably wallowed in the glory of his social prominence. And Cora wallowed in anxiety each year until the first guest arrived.

NINETEEN

"I can't find my pills!" Cora wailed, her hands shaking as she picked up each orange-brown prescription bottle in the medicine cabinet and read its label once again. The tissue she clutched in her hand was wet from her sweating palms.

"Help me find them, Annie," she implored, and she sat down on the step stool in the middle of her bathroom floor and clutched her knees in a bear hug.

"Okay," Annie said. She tucked her straight black hair behind her ears, adjusted her tortoise shell headband and walked over to the medicine cabinet. "I can't reach it without the step stool, Mom," she said hesitantly, staring at her with an apology in her eyes.

Out in the yard, liquid Spanish rolled off the tongues of the migrant workers on the premises. Loud mariachi music played through a scratchy speaker on a silver portable stereo perched on two ragged sawhorses out in the yard. A circular saw whined in the distance and hammers punctuated the atmosphere with exclamation points.

Although they had grown up with the event, Annie, Davis, and Daniel were amazed each year at the transformation of the place. Annual expectations for the party had become more intense and preparations had grown more elaborate. At first a somewhat private affair, the kids were not a nuisance. However, it had mushroomed to the point that last year a professional fireworks *display had been added. Davis and Daniel subsequently had been sent back home to their rooms for pilfering some of the pyrotechnics.*

This year, Daniel had been dismissed to his father's house for the weekend, and, if there had been a place to send her, Annie would have been shuttled off as well. However, there was no place but home for the nine-year old girl. She survived the week by doing chores and by steering clear of Mom, who had opted to embark on a weeklong Valium-bender in the name of anxiety.

The adults had hoped to send Davis to church camp for the week, but with that session full and a promise of inclusion already made to the eight-year old boy, they would go ahead and send him, the week after the barbeque.

The stage was being set to catapult Sanford's Mossy Horn Sanctuary into what Frank Sanford had hoped it would become the first year he'd cut the trees: a cash cow that gives birth to the golden calf.

Cora yielded her perch on the step stool, resting on the edge of the bathtub, while Annie climbed atop the stool and searched the cabinet for the specific pill bottle that Mom required. Based upon the number of prescription bottles, it appeared as though the Sanfords were not a healthy clan. It didn't take long before Annie found the bottle of Valium and doled out a dosage to her grandmother.

"Now, if I just had a finger of Glen Livet, I think I might be able to make it through the afternoon," Cora said, crushing the paper cup in which Annie had served her water.

"I can get that for you, if you want me to," Annie said.

"Please do, honey," Cora said, standing. "And bring it to the bedroom. I am so exhausted that I might take a nap before I start working on the flower arrangements."

Annie nodded her understanding and headed for the kitchen, obliviously carrying the bottle of pills with her as she went. It was two-thirty in the afternoon, which was only a little early for Mom's first cocktail. Annie dutifully poured the single malt scotch into a crystal high ball, one finger, and then another, just as she'd been taught. Then, with a clink-clink, she added two ice cubes before delivering the toddy to her grandmother.

Cora was reclining in the king-size Italianate mahogany bed. "How will I ever get everything done by Friday?" she lamented, graciously accepting the drink.

"Pawpaw and Daddy will get everything done," Annie assured her.

"You go and clean your room while I rest, and then we'll decide what to tackle next, when I feel a little bit better," Cora said.

Annie obeyed her grandmother by retreating to her room, which was already spotless.

TWENTY

"I don't know when they'll be having another one of those," Davis said.

"You're kiddin'," Chip said. "They quit doin' it? How come?"

"My grandparents passed away recently; so I don't really know what the plan is for this summer."

"Oh, man, sorry to hear that," Chip said. He looked down at his note-pad. "Well, um, I'll get these cheese logs in. What about you?" he asked Jennifer. "What can I get you to drink?"

"Water's fine."

"All right, then. Y'all look at the menu, and I'll be back in a few."

Chip went back inside the restaurant, and Davis leaned back in his patio chair and finally made eye contact with Jennifer. He raised his right eyebrow and grinned at her sheepishly.

"Sigma Chi, eh?" she said, turning the coaster over and over in her hand. "I guess that would explain the tattoo."

"Yep," Davis said, nodding, his lips pressed together. "You know, I don't much think about that indiscretion any more, except when people walk in on me when I'm sleeping half-naked." He sat up, reached back, and scratched in between his shoulder blades as though the mention of it caused him to itch.

"I thought about a tattoo, once," Jennifer said.

"Yeah?"

"Yeah. A girlfriend and I were going together to get flower tattoos, but I chickened out."

"Why?" Davis asked. He too fiddled with a coaster that Chip had left behind.

"I decided that a gardenia on my butt at nineteen would not be quite so sexy when it morphed into a magnolia by the time I turned sixty."

Davis snorted and then reclined in his chair, looking up at the sky.

"So, you were at State?" Jennifer continued.

"Yeah, I did time here."

Hearing that analogy, she looked at him quizzically. She wanted to ask questions, but waited instead to see if he would say more.

"I guess I needed to prove I could do it, you know, to my father," he said, staring into space.

"Do what? School? Of course you could *do* it. I just thought you…" Jennifer stopped short of saying more.

"*Stay* in school, with all the drinking and parties and stuff."

Jennifer silenced herself and let him decide what he wanted to say.

"I'd only been out of rehab a year. I left Bedford right after graduation and took some summer school classes. Trying to sneak up on the social stuff, I guess. Mostly, I just wanted out of Bedford.

"Anyway, I rushed Sigma Chi in the fall. My father and Pawpaw are both Sigma Chis, so it wasn't like they couldn't let me in. I thought I'd be able to handle it, cold turkey." He paused. "Anyway, I couldn't, and I didn't want to admit it to my father. And it just sucked that he was here, on campus, and…." Davis trailed off and then sat up abruptly to look her straight in the eye. He leveled his gaze at her and squinted intently. "Do you know the probability of running into one person at random on a campus of fifteen thousand people?" He didn't wait for her response. "It's pretty high. Pretty freakin' high." He slumped down and sighed.

Jennifer stared at the clouds that were tinged orange and pink by the setting sun. The silence was awkward. "Red sky at night," she offered.

"Sailor's delight," Davis completed her thought. Davis placed his coaster on one corner, and held it still with his pointer finger, balancing it on the crosshatches of the metal tabletop. With his free hand, he thumped it across the table and sailed it just passed Jennifer's ear and into the flow-erbed.

"Hey!" she exclaimed. He grinned at her.

"So, what was your major?"

"History, with a minor in criminal justice," he said, almost monotone.

"No, really."

"Really. What? Do you think it's not me?"

"Davis, I honestly don't know what *you* is anymore."

"I doesn't either," hc said, and he winked at her.

She half-laughed, half-smiled at him, trying to see if he'd give up any more information. "Did you sit for the LSAT?" she asked.

"Didn't get that far. I quit after my freshman year, and I didn't go back." He inhaled heavily through his nose. "I could've gone to Bedford State, but that'dve been worse. Dang *thirteenth grade,*" he scoffed, and a sort of stifled chortle came from the back of his throat.

"Yeah."

"Out of the frying pan, you know."

"Yeah."

"So I moved to Yazoo and started working nights for a security com-pany in their monitoring center. Did three years there. It was pretty easy time. I didn't know anybody, and I didn't have anybody asking me to go out for a few beers after work."

"So that's how you got into the security business?"

"Yep. Saved all my own money and most of what Danny Robert sent me."

Her surprised look made him explain further. "Yeah, Danny Robert felt guilty about my not graduating, so he kept sending me money."

"Danny Robert felt guilty?"

"Yeah. I think Danny Robert's still mad at Pawpaw because he wouldn't pay for his school after he got custody of Annie. Danny Robert didn't finish either.

"It doesn't make any sense, but I guess he's trying to make up for my father not paying for anything for me. Well, except that I got a tuition break because he worked at the university."

"So, how many hours do you have?"

"Forty-eight. Need eighty more to graduate. It just won't happen. I'm too old and set in my ways."

"Yeah, right," Jennifer said. She looked up as Chip returned to the patio with the plate of appetizers.

"Okay, these are reverse-blow hot, so be careful," he said, placing the plate between them. "So y'all want to eat real food?" he asked. Jennifer eyed the fried cheese sticks that were almost as big around as half dollars and unrolled her silverware from the white cloth napkin.

"What's good?" Davis asked.

"Everything."

"We'll have two of that, then."

Chip smiled. "How about a Reuben?"

"Two?" Jennifer added.

"Okay, two it is." Chip returned to the kitchen and left them to their fare.

"So, these are jalapeno?" Jennifer asked, spearing one with her fork.

"Yeah, but they're not too hot—spicy-hot anyway."

Davis reached for one with his hands and bit directly into the hors d'oeuvre, stringing cheese and sucking in air to cool the molten lava. He adeptly wrapped the elastic strand around his index finger and pulled it from his chin, dropping the remaining portion onto his plate. He drank some water and then sat back in his chair. "Well, I won't be tasting anything for a couple of days," he said, as he finished the remnants that remained in his mouth.

"Fools rush in," Jennifer said, as she cut hers into bites.

"Woman, don't make me smack you."

Jennifer shrugged, stabbed a portion of cheese, blew on it, and with a flourish of her fork, took a bite. "Mmmm," she closed her eyes and savored the buttery, hot concoction. "When did I eat last?" she said, opening her eyes.

"Pie at breakfast."

"Hmm. That's why my stomach has been complaining." She took another bite, this time dipping it in a side of ranch dressing. "Yeah, I think I could eat my weight in these."

"So, did you see the Billy Gibbons look-alike at the bar?" Jennifer asked. Davis was braving another cheese stick.

"Oh, yeah. He's a campus icon. He's been here as long as I can remember coming to State. He's a photographer for the school, I think, or something like that—almost always has a camera around his neck. Rides a ten-speed everywhere he goes."

"I heard him talking photography when we walked in."

"Or maybe he works for the *Starkville Daily News*." Davis shrugged as he ate.

"Really?"

"Yeah, maybe."

"If he does, maybe he has access to a power cord that would fit my laptop. We patterned our newsroom off of their setup."

Davis looked up. "You know, he might." He stood up and pushed back his chair, dropping his napkin next to his plate.

"What are you doing?"

"Asking him."

"You know him?"

"No, but I figure he probably knows of my father."

"Oh."

"Wait here; I'll be right back."

Jennifer watched as Davis ambled into the dining room and up to the bar. She could not hear the conversation, but watched as Davis shook each of the men's hands and explained their plight. She could see nods and smiles, a second round of handshakes, and then Davis returned to her side.

Her eyes followed him as he returned to the patio, and when he got close enough she offered an inquisitive, "Well?"

Davis returned to his seat. "Well, he doesn't work there."

"Dang."

"But they know somebody who does."

"Cool."

"Yeah, he said he could get us in over at the newsroom after we eat."

"No lie?"

"No lie."

Chip arrived with the sandwiches, and they ate them hastily. Within twenty minutes, Davis, Jennifer, and their boot-clad benefactor were on their way to the office of *The Starkville Daily News*.

They arrived to find two people inside the newsroom on this Friday night. They were greeted cordially, and Jennifer was permitted to plug in her laptop and get to work. Davis delivered their newfound friend back to his perch at the bar, using Jennifer's car while she worked.

He returned to the newsroom and wandered around for a bit. Finally he sat down beside her in a swiveling office chair and propped his feet on a desk while she designed the pages of the next week's edition.

After forty-five seconds, Davis pulled his feet down and spun the chair around twice, holding his legs out in mid air.

"What are you doing?" Jennifer asked, not looking away from her computer screen.

"I'm bored."

Jennifer stopped pointing and clicking for a moment to look at him. "You're bored?" she asked.

"Sorry," he said, sheepishly. "I'll stop."

She smiled and went back to her work. "I'm going as fast as I can."

"I know," Davis said, and he stood up and walked to the front window of the building. Crossing from North Montgomery Street and heading toward the front of the building was a blind man walking with a red-tipped, white cane, moving it precisely from side to side as he proceeded. He was tall and thin, balding and clean-shaven, maybe forty years old, and wearing a Kelly-green button-down shirt with blue jeans.

Davis continued to watch as the man made a left-hand turn onto the sidewalk in front of the building, and then paused for a moment, feeling from right to left and then back again. The sidewalk was in disrepair, and his footing was unsteady, so he once again stopped. To his left he felt a strip of grass, a decorative border between the sidewalk and the street that confused his orientation. He stepped back out into the street and felt again from right to left, but he could not locate any physical clue as to where the sidewalk began. He turned ninety degrees and walked a few paces and then stopped. He turned another ninety degrees and tried again.

By now Davis was beside himself and called out to Jennifer, "I'm goin' for a walk. Back before you're through." Jennifer dismissed him without a thought as she continued to pull ad copy from saved files and drag it onto her layouts.

Davis burst out onto the sidewalk and called out, "Hey, need some help?"

The man replied, "No, thanks, I've got it," and he made another right-angle turn and headed five paces, searching for the sidewalk.

"Hey man, you're out in the middle of the street," Davis offered.

"No I'm not," he replied. He continued to search with his white cane until he found the grass, this time, to his right. "See, here's the grass," he said, and he started walking toward downtown, against traffic, out in the street.

Davis let him walk a few paces before he tried again. "Where you headed?" he asked.

The man stopped again, pulling his cane up parallel to himself and folding both his hands over the top of it. "Well, if you want to know, I'm going to Cheers," he said.

"Yeah? Well Cheers is the other direction."

"It is not. I'm headed east on University Drive, am I not?"

Davis replied, "No, you're not. You're headed west on University Drive."

The man first appeared shocked and then crestfallen. "West, eh? But, the grass," he said, feeling for it with his cane.

"Yep," Davis said, jogging to catch up to him. He approached him and put his right hand on the man's. "Hey, man. Davis Sanford. Five-foot eleven inches, hundred fifty pounds, soaking wet." He introduced himself.

The gentleman extended his right hand as a welcome. "Bob Leach, six-foot five, or so I'm told, and too fat to comment on weight."

Davis chuckled. "You want me to drive you to Cheers? I've got a car right here. I'm waiting on my girlfriend who's working inside the newspaper office."

"I'd prefer not to get in your car," Bob confided. "I know this isn't East Rutherford, but I'm just now getting used to the small-town thing, and I'm still a little leery."

Davis tried to pinpoint his accent. "New York?" he asked.

"Jersey," he countered.

"You teach at the university?"

"What else is there for a blind man from Jersey to do in Starkville?" They both laughed. Davis thought a moment.

"Well, I've got some time to kill. I can walk you over to Cheers."

"I'd be grateful," Bob offered, and Davis turned the two of them around and offered him his right arm. "Okay, this sidewalk is a mess, so I'll try to tell you when to step lively."

"I'm all ears," Bob retorted.

The two picked their way down University Street and made a right on Maxwell, back toward the Cotton District Grill.

"What's it? About a mile to Cheers from here?" Davis asked.

"Feels like it," Bob replied.

"That's a long way to walk in the dark."

"Everywhere I go is in the dark."

Davis was embarrassed at the reply. "But, when it's dark for everybody else, then *they* might not see you," he suggested. "Which I guess isn't that big of a problem as long as you are on the sidewalk. But, like, here, there's no sidewalk," Davis said as he and Bob trudged up the hill. "I mean, Cheers is an awful long way to go, especially when you can get a beer right here," and he stopped in front of the restaurant at which he'd just dined.

Bob protested, "But there's the St. Patrick's Day party at Cheers tonight. I guess I'm just a little too Irish to miss it."

Davis paused, and then said, "St. Patrick's Day is Saturday."

"Right. Today." Then he added, "They've been advertising on the radio that the St. Patty's Day celebration is Saturday night."

The two men continued to stand on the side of Maxwell Street. The streetlights were starting to flicker on. "Yes," Davis said. "But *tonight* is *Friday* night."

Bob let this sink in for a moment and then said, "Well, crap."

"How 'bout an ice cold brewski, right here at the world famous Cotton District Grill?"

"How about it?" Bob asked motioning for Davis to lead the way. "You will join me won't you?"

"No, I do need to go, but I can hook you up with a couple of fellows who can enjoy your company," Davis offered. He opened the door to the establishment and ushered Bob inside. He escorted him to the bar and settled him in. "Anything else I can do you for?" he asked.

"No, thanks very much, though."

"Well, all right then. I'll be headin' back."

"Be careful out there. I hear it's getting dark."

"As long as I don't close my eyes, I'll be okay."

TWENTY-ONE

Annie wove her way between Mossy Horn guests the night of the Fourth of July. She carried a stack of empty Dixie cups in one hand and a pile of used, heavy-duty paper plates in the other, as she made her way to the back kitchen to drop off the final remains of dinner. The thirty potential new guns for the place and their dates had finished eating, and the night was just starting to warm up.

The pre-recorded music was coming to an end, with Hank Williams, Jr.'s nasal rendition of "All My Rowdy Friends Are Coming Over Tonight." The B-Flats out of Memphis were finishing the last of the microphone checks, preparing for three sets of country cover tunes, starting at nine o'clock.

Annie pushed open with her hip the back door to the kitchen and met her father coming out as she was going in. A Marlboro hanging from his lips, a lighter in his fist, he stopped lighting the cigarette to help Annie take her load to the garbage.

"Thank you for all your help tonight, honey," he said, ruffling the top of her hair with his palm.

"I like to help," Annie said, smiling up at her dad.

They dropped the garbage into the waste can at the end of the kitchen counter top. Danny Robert bent down on one knee to look at Annie's stark, blue eyes. He took the unlit cigarette from his mouth, folded it down into his palm, and then, using the same hand, he tucked a rumpled strand of hair behind her ear. He smiled at her and said, "Now baby girl, I need for you to do me a favor."

"Okay, Daddy."

"I need for you to stay in your room and out of the way tonight. There's too many people around here that we don't know all that well, and ever'body's getting' on into the sauce."

Annie nodded and listened.

"It's almost your bedtime anyway, so just get your pajamas on, and I'll come back to check on you in a little bit. There's a fella out there that I got to take home. He's getting' a little rowdy, and it ain't even started yet."

"Okay, Daddy," Annie repeated.

"Now, I got to go to Starkville. I'll be back quick enough, but I don't want you out there without me."

"Okay, Daddy."

"Now get on in there, and I'll come check on you when I get back. You'll be asleep by then, but I'll come kiss you goodnight."

Annie kissed Danny Robert on the cheek and headed toward her room after a hug and a pat on the back from her father. In turn, he left the kitchen to rendezvous with Bobby Jack for the nearly two-hour taxi ride and return trip home.

In the front kitchen, Frank Sanford stood in the butler's pantry, filling his arms three deep with liquor bottles to take out to the open bar in the back yard: bourbon, scotch, and gin in one arm; rum, vodka, and tequila in the other. He was already half-tight himself, but he'd learned from experience that the more liquor that flowed, the more likely he was to sign the full lot of guests to at least a one-year lease. On his way back to the revelry, he spied Cora's prescription bottle sitting next to the sink. He placed two of the fifths on the countertop and dropped the drugs in the pocket of his khakis before reassembling the bottles for this liquor run.

The band was starting into the first set as he traversed the living room and traveled through Danny Robert's wing on his way outside. Annie's door was open, and the light was on, so he stuck his head inside.

"Where's your daddy?" he asked, looking in on Annie, sitting up in a twin-size bed, tucked underneath a pink and white crazy quilt, reading a

Nancy Drew mystery book, a glass of sweet tea on the nightstand at her left elbow.

"Him and Bobby Jack had to take somebody home," she replied.

"Dang it," Pawpaw replied. "Did he say where?"

"Starkville."

"Mmmm. Must've been Scott Jefferies. He was half gone when he got here."

Annie did not have a response, but just looked at her grandfather.

"All right. Stay here, honey. I'll come check on you after while."

The libations continued to flow as the band broke into their first selection, an old David Allan Coe tune. Finding herself unable to ignore the celebrations outside her bedroom, Annie closed her book and laid it on the bed beside her. She looked at the windup alarm clock on her nightstand and supposed her father and uncle were less than halfway through their trip. She was sleepy but still intent on remaining awake until their return. She wanted to go out to the living room, snuggle up on the sofa in a thick, cotton afghan, and watch music videos. Already dressed in her summer, sleeveless nightgown, she stood up, reached for her housecoat that hung on the back of her desk chair, and donned it.

Taking her tea glass with her, she peeked her head out the doorway of her boudoir. She looked to the right toward the kitchen and then to the left toward the living room. There was no one in the big house, so she scurried down the passageway to the vaulted trophy room. She veritably leaped around the corner and cozied herself into the right-hand corner of the deep leather sectional. She parked her glass on the end table and pulled the throw that was draped over the back of the sofa down onto herself. She then stretched her arm to the coffee table, where the television and satellite remotes lay.

Settled in, she turned on the tube and punched in the satellite channel for MTV. It was not long before she could hear the songs in the back of her mind, even though she was unable to keep her eyes open. She shrugged once and then again when Pawpaw leaned over to awaken her.

"Annie," he said, gently shaking her.

"I'm awake, Pawpaw," she insisted.

"I know you are," he said, his drawl becoming more of a slur as the night progressed.

"I've got my homework done," she said in a half-asleep stupor. "I can watch TV. I've got my homework done."

Pawpaw smiled at the thought of a child who dreamed about homework in the middle of the summer.

"I know you do, baby," he said, relenting. He looked down at her tanned and bare legs sticking out from the blanket. "Well, let's cover you up, honey," he said, adjusting the throw

"But I'm not sleepy," she insisted, still in a fog, but sitting up now. "I'm hot," she continued, trying to unzip her house robe. She was becoming agitated.

Pawpaw looked around the room for assistance with the girl. There was none, as the family was still scattered across three counties.

"Okay," he said, stepping back. "You just watch TV, and I'll be back in a little bit to check on you."

Annie returned to her limp state of repose after hearing assurances from Frank that she could continue to "watch" TV. He turned and shuffled down the hall, reaching into his pocket for a cigarette.

He figured that after one more set from the band, anyone who had not signed a lease would have to be pressed about the issue before he had the opportunity to escape. Frank needed to win commitments from twenty of the guests in order for his five-year plan to stay on track. If all thirty were to commit, he'd be in a quandary, with too many guns for the management plan. If fewer than twenty signed on, he'd lack the cash flow to add the stands in the planned high-fence area. Seventeen had already signed contracts. He needed three more to make the year work. Eight more would be perfect, but until at least three signed on, he was unable to think of much else.

He reached for the doorknob, but stepped back as the door opened inward upon him. Davis's mom, Brenda, greeted him with a smile and a stack of papers.

"We got 'em," she said, waving the contracts above her head in one hand, car keys in the other.

"Got 'em?" Frank countered.

"Twenty signatures, on the dotted line."

Frank was noticeably relieved. He reached in his pocket for his lighter, fumbling past the Valium. The smoke bobbed up and down between his lips as he tried to light it and talk at the same time. "I won't lie to you that I was a little nervous tonight. Thank God we got 'em."

"No, thank me," Brenda said, moving past him to sit down at Danny Robert's kitchen table, her car keys clattering on its surface.

"Whatever," Frank said, taking a long drag and then blowing it out the side of his mouth. His staggering began to morph into a swagger. "Drinks all around," he said, and he began looking in Danny Robert's refrigerator for refreshment.

"You don't need another drink, Frank," Brenda said, looking down at the paperwork and recounting the documents.

"How many other John Henrys are thinking about signing?" he asked, standing up from a beer-retrieving crouch.

"John Hancock." Brenda said. "Dammit Frank, for a smart man, why is it you can't remember that John Henry was an illiterate, steel-driving man? Whaddya think? They all put a big X on the dotted line? That's what a John Henry *would be."*

"Yeah, yeah," Frank said, opening the Budweiser and taking a sip. He waved her off. "How many more?"

"Well, Scott Jefferies is toast. He's so pissed we took him home that he'll probably never sign."

"Well, the last thing we need around here is a real drunk."

Brenda paused, but said nothing.

"And the Farleys I think came just to see the setup. I overheard 'em twice talking about some land up in east Webster County. So that's three total that I don't think are gonna come on."

"Well, we need to dissuade two more. Any other drunks we can throw out?" Frank laughed at his own joke.

"Other than you, I can't think of any," Brenda countered.

Frank held his beer can in his right hand between his thumb and ring finger. The last half of his cigarette burned between the first two digits. He leaned heavily on his left shoulder on the doorjamb to the galley.

"Bobby Jack always was drawn to women with smart mouths," he reflected aloud.

"Look, Frank. Here's the paperwork. I got a sitter at the house with Davis, and I got to get back at a semi-decent hour." She stacked the paperwork with several short raps on the kitchen table. "And if you no longer require my services, I'd like to head that way."

"Go on," he said. He walked to the kitchen sink and stuck his half-smoked cigarette under running water before dropping it in the garbage. He crossed the room with his hand extended to receive the contracts, and Brenda handed them to him.

"Don't drink anymore tonight, okay, Frank?"

"This is my last beer," he said. "I'm taking these down to the office, and then I'll give the signal to start making coffee."

"Okay. I'm outta here. Tell Bobby Jack I went home."

"Will do," Frank called over his shoulder, as he walked toward the basement stairs. Brenda exited the back door, and Frank crossed the living room floor enroute to the office. Annie was sitting up, watching MTV.

"You should be in bed," he called over his shoulder.

"Can't sleep," Annie replied, staring at the television. Her elbow was perched on the arm of the couch, her chin propped on her fist.

"That's funny," Frank turned and looked at her, "coming from the girl who was talking in her sleep five minutes ago."

"I've been awake," Annie insisted, breaking her stare to look at her grandfather. "I'm sleepy; I just can't go to sleep."

Frank stopped for a minute, and then reached into his pocket. "Here," he said, opening up the bottle of pills. He poured one out into his mammoth hand and looked at it. It was just a small, white pill with a score down the middle. He put it to his mouth and bit it along the score with his front teeth. One half he offered to Annie; the other he swallowed. "Take this, and you'll be out in no time."

Annie looked up questioningly at him and reached to take the pill from his open palm. "Go on," he said. "It won't hurt you."

Annie did as she was instructed, hesitantly putting the pill in her mouth and reaching for a watered-down glass of sweet tea that sat beside her.

"You'll be out in no time," he said again, and continued to make his way to the office. "I'll come back to check on you in a few."

Frank made his way down the steps, through the lounge, and past the pool table, to the bookshelves. He moved the Masonic Bible covering the latch that gave entry to the office. The shelves creaked on the spring-loaded hinges and then rolled back from the force of his arm.

Once inside, Frank decided to enter the new names into his new computer. He sat down at the desk and heaved a sigh. His bones ached, and he needed to relieve himself. He powered on the Commodore 64 and watched the small green light flash on the external floppy drive.

As soon as the device booted up, he opened the word processing software package and looked down at the stack of contracts. He focused and refocused on the writing on the page. It was too small and blurry to read. Exasperated, he put it on the bottom of the stack and tried the next one. It was no better, nor was the next one.

He muttered, "Damn drunk," switching off the computer and rising, leaving the pile of paperwork on his desk. He exited the office, closing the secret door behind, and mounted the stairs to the living room.

Annie was still on her same corner of the couch, eyes glazed, staring at a racy music video. Frank looked at her and then at the television, and then back at her. "You like that?" he asked as he sat down on the couch beside her.

Confused and tired, Annie looked at him and said, "Hey, Pawpaw. What are you doin'?"

"Putting you to bed, sweetheart," he said, and he lifted her up off the couch and carried her up close to his chest, her long legs, dangling and limp. He struggled a little with his drunkenness and her weight and offered, "You are getting to be such a big girl."

She did not respond, but rested her head on his shoulder. He carried her around the corner of the couch and down the hall to her bedroom on the right. Only her night table lamp was burning. He laid her in her bed and stood back up to gaze at his granddaughter. She lay still in her house robe, legs askew and uncovered.

Frank went to the door and pushed it to before returning to her side. "Sit up, baby girl," he suggested. "You don't need to sleep in your house robe."

Annie groggily obeyed, and he unzipped her and pulled her arms from the garment. She smiled vacantly at him.

"I wanted to stay up until Daddy got home," she said.

"He'll be home soon enough," Frank offered, and he gently helped her remove the robe and lie down. He started to cover he small frame with the pink and white quilt, but stopped as he continued to gaze at her. He leaned over and gave her a half-hug of sorts, his face and shoulder to hers. She half-sat with an attempt to peck him on the cheek, before missing and trying to lie back down.

Frank held her up saying, "You want a kiss? That's not a kiss. I'll show you what a kiss is." And he pressed his lips to hers, holding her up close to his giant frame. Annie stiffened in confusion as Frank discovered her tongue with his own. He moved his hands across her back and down to her small bottom where he squeezed her hard as he continued to explore her mouth.

Annie pushed him away and moved as far away from him as she could. "What are you doing, Pawpaw?" she asked him. Her speech was slowed but scared. She awkwardly reached for the hem of her gown and tried to pull it down past her knees.

"Just showing you what a real kiss is like," Frank said. He patted her on the shoulder and slowly moved his hand from there across her chest, and she stiffened once more. "When you're older, you'll like that, too."

Annie's ears were ringing and her face began to flush. Before she could resist again, the door to her room swung open. Brenda stood there with her keys in hand.

"Forgot these," she said, holding them up.

She looked from Annie to Frank, and then back to Annie again.

"Everything okay here?" Brenda asked.

"Oh, yes," Frank answered. "Just putting the little one to bed."

"I saw the light and wondered if the music was keeping you up," Brenda offered to Annie. "If you want, you can come and stay at our house. Davis would like it." She continued to look back and forth between grandfather and granddaughter.

"I would like that," Annie offered, and she attempted to rise from her bed. Frank stood up out of her way and she stumbled, one leg almost collapsing on her first step.

"You okay, baby?" Both adults reached for her in unison, Brenda rushing across the room to assist.

Annie quickly grasped the back of her desk chair and held on with her left hand, pushing Frank away with her right. "I'm okay," she said, focusing on staying upright. Frank moved aside and allowed Brenda to help her.

"Here, let me get your housecoat, and you can just come on like you are." Brenda helped her step into her robe and zipped it up for her while Annie continued to hold onto the chair. Frank stood looking out the window, his back to the women. He shoved his hands deep in both his trouser pockets and grasped the bottle of pills.

Brenda smoothed Annie's coal-black hair and smiled at her. "You want me to carry you?" she asked.

"I'll carry her," Frank offered.

"I can carry her," Brenda retorted, and hoisted the child up onto her hip. She shifted Annie to her chest, and Annie wrapped her legs around her aunt's waist. The smell of cigarettes and bourbon wafted up from the child when Annie buried the bridge of her nose into her caretaker's neck. Brenda bristled at the smell and cut an eye at Frank, who was staring awkwardly at the doorway.

"Is everything okay?" she asked Annie again, craning her neck down to try to look at her face.

"Fine," Annie mumbled. "Sleepy."

"Okay," Brenda answered, unsatisfied. "Okay. Just close your eyes, and everything will be okay."

Annie shook her head. "I won't close my eyes. Then everything will be okay."

Brenda held her tighter, shooting a glare at Frank, before she headed for the car.

TWENTY-TWO

Upon their return home from the metropolis of Starkville, Jennifer had excused herself to continue working on page layouts in the basement. The Starkville journalists, who had so desperately wanted to go home, had graciously lent a power supply with Jennifer's promise of a return. Annie dozed on the couch in the trophy room, her back to the corner of the leather couch, CMT flickering on the television, sweet tea languishing in a watery glass nearby.

Davis opened the refrigerator a half-dozen times, paced the floor for twenty minutes, and finally decided to go to the skinning shed to reexamine the meat grinder. Danny Robert had just loosed the hounds after their evening repast of waffles, and they milled about the back yard, noses to the ground, tails wagging, with a smattering of scratching interspersed. Davis wove his way though the pack and up onto the concrete pad that was the skinning shed's floor.

The day had capped off at a pleasant seventy-two degrees, but, with the sunset at just past six o'clock, the temperature was nearing sixty. His short-sleeved shirt was insufficient outerwear, and he looked around the shed for a jacket or shirt that he could don. He located and put on a large, quilted, flannel work shirt, hanging on a hook near the freezer door, ostensibly for work inside the walk-in unit. As it was quite large for his small frame, he rolled up the sleeves, not only to expose his hands, but also to hide the dried bloodstains on the cuffs.

Dogs of mixed ancestry lounged in the thinning grass beside the shed. Pinky followed him close by, watching his actions, hoping for a treat, be it a deer hoof or a turkey head. She was indiscriminate. Davis tolerated her presence underfoot and began looking at the meat grinder again. He plugged the machine into the electrical outlet above the bench and flipped the switch. After a click and a whine of the engine, Davis quickly turned it back off and unplugged the unit.

On the outside of the polished steel machine, a large placard was affixed: "Warning: no user serviceable parts inside. Opening of this unit by anyone other than a factory-certified repair person voids the warranty." He looked down into the feeder tube of the unit, attempting to see its works, but recoiled at the smell of rotting meat. He thought for a moment and then, looking around for a water hose, he found one coiled in a retractable case next to the spigot. A high-pressure attachment was affixed to one end.

Davis first moved the unit to the skinning shed floor, then turned on the water, before pulling a length of hose from the reel. Using the highest pressure available, he rinsed the inside of the unit from the topside, waiting to see what might emerge from the extruder's end. Large hunks of week-old meat emerged, and Davis quickly washed them to the edge of the concrete pad and out into the yard, where the dogs began to fight over them.

He looked around again for a shop rag and found one in the right-hand drawer of the worktable. He wiped down the unit, drying off every drop of water he could reach, then moved the grinder back to the tabletop, where he plugged it in to the wall. Again he turned it on, and this time the machine ran smoothly. Davis smiled, satisfied, and turned the machine off before unplugging it.

He gazed across the yard at the back of the house. The main kitchen was dark, as was the back one. No one was sleeping in the master bedroom; so it, too, looked out darkly across the yard. Davis buttoned up the flannel work shirt and shoved his hands into the pockets of his jeans. He started to walk across the backyard diagonally, toward the carport.

He cut through the carport between Jennifer's car and Danny Robert's truck, Pinky at his heels. Davis wrapped around to the right and gazed for a moment into his grandparents' front yard. In the darkness the heads of thousands of daffodils bobbed and swayed with the light southwesterly breeze. And while trees surrounded the house on its periphery, daffodils notwithstanding, the only other flora on the immaculate front lawn was a two-hundred-year-old, five-trunk oak tree.

Its shadow, cast by the glow of the front porch floodlights, loomed out toward the surrounding woods. Davis approached the old tree, looking up for the one long branch upon which fifteen years earlier he and Annie had formed grooves with two tire swings mounted on nylon ski rope. That limb appeared to be gone.

He felt the bark of the old tree, moving his palms around, searching for a toehold to make the climb. He found the first one, substantially lower than he remembered it, and quickly pulled himself up into the arms of the giant oak. Pinky sat down at the foot of the tree and watched him climb.

When Davis was twelve, he'd hammered two boards into the behemoth tree, connecting two of the trunks into a haphazard ladder, giving him added height and surveillance capabilities. One of the boards was still there, although he dared not put any weight on it. He simply dug his heels into the tangential trunks and hoisted himself as high as he could climb.

A breeze was kicking up, and Davis shuddered, sitting in the damp night air. As his eyes adjusted to the night, he surveyed the yard starting with the perimeter, working in, until he finally focused on the tip ends of the branches of the great-granddaddy oak in which he sat. Not one that he could see displayed a live bud or other sign of life. He turned in dismay and looked at the opposite side of the tree.

It was too dark to see without moving, so he swung around and pulled himself to the far side. There was no sign of life there, either. The old tree was either dead or dying, as best as he could discern. He sat just a moment more, and then climbed down. Pinky rose to greet him, and the two meandered across the yard, even the dog taking care not to step on the daffodils.

This time they walked around the back of the dog pound, and Pinky kenneled on command. Davis issued two short chirps for whistles, and the remainder of the pack encircled him, awaiting their turn to repose. Once all the dogs were inside, Davis fastened the door for the night and walked back up to the skinning shed, stopping short at the track hoe.

He stared at it for a moment, then walked over and mounted the machine. It had been many years since he'd used one about the place. This was not the same model or make that Marcus had taught him to drive. He sat and stared at the levers, noticing that the key was still in the ignition. The house was quite dark when he looked across the way; so, he started the engine and waited.

After a few false starts, Davis was able to turn the lights on, ease the tractor forward from its parking place, and drive it down the small slope past the doghouse and around to the front yard. He chose the path of least resistance in regard to the daffodils, plowing under only a few hundred before arriving at the old tree. He turned one hundred eighty degrees and maneuvered the heavy equipment so that the backhoe attachment dropped down just underneath the spot where, a lifetime ago, Annie and he had worn the grass away with the swings. He spun the seat around, extended the hydraulic legs, and began to dig.

The tearing and ripping of roots was almost drowned out by the sound of the engine. Davis dug down, pulled up, swung to the left, and dropped a scoop of slimy, wet mud. He swung back, and then he dug down again, pulling up, swinging to the left, and dropping another scoop, this time not as wet as the first. Within three minutes he had formed a haphazard rectangle, roughly two scoops wide and six feet deep.

He was in the process of repositioning the tractor to make another pass at a second hole, when he realized that someone was calling his name. He looked down and to his right and saw Annie standing there, hair disheveled, feet bare. He turned off the engine and smiled at her.

"Hey," he offered, a little too loud, now that the engine was off.

"What are you doing?" Annie asked, in disbelief.

"Herschel said *Cletus* couldn't dig the graves. Didn't say that we couldn't."

"You have lost your ever-lovin' mind," Annie said, hands on her hips. "You're gonna get that tractor stuck out here in this mud, and we'll never get it out."

"It's not that bad," Davis offered. "Now go on and let me finish this before I mire down."

Annie stalked to the house, flinging her hands up in the air two separate times during her monologue to herself. Within three more minutes Davis had fashioned another reasonable facsimile of a grave. He spun the seat again, pulled in the legs, put the tractor in drive, and crushed another hundred or so daffodils on his return trip to the shed.

He negotiated the equipment back into its parking spot, turned off the lights, killed the diesel engine, and climbed down. As he turned the corner in front of the tractor, a glint of light caught his eye, and he turned to look. On initial, cursory inspection, he saw nothing, so he moved closer to examine what might have attracted his attention.

The carport for the tractor had been an addition to the skinning shed. As happened with most things at the Sanford estate, the entire setup had been built in phases. The roof to the garage was held up by four round metal posts at each corner of a concrete pad poured just for this purpose. And, this concrete pad was not completely flush with the concrete pad that served as the skinning shed's floor; a slight step down, of half an inch or less, marked where one ended and the other began.

Over the years, the two sections of concrete had rubbed together in the winter and pulled apart in the summer, leaving a gap that caught all sorts of odds and ends. The bauble that caught Davis's eye was purple and gold. He bent down to pick it up, and then realized he was holding Marcus's class ring, covered in dried blood, both inside and out. He turned it over in his palm, then carefully dropped it into his pocket.

He now moved slowly from the tractor shed back to the walk-in freezer, where he slowly unrolled the sleeves of the work shirt. He looked down at them again as he removed the garment, and he scrutinized the stains more carefully. These were not old stains that had been left over from a washing, but rather were fresh ones that had never been laundered. A dried and flaky caking of blood covered the frayed shirtsleeves.

Davis hung the shirt back on the hook where he'd gotten it. He looked around at the skinning shed. He did not know what game was currently in season, but he began to look for signs of any other butchering that might have taken place during the past week. Everything appeared to be in order. He reached for the freezer door and opened it, only to be taken aback by the smell. No cool air emanated from inside. He looked around the back of the unit, and for the first time he noticed that neither the fan nor the compressor was running.

He moved back around to the front of the freezer and opened the door again, this time, holding his breath. Stacked on the shelves of the unit were two-pound tubes of ground meat, indelibly marked *wild boar*. All the tubes were soft, and blood dripped from them into the center of the freezer, forming a pool. His curiosity satisfied, Davis stepped out, shut the door, and walked quickly away from the area to get a fresh breath of air. He leaned over and clutched the top of his pants, gasping, trying to keep his stomach from turning over.

It wasn't hog season, but landowners were allowed to shoot just about any animal that presented a threat to person or property, regardless of the time of year. Davis looked up and saw that the big kitchen light was on. Annie and Jennifer appeared at the back door off the kitchen, and Jennifer called out, "It's colder than a grave digger's...."

"I'm coming!" Davis called, and he made his way back inside.

TWENTY-THREE

The ladies met Davis at the door with a cup of hot cocoa. He greeted them and smiled a crooked, thank-you grin. "It's a little chilly out there," he offered.

"See," Annie turned to Jennifer and said, "He's clearly lost it."

"I've got some good news and some bad news," Davis said.

"Okay," Jennifer said.

"I assume the good news is that you dug two graves in the front yard?" Annie asked.

"Yep, that's the good news."

"Graves that we can't use," Jennifer added.

"I'm getting that notary first thing in the morning," he announced.

"How?" Annie asked. "Hank Jacobs don't come down the hill, ever."

"I'm just gonna take a notary up to him, then."

"Right," Annie scoffed.

"On the Lord's Day?" Jennifer added.

"Annie, I'm not gonna bury them at the Presbyterian Church unless we absolutely have to."

Annie just stared at him. "Okay," she said. "And, now is the bad news that you hit the gas line to the house?"

Davis looked concerned for a moment, "No, I don't think so. I-I mean, I don't think I hit the gas line."

"You didn't, you doof," Annie consoled him. "What's the bad news?"

"Like we need anymore bad news," Jennifer said, pouring herself some hot cocoa out of the boiler on top of the gas stove.

"Well, the bad news is that the walk-in freezer out there isn't running."

"You're kidding?" Annie said, setting her tea glass down on the counter. "There's a four-hundred-pound hog in there." She went to the window to look out.

"Um, there *was* a four-hundred-pound hog in there. Now there are four hundred pounds of trichinosis in there." He took a sip from his cup. "And it smells mighty fine, too. *Mighty fine.*"

"That is *not* something I had planned on dealing with tomorrow," Annie lamented.

"I'll take care of it in the morning," Davis said. "But right now, I need to check my messages at home and *get a bath*. I smell like a wet goat."

"Is that what wet goat smells like?" Jennifer asked.

"Woman."

"I'm gonna use the shower in the basement, if that's all right with you ladies."

"Fine by me," Annie said. "Honey cleaned it yesterday."

"Like that matters to me," Davis said over his shoulder as he headed for the basement.

"Do you want me to get you some clothes from upstairs?" Jennifer called after him.

"Would you?"

"I think I can manage it," she said.

As Davis descended the steps, Jennifer climbed to the loft to get his bag. Remembering the gator this time, she skirted it cautiously. She picked up his things and returned to the basement to find Davis, not in the bathroom, but back inside the vault, turning on Pawpaw's computer, sans shirt.

"Is that wet goat I smell?" she asked upon entry.

"I'm letting the water get hot in the shower," he said.

Davis sat down in Frank's chair.

"I've been thinking," Davis said.

"Ooh, don't hurt yourself."

Davis smiled without looking at her, and then navigated the web browser to a search engine. He typed the words *arsenic* and *Bangladesh* into the dialog box and pressed *Enter*.

"What are you doing?" she asked.

"Thinking."

"Should I go turn off the water in the shower?"

"Probably."

Jennifer did so, and then returned. Davis was busy reading an article. "Listen to this," he said. "Studies have linked prolonged exposure to arsenic with cancer, diabetes, and thickening of the skin, liver disease and problems with the digestive system. Arsenic is a known carcinogen. Arsenic poisoning has been associated with nervous system disorders, tingling or losing sensation in the limbs, and hearing difficulties."

"Yeah?"

Davis continued scanning. "Blah, blah, blah," he skimmed over irrelevant data. "At low concentration levels, it is thought to take between eight and fourteen years for the physical symptoms of arsenic poisoning to emerge." He scanned some more. "Blah, blah. Oh, wait. Listen to this: The first outward manifestation of arsenic poisoning is melanosis or dark spots occurring on the chest, back, limbs, and gums."

Jennifer leaned in to read along with him. He pointed to the screen where he read: "In advanced stages, wart-like skin eruptions develop on the hands, feet, and torso, which can lead to skin cancers, loss of circulation, and eventual gangrene, indicating amputation. Chronic arsenic poisoning results in enlargement of the liver, kidneys, and spleen, and often develops into tumors, including lung, skin, bladder, and prostate cancers."

"What are you thinking, Davis?"

"Here's more," he said, pointing to another paragraph. "Signs and symptoms of acute arsenic poisoning. Okay, wait. Look here. Initial symptoms include—no, no. Not that," and he continued to scan. "Look, vomiting and diarrhea, stomach cramps. Blah, blah, blah."

Jennifer jumped in, pointing two lines below. "Circulatory collapse with liver and kidney failure, irregular heartbeat, breathing difficulty, and fever." She continued to read aloud, "Death usually occurs within a few hours. In some cases death follows a few days after the kidneys fail."

Davis looked over his shoulder at Jennifer. "Hank Jacobs may be crazy, but he sure did peg ninety-five percent of the arsenic poisoning symptoms."

"So, you think the government has been poisoning your grandparents?" Jennifer tried to be light-hearted.

"No, but I do know that arsenic killed Mom. And I'm starting to wonder if diabetes killed Pawpaw." He continued to stare at the computer screen.

"That's what Annie said. That he was diabetic."

"Was he? Hank said he wasn't."

"Hank also said his mama died when he was in Ko-rea."

"True."

"Davis, you haven't slept much. I think you are reading a lot into a bad situation."

"Maybe I am, but there's something else."

"I'm listening."

"Pawpaw said there was a letter for Mom." He paused to see what Jennifer would say. When she stared blankly at him, he added, "I haven't found any letter."

"Okay?" Jennifer said hesitantly.

"There *was* a letter, Jen. There had to be, in that envelope. Otherwise, I'm not sure Mom would have thought to shoot herself full of worm medicine." He swiveled the chair around to look at Jennifer directly.

"Okay," Jennifer said slowly. "So, where is it? The sheriff's office?"

"No, there wasn't a letter when she got here. She took the needle and vials, but that was it."

"So, sometime between the time we got down here and found her and the time the sheriff got here, somebody took the letter?"

"That's what I'm thinking," Davis said.

"Why?"

"Well, I don't know."

Jennifer shook her head at Davis and grimaced, squinting her eyes in confusion.

Davis stood up and dug into his pocket, pulling out the ring. He held it out for Jennifer to take and she opened her hand.

Looking down at the bauble that lay in her open palm, she looked back at Davis.

"Whose is this?" she asked. She closed her hand around it, transferring it to her fingers to grasp, and inspected it closely.

"Marcus's," they said in unison.

"Covered in hog blood?" she asked, wrinkling her nose at the idea of what she held.

"Maybe."

"Or *maybe his own!*" Jennifer said melodramatically, raising her eyebrows and widening her eyes. She then handed it back to Davis.

"I'm not kidding, Jennifer."

"I am," she said, and started to walk away.

Davis grabbed the back of her shirt and stopped her.

"Listen, just humor me."

"Okay."

"Marcus and I used to go to a place called "The County Line," up by Winston County."

"All right."

"That's where he always goes. That's where his friends are."

"All right."

"And we're going there tomorrow to find him."

"What will Annie think about this?"

"We're not tellin' Annie."

TWENTY-FOUR

It was still dark on Saturday morning when Davis awoke to the strange sensation of someone staring at him. "You sure sleep hard," Annie noted aloud. She was reclining in Mom's chair, her feet up on the ottoman. Davis rolled over on the couch and propped up on one elbow. He could smell coffee.

"What time is it?" he asked, noticing the still-dark windows.

"Four-thirty, *slacker*," Annie said, and she took a sip from her cup.

"Is that all?" he countered, digging his fists into his eyes.

"Come on," she said, rising awkwardly from her seat.

"Where?"

"I've loaded the back of the truck with that bad meat. We got to haul it out of here."

"Haul it out of here?"

"Yep. Country folk like us don't have curbside pickup, you know. And it's against the law to dump meat in the convenience center. Bears, you know."

"There ain't any bears around here," Davis said, finally sitting up.

"The heck you say. Somebody ran over one in their car up in Sardis a couple of years ago."

"That was Sardis."

"Don't back-talk me," Annie said. "We have to get this meat out of here before it ruins the whole place. I don't want buzzards or coyotes at the funeral.

"Except Aunt Vera?"

"Yeah, except Aunt Vera. She's the only buzzard invited."

"I told you I was gonna take care of that today."

"Yeah, well, after you went off to get rid of the wet-goat smell, I went out and flipped the breaker on the freezer. That's all it was. So's least ways it was close to frozen again this morning and not oozin' all over the place."

"You loaded four hundred pounds of hog into the truck by yourself?"

"Well, it sounds like a lot, but it come in two-pound packages, Davy."

"I said I would get it," Davis sulked.

"I know you did. But *I* got it, and now we got to get it out of here."

"Where? And why now?"

"Oktoc Creek, 'cause if we get caught dumpin' it, it's a big fine. Got to be outta there before daylight."

"I got to brush my teeth," he said, staring around at the room, trying to awaken fully.

"Get some coffee instead. You're gonna need it for this."

*   *   *   *

Annie stood two feet from the edge of Oktoc Creek, an oxbow off the Noxubee River. Davis lingered behind at the tailgate, loading the last of the meat into an empty cooler, not anxious to join in the actual work. The eerie, still darkness of pre-dawn enveloped them even within the shaft of light cast by the truck's headlights. She turned, shaded her gray-blue eyes against the deluge of light, and commanded, "Get your gloves and your case knife and get over here." She was already busy ripping through the plastic sheathing on one package of the semi-frozen meat. A large pile of packages lay on the ground by her feet. She pulled the wrapper from the two-pound lump, dropped the trash in an empty cooler behind her, and then lobbed the meat into the creek.

Davis dumped the last of the packages into the pile, then pulled out one for himself. They worked quietly and quickly for twenty minutes before Annie began to talk.

"I'm gonna tell you a funny story that Mom told me a long time ago," she said.

Davis shrugged his shoulders. "Okay, give."

"This story is about a goose, a cow, and a coondog."

"I always liked a good barnyard tale," he said, peeling the plastic away from his fiftieth package.

She glowered at him and continued to open the rancid ground meat and toss it into the water. "Okay, so the story goes like this. There was this goose, and he decided he didn't want to fly south for the winter. Figured he'd just stay where he'd been all summer. It seemed nice enough.

"So, November and December go by, and January hits. It really starts to get cold, so cold that he decides he better try to get a little farther south after all. So he starts to do that migration thing." She wiped hair from her face with her forearm as she continued to dissect the trash.

"Well, it starts to rain, and then it gets colder and colder and colder, and the rain on the wings of this goose starts to freeze up and get heavy. It's so heavy that he has to make an emergency landing in a cow pasture."

"And this is where the cow comes in?" Davis asked, holding his package at arms length as he peeled. He choked back a gag as he looked down at what he held and then tossed it into the creek.

"Yep. So anyway, the goose is upset because he realizes he is too late. He figures he's a dead duck." She smirked at her own joke. "And so he starts to honk and squawk and complain. And so, this cow comes up to the goose, looks at it the way stupid cows do, you know? A kinda dull look."

Davis nodded his head, letting her rant. Her elfish features were flashing in the headlights.

"I can't get this one," she said, handing him another two-pound package of hog meat.

"Just use your teeth," Davis suggested, but took the meat anyway.

"Anyway," Annie faked a look of fiery disdain. "So the cow turns around after she's gotten bored with the goose. You know, like after three seconds, and promptly proceeds to take a dump right where the goose is layin', all frozen."

Davis raised his eyebrows at the turn of events in the tale.

"Well, now the goose is really pissed. And he honks some more. But, lo and behold, the goose realizes that all that hot poo is melting the ice off of his wings, and he's gonna be able to get out of there after all. But, all the squawkin' and complainin' he did had let the dog know that he was there. So the dog comes over to take a look.

"And you know coondogs and geese." She threw another handful of meat into the lake. Davis paused as he thought he saw movement just outside the periphery of the headlights' beam. He stared harder and realized that the water fifteen feet from shore was starting to move.

Annie continued peeling and shucking her packages of meat, skillfully working, reaching for a new package every twenty seconds. "So now, the goose is thinking he's screwed again. That dog's gonna get him for sure. But, instead of biting his head off, the dog goes to licking all that crap off the goose." She pauses to look at Davis. "Crazy, I know," she said.

"Smells bad. Must be good. Dogs can be kinda gross," he offered as he tossed more meat into the water. He started to reach for another package. They were softening again and dripping a combination of blood and water. His gloves were soaked, and he pulled his cold, wet hands from them and wiped them on the seat of his pants before continuing to assist her. The night around them was quickly lifting, as a shadowy gray dawn crept up from behind the cypress trees that enclosed them.

Annie continued her story. "So, now the goose is happy again. He's thinking he's gonna get out of here and not have to deal with the crap. And it looks like the goose might be right. He's almost completely cleaned up of all the cow patty, when in one big lunge, the coondog reaches over and snaps the goose's neck with one bite." Annie reached for one of the last two packages, but watching the water, she changed her mind.

"Better back up now," she said, scrambling up the wet grass for the levee road, dragging the cooler behind her. Davis looked up from his package, saw the boiling water and virtually leapt backward. He landed squarely on his hindquarters, almost four feet behind where he'd previously stood, just in time to see five feet of alligator go into a death roll. He continued to crab-walk backward up to the gravel path where he finally stood warily beside his cousin.

"Awesome, ain't they?" Annie asked. "I wasn't sure we'd see any today," she added. Most alligators as far north as Mercy were still in a torpid state, lying at the bottom of the river. "They're usually not real active for another couple of weeks."

"Yeah," he said, wiping his palms on his shirttail. "I guess you could say that we're lucky."

"Okay, so what was I sayin'?"

"Uh, 'broke the goose's neck.'" Davis said, but then added, "Is this far enough away?"

"We might ought to get in the back of the truck," she suggested. Davis hoisted Annie into the back, and. before he followed suit, he daringly, and against his better judgment, grabbed the last two packages from the bloody grass at the creek bank. Making a sprint for the truck, he vaulted himself into the bed, and handing one package to Annie, they opened and added them to the feeding frenzy below.

"Okay, so what was I sayin'? Broke the goose's neck. Yeah. In one bite." And then she fell silent, watching the reptile eat.

"And?" Davis said.

Annie continued to stare at the brown water as another gator appeared on the scene. "And. And what?" she asked.

"The moral?" Davis asked. "There's got to be a moral," he said, keeping his eyes on the bloodbath below them.

"Sure. The moral of the story is this: not everybody who dumps on you is the enemy, and not everybody who cleans up your messes is your friend. And since it's impossible to tell what anybody's motives are, when you find yourself in a situation that you don't want to be in, it's just better to take the crap, shut your mouth, and fly south when the time is right."

Davis looked at her golden skin, onyx hair, and frail body. She looked tired. Bruises on her left shoulder, tell-tale signs of Marcus's anger, showed plainly in the sleeveless shirt she wore, even in the early white light of dawn. Her stomach had grown, it seemed, dramatically, since he had arrived. Davis reached out to touch her shoulder, and she withdrew.

"Why did you let him do that to you for so long?" Davis finally asked the question that had been plaguing him for years.

She sat down on the wheel well and crossed her arms over her chest. "I guess it's all in what you get used to, you know?"

"You can get used to being beaten?"

"Well, no. Not really. But, it could've been worse. You know, five years is a long time—"she began.

"A long time to put up with that crap? You're right." The water in the creek had slowed to a simmer.

"I was *gonna* say, 'A long time to just throw it all away,'" Annie replied, standing up and dusting off her hands, matter-of-factly.

"I know what you were *gonna* say, and that's just crazy." He then fell silent, pondering the situation. He added, "He doesn't know how lucky he is that he hasn't bothered to show up yet. You know I'd find a way to hurt him." Davis looked at her sternly. He meant what he said.

Annie stepped up to her cousin, squared his shoulders with her petite hands and returned his stare: "I always kicked him in the shin," she said somberly. "He's got a pin in his right tibia from a motorcycle accident."

She winked and smiled, and then added, "Get me down from here, city boy. We got to get out of here before the park ranger catches us." He helped her down and guided her quickly to the driver's side before he circled around the back way to climb inside as well. Grabbing up the cooler before he climbed in, he tossed it, along with two hundred bloody meat wrappers into the bed of the truck.

Annie pulled her door closed, and Davis followed her example. He shook his head and asked, "Have those always been here?"

She laughed and nodded as she put the truck with the over-sized tires and lighted running board into drive and pulled away from the scene of the crime.

TWENTY-FIVE

Annie and Davis pulled back into the front yard of Sanford's Mossy Horn Sanctuary at half-past six, to find Danny Robert standing on the porch, smoking a cigarette. As Annie maneuvered the white Ford pickup across the gravel drive, Danny Robert flicked his cigarette butt into the flowerbed and descended the steps to the yard. He hailed the pair, and Annie slowed the vehicle as he approached.

Stopping in front of the Sanford home, Annie lowered the window on the driver's side, and she and Davis looked out at her father.

"Where y'all been?" he asked, and he spit the remains of the taste of cigarette onto the drive.

"Freezer crapped out on us," Annie said.

"What?"

"Threw a breaker," Davis added.

"What freezer?"

"The big 'un," Annie said, nodding toward the skinning shed.

With the situation understood, Danny Robert looked crestfallen. "So, where y'all been?"

"The creek."

"Already?"

"Must've happened days ago, Daddy. It was startin' to smell somethin' awful, and with the funeral and all," Annie trailed off.

"Yeah," Danny Robert said. "I been studyin' on them holes out there," and he nodded toward the monstrous oak.

"That's Davis's doin'," Annie tattled.

"You get Hank Jacobs to sign?"

"Not yet, but he's gonna today."

"Well, I hope so, otherwise we got a nice start to a pond." Danny Robert sucked at his teeth then scratched his head. "All right, then," he added, stepping back from the truck for Annie to continue to the parking area out back.

Danny Robert hitched up his jeans by the belt loops and ascended the steps to the porch. He stood for a moment, watching them go around the corner, then entered the house from the front. Moments later he greeted the two in the main kitchen.

"Where's Jennifer?" Davis asked.

"She said she was goin' downstairs to do some work," Danny Robert explained. He walked over and absently kissed the top of Annie's head. Staring around the room, he commented, "Flowers look nice."

"Don't they?" she responded.

Everyone was quiet for a moment, and then Danny Robert asked, "Too early for gators?"

"Naw, Daddy, you shoulda seen 'em this mornin'. Two of 'em, and one of 'em had to be five foot."

"You lie."

"Not about that, I don't."

"She's not kiddin'," Davis backed her story. "I 'bout soiled myself." He laughed and reached into the refrigerator, looking for something to eat. The electronic, pink plastic pig lit up and oinked at him from the back of the top shelf.

"You ain't gonna sit down and eat smellin' like that, are you, boy?" Danny Robert asked.

Davis stopped short of reaching for a package of deli sliced ham and looked down at his hands. He was covered in blood and mud, and remembered he had yet to shower.

"What? You think I should wash?" he asked.

"Boy, get out of that ice box and go get cleaned up. I got to go get Honey, and she can cook you something when we get back."

"Go get her?"

"Yeah, her husband done run off with the car again. Can't get over here."

"Dang, no account husbands," Annie said.

"Men!" Davis exclaimed, and he headed for the basement to shower.

Down the two-toned steps and around the corner, Davis nearly collided with Jennifer as he made the turn past the Wurlitzer.

"Whoa!" Jennifer exclaimed, startled by his return.

"Where've you been?"

"Dumpin' hog meat out at the Refuge." He held out his hands for her inspection.

"Gross," she pronounced, recoiling.

She turned to walk with him and said, "I thought we were going to look for Marcus today."

"We are," Davis said, "But no reason to start looking before noon. Besides, I thought you thought I was full of crap last night."

"That was last night," Jennifer said.

"What, you've had a change of heart?"

"A change of circumstances."

Davis stopped walking and looked at her. "What?"

"Go wash your hands, and then come in here and look at this." Jennifer left him standing there as she limped across the floor and into the vault.

"What?" he followed after her, not bothering to do as he'd been instructed.

"Well, I finished my ad layouts, and I was sitting here watching them go out on email, and I started thinking about that letter you were talking about."

"Yeah?"

"Well, I started to wonder if it was a hand-written letter or a typed letter. Looking at the hand-writing on this envelope, I wondered how long of a letter your Pawpaw would have been able to hand-write."

"I hadn't thought about that."

"So, anyway, I hope you don't mind, but I started looking on the computer for it."

"And you found it?" Davis asked, hopefully.

"In the recycle bin," Jennifer said, and she started navigating to the file. "File name, 'My Dearest Cora,' file original location, 'My Documents,'" she added. "File created date, January seventeenth."

She double-clicked the file icon with the mouse, and read some more. "File deleted, March fifteenth." The two exchanged excited glances. She clicked Restore, then clicked OK. Navigating again, she found the file and opened it with the word processing software.

They leaned closer together to read:

My Dearest Cora,

It's been a wonderful ride, hasn't it? Who would have thought from our days in school that we'd be where we are now? I'm not sure how I lived through the drive from Tuscaloosa to Columbus twice a week. I got more speeding tickets in Reform, Alabama, in those two years than I got the rest of my life. But, we survived it.

Cora, you have been a saint to me. Through thick and thin, you've been a loving wife. I couldn't have asked for someone better than you to be my lifelong partner. For better or worse, for richer or poorer, you were there—in sickness and in health.

And I'm sad to say that there's been more sickness than health these last four or five years. I'm not going to survive it, you know. I've not been the best husband or father or grandfather, but I've done the best I can. I know you forgive me, but I also know that there are others in the family who don't.

I can't say I'm proud of all the things I've done along the way, and I can't say I'm sorry, either, but I can say this: I loved you all, and I did everything I could to provide you with a lifestyle you could be proud of. I was a hard-ass, and I know it. But the place would never be what it is today if I hadn't been the person I am. I guess what I'm trying to say is that I'm human, and I'm flesh and bone, and I'm a dying man.

As we agreed, I'm leaving everything to Annie and Davis, in trust, with a life estate to both the boys. Bobby Jack is the executor, and he knows that I've stipulated that they can't sell out or cut the trees for another ten years. That will help take care of Davis and Annie. And, now I'm asking you to do one last thing for me.

Inside this envelope is some medicine. Annie's been giving it to me for years now. It's pretty powerful, but it can bring you home to me. You will need to use all of it to make sure that it works; otherwise, you might just end up sick.

Just think about it and decide. When you are ready to see me again, I'll be just a few minutes away. I love you, and I need you.

Your husband and friend,
Frank

Jennifer sat back in the chair, and Davis stood slowly from his half-crouched position. They said nothing to each other, and time moved in a surreal slow motion as Jennifer reached across the desk to get the phone, handing it to Davis to dial.

Davis did so, waited, and answered. "Aunt Vera? Is Cletus there?" He paused, listening, then added, "That would be nice. Annie'll be here all day. You can come on anytime."

He hung up, then dialed Cletus at work.

"Cletus there?"

Jennifer could hear a woman's voice on the other end. She listened intently.

After a pause, Davis said into the phone, "Hey, man. Davis. Yeah, um, Pawpaw still on ice?"

Jennifer stood so that she could be closer to the conversation.

"Hmm."

She thought that sounded bad.

"Well, how far along are you?"

Jennifer leaned in to try to hear Cletus's response.

"Well, I'm thinking Artiss might want to come by there in a bit."

More indiscernible chatter could be heard coming from Cletus's end.

"Yeah. Your mom's bringing it by this afternoon. All right. We'll let you know this afternoon, I'm sure. Me or Annie, one."

Davis hung up and looked at Jennifer.

"Too late?"

"He's already pumped him out."

"What about a skin sample or something?"

"I don't know. I'm calling Artiss next."

"What's his mom bringing by?"

"Dinner."

"Oh, that's nice."

"You think? You've never eaten at Aunt Vera's."

"Aunt Vera's coming?" Annie said, standing in the doorway.

Both Davis and Jennifer looked up, startled.

"Boy, I thought you were gettin' a shower," she added.

"I was, before Jennifer distracted me with a question about the layout for my ad that's running in next week's paper," he said.

Jennifer tried to look nonchalant as she sat back down and powered off the Sanford machine as quickly and discreetly as possible.

"On Pawpaw's machine?" Annie asked, confused.

"She's a city girl," Davis said, crossing the room to meet his cousin. "She forgets she can't surf the web on one machine while doing email on the other. Only one connection out here in the sticks."

"Yeah, sorry," Jennifer said. "I thought you could see it in the online mockup we have, but I forgot that I was using the only connection to send the file back to the office."

Annie sighed and agreed. "Yeah, we're not too technical out here." She then turned to Davis and said again, "Aunt Vera's coming?"

"Yep. She's bringing her tuna casserole and Jell-o salad."

"Great," Annie said, drolly. "Did she call? I didn't hear the phone."

"No, it was Cletus. I picked it up on the first ring," Davis said. "Maybe you were outside?"

"No," Annie said, thinking back. "Maybe I was in the bathroom."

"Well, now, that's a stretch," Davis said, laughing, escorting his cousin from the room.

"You gonna shower today?"

"Maybe. Are you?" He kidded her as they crossed the room.

"I scrubbed from the elbows down. I'm okay, I'm thinking," she said.

"Well, I'm gettin' in the shower now, and then me and Jennifer are goin' in to town to kidnap Hank Jacobs."

"What?"

"We got to have a funeral before Monday, Annie."

"I been tellin' you that," she said.

"So, we're takin' Hank to Mr. Bowdrie to get his signature notarized."

"I thought he said he wouldn't sign before Monday."

"Well, depending on when we catch Hank, and what state of mind he's in, we can make it be whatever day of the week we want it to be," Davis said, digging in his duffel bag for clean clothes. "We've just got to convince him."

"Sounds dangerous," Annie said.

"Danger is his middle name," Jennifer offered, stepping out of the vault and into the room with the two.

"You through working?" Davis asked.

"For now. Nothing more to do until Charlotte sends more copy, and I don't expect to see any before tonight."

"Good. Let me clean up, and we'll get out of here."

"Dad'll be back with Honey any minute," Annie said. "Don't you want to eat?"

"We'll grab a sandwich in town."

Annie relented and returned upstairs. Davis smiled feebly at Jennifer before ducking into the bathroom. Jennifer sat on the couch until he emerged and they could leave.

TWENTY-SIX

A cleaner version of Davis emerged from the back of the Sanford home, county papers in his pocket, cell phone in his hand, and Jennifer in tow. He spoke a few words, hung up the phone, and put it down upon the padded chaise on the back patio.

It was already a quarter past ten, and he felt a sense of urgency to get the paperwork finished. Upon remembering that the four-wheeler was no longer in the bed of Annie's truck, he revised his plan of attack, checked the battery in the golf cart, and loaded himself and Jennifer onto it, choosing to take the path through the woods to the Jacobs place. He considered that a circuitous route to the old man's manor might aid in the ruse he was about to employ.

"I thought Danny Robert said the bridge was out between here and there," Jennifer protested as she climbed into the golf cart.

"It's not really a bridge," Davis explained.

"Let me guess. It's really two dead trees, lying across a gorge, raging white water two hundred feet below."

"Sarcasm will get you nowhere," Davis said to her, throwing a shovel onto the back of the cart.

"You're living proof," she replied.

Davis ignored her rebuttal and said instead, "See, it's two pallets that I put down side by side, then ran four landscaping timbers in between the slats. Then I took some pole barn nails and drove 'em into it," he said, hammering out a charade.

"Then I dug out the side of the ditch on either side and buried the part of the landscaping timbers that stuck out." He waved his arms and simulated the digging of holes as he spoke.

"Then I ran a couple of pieces of corrugated metal sheeting over the top," he said, a note of assuring finality in his voice.

"*You* put down? When was the last time *you* were here?" Jennifer said. "How deep is this ditch?" She peppered him with queries.

"Not deep enough to kill us," he said. "Break a few bones, maybe, but definitely not kill us. Definitely not kill us," he repeated in his best Dustin-Hoffman-as-Rainman impression.

"Why do I hear 'Dueling Banjos' playing in my head?" she asked. Davis playfully scowled at her, started the golf cart, and headed toward the Jacobs place.

As the cart puttered along the two-mile junket, Jennifer and Davis stared straight ahead. Loblolly pines, fast approaching maturity, surrounded them. Had the Sanfords been in need of cash, liquidity surrounded the estate. Neither passenger nor driver cared to speak of the letter they'd read or the feat they were setting out to accomplish.

Less than a mile out from Frank and Cora's back yard, they came to a ditch, Davis's makeshift bridge lying sideways in the gully. Upon their approach, Davis let up on the accelerator on the golf cart, and it sputtered to a stop, two-cycle engine fumes bringing up the rear. He dismounted and surveyed the damage. Years of erosion had simply washed away the place where he'd laid the bridge as a teen.

Returning to the cart, Davis retrieved the shovel and approached the project again.

"Why is it, again, that we're coming this way?" Jennifer asked, walking up to the side of the ditch with him.

"Annie and I used to come this way all the time. I'm banking on two things. First, that Hank's got a date with Mary Jane, and second, if the date's going well, that he'll take ol' Dave and Annie up on an offer to buy him a cheeseburger in town."

"Mary Jane who?" Jennifer asked. "And why would he think I'm Annie?"

Davis looked at his girlfriend, bemused by her innocence. "*Where* did you go to school, again?" he asked her.

Within twenty minutes Davis had dug the holes and hoisted the bridge back into place, only a few feet farther downstream from the spot on which he'd originally engineered it. He walked across it twice, even jumped up and down in the middle, but still did not convince Jennifer to ride the golf cart across. Choosing instead to walk across, Jennifer held her breath and refused to look while Davis drove the cart across without mishap.

Moving along again at a rugged but rapid clip, the two approached the back boundary of Hank's property within minutes. Davis applied the brake until the engine died, set the parking brake, and looked over at Jennifer. "All right, Annie Mae," he said. "Play along, if you know how."

Jennifer grimaced, but arose and followed Davis to the back steps of the single-wide trailer. He ascended the steps and knocked. Waiting and hearing nothing, he knocked again. A few moments later, the two heard a clamor inside. Davis paused, then knocked a third time. Finally, a muffled "Who is it?" came from the other side of the door.

"It's Davis," he replied, looking to Jennifer and giving her a wild-eyed grin.

Standing at the bottom of the steps, Jennifer studied the back elevation of the trailer and noticed something green out of the corner of her eye. Farther down the abode was a window, presumably over a kitchen sink, green light emanating from within. A moment later, and the door opened; two moments more, and the smell of marijuana enveloped them.

"Davy, my man," Hank said, extending his maimed hand in greeting. Davis shook it heartily, and smiled. "Come in, come in," Hank began, then stopped short at the sight of the girl. "Or maybe we should go outside," he said, pulling the door shut behind him and standing on the small landing with his visitor.

"Whatcha doin' here?" he asked.

"Oh, I came to see if you'd be up for runnin' down to the market with me for a burger and fries."

Hank looked around, not making eye contact with either visitor. He said nothing at first, then felt the pockets of his cutoff fatigues and said, "I don't have my keys or my wallet."

"I got keys and a wallet. You just get your shoes," Davis suggested.

Hank looked down at his bare feet, and then looked back up at Davis. "You're right." He opened the back door and disappeared inside, surreptitiously closing the door behind him. Davis looked to Jennifer, who had wandered farther down the trailer toward the kitchen window. She was oblivious to Hank's doings, but was instead fixated on the window. She silently beckoned Davis with her finger for him to join her.

He began to work his way toward her, but within seconds Hank reappeared, boots in hand, and sat on the top step to don them. "A burger and fries, eh?" Hank said. "To what do I owe the honor?"

"I don't know. We hadn't seen each other in a while, and I thought we could catch up on basketball talk," Davis offered, walking back toward the steps, Jennifer following behind. "Hadn't heard much out of the recruiting class for next year."

"Oh, they're all a bunch of idiots up there in Starkville," Hank said, nimbly lacing the old Army-issue boots.

"You think their power forward's gonna recover from that torn ACL before next season?" Davis suggested.

"Not a chance, from what I hear. I think they'd be best to try for a medical red-shirt and focus on that Jesus boy outta Sturgis. Got to be the most goddam sacrilegious thing I ever heard of. Namin' a kid *Jesus*," Hank said, lacing his second boot.

Jennifer said, "Lots of people do it in Latin countries, as a name of honor."

"Yeah, but they don't *pronounce* it that way," Hank said, standing and descending the steps.

"Well, don't they pronounce it like they do in Spanish?" she asked, joining the men on their way toward the golf cart.

"Exactly," Hank said. "It's one thing to call your kid *Hay-soos*, and it's completely different to call him *Jesus*."

Jennifer started to say more, but Davis glared at her so that she abruptly closed her mouth and climbed onto the back of the cart and stood up next to the shovel.

Oblivious, Hank took the passenger's seat and Davis slid in to drive. "Hold on, y'all. Haven't tested the brakes on this thing," he admitted.

Jennifer rolled her eyes and held on tighter. Davis punched the gas pedal to release the emergency brake and the engine started. They eased across the side yard, crossed to the front, and navigated the minefield of crosses before they started their descent.

Between the parking area below and the trailer atop the hill, the driveway was rutted and washing, and Davis carefully maneuvered his way down the incline. Jennifer read the inscriptions on the handmade crosses as they bumped and slogged their way downhill. Davis and Hank spoke of Mississippi State basketball, zones, and man-on-man. Their conversation became mere background noise as she tried to think through the letter they'd discovered and exactly what it meant about Annie.

She did not have much time to ponder the situation before she could feel their momentum increasing. The driver's anxiety was soon augmented by their speed, and Jennifer braced for impact. Davis gripped the steering wheel and slammed on the brake pedal. His shouts to his passengers were superfluous, as both Hank and Jennifer knew that they were in for a crash landing.

They passed the parking area at a frenetic pace and seemingly plummeted the last fifty yards to the abandoned railroad bed. Davis turned the wheel hard to the left. The three held on tightly as the cart slid sideways over the ruts they'd made the day before and out onto the white gravel. All were silent for just a moment, then Davis, realizing everyone was okay, released his grip on the steering wheel.

He sniffed, wiped the sweat from his upper lip onto the back of his hand, and said in a somewhat shaky voice, "The things we do for a cheeseburger."

Hank laughed out loud and slapped his knee. Jennifer loosened her grip and sank down to a squat on the back of the cart.

"You okay?" Davis asked, swinging his arm over the backseat and turning his head to check.

"Fine," she said, somewhat queasy. "Let's just go."

Davis faced forward and restarted the cart. They puttered along the track the two hundred yards toward Mercy Station Market, Jennifer recovering, and Davis and Hank engrossed in more basketball talk.

Parking next to the gas pumps, the trio ambled inside for a bite to eat. The establishment was low on patrons for a Saturday morning, it not yet being lunchtime, and the breakfast hour having passed. This worked out well for Davis, as he feared that Jacobs had become agoraphobic in his old age. Hank looked around the place suspiciously. He scratched his chin, then asked, "How long's this place been here, Dave?"

"How long?" Davis asked, surprised. "Hank, you and me used to come here every Friday when I'd come home for the summer." Davis stretched the truth about the past. It was true that he often saw Hank Jacobs on Fridays, but it was usually to pick up a small plastic bag from the old man before Davis and his friends made their Friday-night rounds.

"We did?" he asked, looking a little confused. Hank eased himself into a straight-back chair at one of the tables, continuing to survey the place.

"Sure. You, me, Annie," and Davis barely nodded toward Jennifer at the mention of Annie's name. "We'd come here and eat bologna sandwiches or cheeseburgers, or," and then he stopped spinning his tall tale.

Two patrons looked over, in shock, at the sight of the creator of the infamous Seven-Up Jesus. No one had seen him in town for at least five years. Davis gave them a hard stare, and they stopped gawking, returning to the remnants of their breakfasts.

Davis pulled out a chair for Jennifer, and she sat between the two men. Davis continued his storytelling. "Sometimes Mr. Bowdrie would break for lunch and come join us," he said. And seemingly on cue, the family pharmacist entered the restaurant, looking more than a little frightened, with a small, rectangular, vinyl pouch tucked underneath his arm.

Davis hailed him. "Well, lookie here!" he exclaimed. "What are the odds?" Davis and Jennifer smiled reassuringly at Mr. Bowdrie as he crossed the room and returned the greeting.

"Well if it isn't the Sanfords, and their neighbor, Hank Jacobs," Mr. Bowdrie said, halting and stiff.

A waitress approached the group and said, "Y'all gonna eat?"

Davis looked up at her, half-annoyed, and said, "Yeah, um, give us a minute."

She disappeared, and Mr. Bowdrie pulled up the fourth chair at the table, placing his notary public tools on the floor beside him.

"How you been, Hank?" Mr. Bowdrie tried to appear calm and casual.

Jacobs looked impassively at the pharmacist, then said, "It's been a pretty good Friday so far."

Davis and Jennifer relaxed noticeably when Jacobs admitted that he'd regressed a day on the calendar. Mr. Bowdrie started to dispute the veteran, but Jennifer adroitly interrupted him with her dining desires.

"You know, I can't think of the last time I had a bologna sandwich." She played off Davis's earlier comments.

"Yeah, with pickles and mustard?" Davis added. The longing tone in his voice gave a gourmet sensation to the menu suggestion.

"On fresh white bread," Jacobs added.

"Got to be white bread," Davis said.

Jennifer tried not to show her distaste for white bread, and, in keeping with the macabre concept of the meal, she added, "Fried."

The three men, in unison, offered wistful sighs at the thought of a fried bologna sandwich. The lady among them tried not to cackle.

By this time the waitress had returned. "Y'all want fried bologna sandwiches?" she asked, having overhead their conversation.

"Yes," the three men announced.

"Rag, beef, or imitation?"

The diners exchanged glances and pronounced in quadraphonic stereo, "Beef."

"Chips, potato salad, or coleslaw?"

They placed their orders, including sweet tea and an extra side of mayonnaise for Hank, and the waitress left them to their business.

Jennifer played nervously with the silk gerbera daisy in the small blue vase in the center of the table. There was no conversation, until finally Jacobs spoke.

"So, when y'all gonna have services for your Pawpaw and Mom?"

Davis was taken aback by the lucidity of the question, but he moved quickly into the reason for their rendezvous. "Well, as soon as you sign off on them papers from the county, I reckon we can decide."

Jennifer smiled to herself at how Davis's dialect became thicker with each passing hour in Mercy. She looked between Davis and Jacobs to see what would happen next.

"Now, refresh my memory about them papers," he said.

"Well, you know Pawpaw wanted to be buried on the old home place, but you got to give us your permission to do it. You know my second cousin, Cletus, is the mortician, and he's not allowed to dig the graves until you give your permission, signed and notarized, that we can bury them on residential property."

"That's right," Jacobs said. "I remember now."

"So, I've got the paperwork right here, and if you want, we can go find us a notary today," he said, staring hard at Mr. Bowdrie to give him his cue.

"Why, do you need a notary?" Mr. Bowdrie asked.

Hank looked at him and said, "The boy here says we do. Why? Do you know one?"

"Well, why, y-yes," Mr. Bowdrie said, somewhat daunted by Hank's direct and pointed response. "I-I'm a notary," he said. "And I always keep my stuff with me, wherever I go," he added, leaning down to get the seal and log from the floor.

"Well, now, ain't that handy?" Jacobs said. "We can get it all done right now, and then eat our bologna sandwiches." Then he mused, "You know, I ain't never heard of no *imitation* bologna. Wonder what they make it from? Fake pig lips?"

Mr. Bowdrie hastily pulled what he needed from the black vinyl bag and placed them on the table. "You have the paperwork, Mr. Davis?" he asked, not looking up.

Davis pulled the paper, folded in quarters now, from the back pocket of his jeans and spread it out between himself and Hank. "This just says you give us permission to establish a family cemetery on our land, and you understand that the cemetery will be on property adjacent to yours." Davis pointed to the handful of paragraphs above the line where Jacobs was to sign.

"You sign here," he said, pointing to the appropriate line and producing a pen that earlier he'd clipped to the placket of his golf shirt.

Hank took the pen, signed in his shaky hand, and Davis then pushed the document to Mr. Bowdrie. The pharmacist placed his seal on the document, signed his own name, noted the transaction in his register, and looked up just in time to see their luncheon arriving.

"Just in time," he said, putting away his things.

Davis took the completed paperwork and refolded it, then shoved it back into his pocket to take to Cletus afterward.

The waitress presented their feast, and the three men smiled down at their plates. Jennifer smiled at Davis, looked down at her entrée, and then closed her eyes.

"Eat up," he said. "This beats a cheeseburger any day of the week."

She kicked him under the table and reluctantly took a bite of her sandwich.

TWENTY-SEVEN

After lunch, Mr. Bowdrie returned to his drug store, and Jennifer, Davis, and Hank headed back down the railroad tracks toward the Jacobs estate. Davis begged the old man to climb the hill alone so that he and Jennifer would not have to traverse it downward again for his return trip to town. Hank was amenable to the idea, promising not to shoot when they passed by later in the day. The couple hoped he'd remember.

The two interlopers returned to town on the golf cart to visit with Cletus, to give him the paperwork from the county, and to discuss the recent disclosures. As they puttered across Main Street, Davis could see him sitting on one of two wooden pews that adorned the porch in front of the funeral home. Cletus draped his left arm across the back of the bench and jingled loose change in his pocket with his right. He smiled and nodded at the shoppers who crossed in front of him until he spotted Davis. He stood and greeted the couple as they approached. He wore a long-sleeved, well-starched white shirt with black dress trousers—his standard uniform when not attending a funeral service.

"Davis," he said. "And this must be the lovely Jennifer." He spread his arms to welcome them, then stood to one side to shepherd them into his storefront.

Jennifer decided that Main Street must be the only commercially zoned area in Mercy, as she had never before seen a funeral home located in a strip of storefronts, placed conveniently between a flower shop and a fitness center. The outside of the building gave no evidence of what lay within. The front room could be seen from the street through the plate glass window, but there was nothing inside save a well-worn, uncomfortable-looking couch and an old school teacher's desk that served as a place both to transact business and to greet mourners.

Farther back in the establishment was a visitation area: a plain room with a single row of folding chairs arranged in a semicircle. There was a white wall, illuminated by a soft pink bulb, adorned only with a small wooden crucifix, and clearly designed to frame an open casket. Behind that room a multipurpose restroom and an embalming chamber comprised the far rear of the suite. Since almost all funerals were held at the decedent's church, there was no need for a chapel.

"It's good to see you, even in these difficult times," Cletus said to Davis, shaking his hand. Almost Pawpaw's age, Cletus had taken over Mercy's mortuary from his father when he turned twenty-one. He'd buried almost everyone who had died in Mercy during the past forty years. He was kind and discreet, and he had a good eye for funeral parlor cosmetics. When he'd turned forty, Cletus was elected coroner for all of Lanier County, and he had not faced any opposition since then. It was an effective matrimony of his skills.

"You as well. You're looking good," Davis added.

"I understand you have some paperwork for me that can get us on our way."

"Yes," Davis said, reaching for the well-creased document that was becoming somewhat limp in all its travels. He handed it to Cletus with a sigh of relief.

The mortician quickly scanned the signatures and then looked up and smiled at the two. "That should cover us," he said, and he moved behind the desk to file it away.

"Now, what did you need to tell me about Artiss?"

Davis looked at Jennifer who started to speak but could not find a way to begin. As she was of no help, Davis dove into his confidence.

"Well, it's like this. I'm starting to be concerned about Pawpaw's cause of death."

"Really?" Cletus said, surprised, looking up from his paperwork. "Here, the two of you sit down." He pulled two straight-back chairs from the wall and arranged them in front of the old wooden desk. "What's the cause for concern?"

"Well, I was looking for a letter that Pawpaw had mentioned right before he died."

"And you found it?"

"Yep."

"And, so what did it say?"

"Well, it seems like Pawpaw thinks—thought—he was being poisoned by a family member."

"*Really?*" Cletus said. "Which one?"

It was no family secret that multiple family members had had words with Frank Sanford over the years.

"Well, it didn't really say *which* one," Davis said, veiling details until he could be certain. "But what is interesting is that he thinks he was being poisoned with the same stuff that Mom killed herself with."

Cletus sat back in his chair and contemplated the situation.

Davis continued, "So, I was wondering if there's any way to find out whether that was really the case, or if he was just paranoid in his old age."

"Hey, I represent that remark," his cousin said.

"Sorry."

Cletus smiled. "I'm kidding." Then he added, "Well, the state requires that on all non-hospice deaths in the home that a blood sample shall be saved from the body until the cause of death can be determined. Most of the time nothing is done with the sample, but it's a requirement."

"But Pawpaw was hospice, wasn't he?"

"Technically, yes, but the paperwork had not come into the coroner's office yet; so, I had to treat it as a standard death in the home, even though everybody in town knew he was a goner."

"You're kidding?" Davis said.

"Nope."

"So, you have a blood sample?"

"At the morgue, yep, I sure do. Have one from Mom, too. I've just been doing this too long to go off and get lazy on one of my own family members."

"Awesome!" Davis said. "So, what should we do?"

"Well, I can call Sheriff Artiss, or you can, whatever you want to do. But I can meet her over at the hospital morgue, and then she can take the samples up to Starkville for analysis."

"We can't do that here at the hospital?" Jennifer asked.

"Not if we believe there's been a crime perpetrated. It has to be a state-certified pathology lab, and Oktibbeha General is the closest one. Any other lab, and we'd have to go through a HIPPA quagmire."

"How long will it take?" he asked.

"Depends on the case load."

Davis moaned audibly.

"Son, I've got to go over to the hospital anyway to get Cora out of storage. Do you want me to call Artiss? She can meet me there in fifteen minutes, and we can put an end to all the wondering."

"I guess so. How come you're so calm about all this?"

"How come? I suppose it's because I've seen all manner of this sort of thing most of my adult life. Not a year's gone by that there's not some sort of foul play in the county that I have to either patch up for viewing or keep on ice until lab results come back. Just comes with the territory. Now, before you go, do we have a time for the services?"

"How quickly can you be ready?" Davis asked, shaking his head at the reality of Cletus's comments.

"Frank's done. I can have Cora ready for visitation tonight."

"Okay, then I think we do the visitation tonight."

"And services?"

"At the house," Davis said.

"And who's officiating?" Cletus asked, taking notes.

"We're just doing a graveside service with the Masonic last rites."

"Anyone gonna speak words?"

"I don't think so," Davis said. "But check with Annie, okay?"

"I'll call her as soon as I get off the phone with Artiss."

"Oh, and don't say anything to—'

"To Annie?" Cletus said. "Of course not. Not until we hear from Artiss."

"Right. So, see if Annie has a problem with visitation at the house, tonight at six. And then services tomorrow as soon as they can round up five Masons."

"I'll get 'er done," Cletus said, punctuating his words with a tap of his pen on his notepad.

"Thanks, Cletus," Davis said, standing and extending his hand.

"It's my job," he said, shaking his hand firmly. The cousins smiled awkwardly, and then Davis withdrew his hand, shoving it into his pocket.

"Okay," Cletus said. "You go do whatever else it is you need to get done before six. Oh, and I'll tell Annie we'll get some equipment out there this afternoon to prepare the gravesites."

"Already did the hard part for you," Davis said. "You just bring the tent."

Cletus raised his eyebrow, but did not question him further. "Six o'clock, now," he said. "I'll see you at the house."

Davis and Jennifer retreated to the golf cart. Davis threw it into reverse, announcing his movements with the standard, shrill beeping. He backed from his parking spot and then looped around Main, back toward Mercy Station Market and the scenic route home.

Up Hank Jacobs's hill, past his trailer, and through the woods to the Sanctuary, Davis and Jennifer traveled. It was a quarter until one o'clock. Davis garaged the cart and without stopping inside the log cabin, the two got in her car and took the civilized route south toward Mashulaville, then headed west for the Winston County line.

Five hours and nine pool halls, package stores, and juke joints later, they had been unable to find Marcus or to obtain a report on his whereabouts during the past week. Disheartened with their failure, and late for the visitation he'd scheduled, Davis turned the car toward Highway 14 to head home.

He and Jennifer didn't say much until they crossed back over into Lanier County. She stared at the pine trees out her window, and then finally suggested, "Maybe he went back to Louisiana."

"Or maybe he's in a shallow grave somewhere on the eight square miles of Sanford property," Davis said. He would not break his solemn stare on the highway.

"Oh, don't say that."

"She poisoned Pawpaw," Davis said. "Surely she's capable of killing Marcus, too."

"We don't know that for a fact," she said.

"Pawpaw knew it," Davis said.

"Pawpaw was talking out of his head when I saw him."

"He wrote the letter in January."

"This is March, Davis. January was not that long ago."

"She poisoned him to death," he said, and he hit the steering wheel with the palm of his hand to punctuate his proclamation.

"Why, Davis?" Jennifer asked him. "You have to ask yourself why she would want to kill him. What was in it for her?"

"Money."

"Baloney," she said. "She had access to whatever she wanted. Just look at you, walking around with that bank roll from Danny Robert."

"Well, something, then."

"What something?" Jennifer asked, incredulous.

"I don't know, but *something*."

"I don't get it. Why would you think that Annie is capable of killing her grandfather? Now that *husband*, maybe."

Davis said nothing, but sulked in his own musings. Then he said, "My mom never liked Pawpaw."

Jennifer looked at him questioningly. "Okay?" she said with an open-ended tone.

"She thought Pawpaw was a dirty old man."

"Okay," Jennifer said, even more slowly. She paused, then said, "Do *you* think your grandfather was a dirty old man?"

"I don't know," Davis offered lamely.

"You don't know, or," and Jennifer paused so that it would sink in, "you don't want to know that Annie could be a victim?"

"I don't know. I don't know. I don't know," he said, emphatically, and he pounded the steering wheel again. "I never would believe her."

"Believe who?" Jennifer asked.

"My mom."

"So, Annie never gave you any indication that—"

"No, never. Annie never said anything that I can think of."

"Do you think she would have?"

"I don't know," Davis said, and he hung his head.

"Okay, you have to drive," Jennifer said, lifting his chin. "Or I can, but one of us has to watch the road."

Davis sniffed and re-gripped the steering wheel at ten and two. Then he reaffirmed, "She killed him, Jennifer. She killed them both. She said, *I'll keep him alive till you get here.* She said that on the phone."

"She's a nurse; that's her job—to keep people alive."

"You'd think."

"Okay, we both have to calm down about this," Jennifer said, admitting for the first time her own reservations. "Cletus has given the blood samples to Artiss, and she should be back from Starkville by now. We can call her if you want," and she started digging in her purse for a cell phone. "Or we can go by there."

"They're not going to be able to do anything with those samples on a Saturday," Davis said, dejected.

"You don't know that. If they wanted to, they could get it done. The important thing right now is that we don't have to wait to bury your grandparents. Nobody knows that we know anything, or I should say 'suspect anything.' The funeral's tomorrow. Let's get them in the ground, and then we can tackle the rest of this after the dust settles."

TWENTY-EIGHT

Alan Jackson sang Chattahoochee on the radio as the ebony-haired teen worked alone in the kitchen. Although it was high noon outside, it was dark and cool in the interior of the Sanford home, and she did not turn on the light. Mom had been in bed for the last two days, unable to stand or walk.

Her father and Pawpaw were returning soon with the new hired man from Louisiana. With her father and grandfather gone two weeks, Annie had been left to her own devices during the last days of their absence, her grandmother taking ill after wrangling loose dogs in the summer heat.

Her birthday arrived that morning with no glory or fanfare, with no one to recognize its coming. She hoped that the going of it would garner some notice once the men returned home.

Annie had kept the dogs up in their kennels, since the main fence around the house was down, and the dogs could not be contained otherwise. She'd kept them fed and their runs hosed out, and she truthfully looked forward to someone coming to relieve her of that duty.

While two weeks off with just Mom about the house had seemed promising, the last few days had held more responsibility that she wanted. Besides, Davis was coming back for the summer, and since Bobby Jack and his girlfriend were off on vacation this week and next, Davis got to sleep in one of the twin beds in Annie's room until they returned.

The baying of the dogs from their kennel foretold the arrival of the men before Annie saw or heard them. She dropped the stainless steel bowl with remnants of chocolate frosting into the kitchen sink, wiping her birthday-cake hands on a dish towel.

"Mom!" she called out. "They're here!" She veritably skipped toward the back of the house and the master suite of the Sanford home.

To Annie's surprise, she found Mom seated, upright, in bed, her legs flung out to the side. She held a shiny, unscathed hand trowel in her lap. She fingered it with her knobby, crooked index finger. She looked up and smiled at Annie.

"Hey, the men are here," Annie said to her, standing in the doorway.

"Come sit next to me, baby girl," Cora said to Annie, patting the space on the bed beside her.

Annie walked over to the bed and sat down. "What's up?" she asked, looking down at the garden spade.

"I want to tell you a story," Mom said. "And I don't want you to say anything until I'm done."

"Okay," Annie replied, looking a little confused. Her grandmother took her hand and began:

"Once upon a time, there was a duck. This duck didn't want to be like the other ducks, so he decided that he was going to forget about migrating south for the winter. It was too much hassle, and he liked it where he lived.

"So, he stayed on at the little pond where the summer had been so comfortable. But the weather turned off bad that year. In fact, it was worse than most winters. So, sensing the error of his ways, he decided to make double time to try to catch up to the other ducks.

"He flew and flew, but he didn't think he'd ever catch up. And then, it started to rain, a cold, freezing rain. And the duck's wings got heavier and heavier with ice, until he landed in a barnyard, unable to fly.

"He knew he was in trouble, and he began to moan and squawk and cry, thinking he was dead for sure. Well, it turns out, he wasn't as bad off as he thought.

"You see, this cow comes up, sees this flopping duck, and relieves herself right on the duck. And, while now the duck is covered in cow manure, the heat is

melting the ice off his wings, and he is going to be able to continue to fly."
Mom looked down at her arthritic fingers and grimaced.

"But, before he gets full use of his wings back," she continued, "the barn cat
spots the duck. You see, because the duck had been making so much noise, first
about being doomed, and then about being saved.

"And this old barn cat comes up to him, and starts to clean him up, just like
he was one of her kittens or some odd thing. She just licks and licks and licks,
until the duck is not only thawed out, but completely clean.

Annie continued to listen to her grandmother as her voice began to grow
more faint. Mom stared down at the trowel and continued her tale, not mak-
ing eye contact with Annie.

"So, now the duck is clean, and he starts to flap his wings to take flight, but
the cat reaches out with her cat claws and just tears at the duck's head, until
the duck is maimed and unable to fly away."

Mom sat and stared unemotionally at the wall in front of her. And then she
looked at Annie and smiled.

Annie smiled back at her, but with a puzzled tilt to her head. "And then
what happened, Mom?"

"W-what?" Cora replied.

"Then what happened?" Annie asked again. She looked up at the doorway
to the bedroom, as she sensed that was where Mom was staring, too.

Danny Robert stood there, grinning, holding out his arms to his daughter.

Annie jumped up and ran to the door to greet him, and they embraced.

Mom placed the trowel on the nightstand and pulled her feet back up into
the bed and the covers up around her neck.

She muttered, "I got you that for your birthday," and she rolled over and
closed her eyes, turning her back to the door, to Annie, and to Danny Robert.

TWENTY-NINE

Davis tried to smile as they pulled onto 490 headed north, the last leg of the trip home. Ahead of them he spied a new, black Volvo with a Mississippi State staff-parking permit on the back window. "There's my father," he said. "Just what I needed." He sighed, but continued to follow him, down the highway, past his own driveway, and onto Sanctuary property, toward his grandparents' house.

The front drive held a 1974 gray Cadillac hearse and a half dozen other cars, including Bobby Jack's. Danny Robert smoked on the front porch and espied their return. He stepped to the front door to say something to those inside as Davis and Jennifer drove around back.

After parking, the two walked around front to join Davis's father and his girlfriend as they emerged from their vehicle. She was tall and thin, her fingers entwined in his. Jennifer gawked at her beauty: long, straight black hair and a dark tan. Fashionable sunglasses covered most of her face; an ankle-length, black linen sheath draped her body.

Before Davis could speak, Annie burst through the front door, the screen door swinging outward and slamming back in her whirlwind.

"Where in the hell have you been?" she asked Davis. She marched past her father, down the steps, and accosted Davis. She had on a black dress and heels, and she carried a potholder in each of her hands that were clenched, defiantly resting on each hip. Annie completely ignored the remainder of the family. "I got me a wake goin' on in there, one that *you* scheduled, and I thought I might be able to count on you to beat your no-account daddy to the event." She shifted her glare from Davis to Bobby Jack for just an instant.

Mary Nguyen gave an exasperated huff and slouched, looking away. Annie fired at her, pointing her finger, "You know, when you're no longer a teenager, maybe you can pull that kinda crap with me, but until then, learn to respect your elders." Annie then turned to Davis and Jennifer and said, "Go in the back way, get into some decent clothes, and help me. I got me two dead bodies in the livin' room, a mortician, and eight other do-gooder-mourners. And I got casseroles ass-high to a giraffe in there, and me and Honey are the only sane folks here."

Davis tried to speak calmly. "Annie, everybody in there's seen me in blue jeans," and he walked past her to the front door. "They can see me in 'em again for the eleven seconds it takes us to get across the room and down the stairs." Annie stood in the gravel drive, hands still on her hips.

"Fine!" she called after him. She glared over her shoulder at Bobby Jack and his concubine. "And put that out before you come in the house," she said to him as he took a drag from his cigarette. He silently dropped the half-smoked menthol on the driveway and crushed it with his heel before following her inside. Danny Robert brought up the rear.

Once inside, they were confronted by the fact that the furniture had been rearranged to accommodate two caskets, which were aligned in front of the massive stone chimney and remained open for inspection.

Cletus greeted them solemnly at the door, standing beside a guest book arranged on a mahogany podium, a small, brass art lamp emitting light in the ever-darkening room. Davis and Jennifer slipped downstairs to change clothes, while the remainder of the family met with the townsfolk and distant relatives who awaited them among the taxidermy.

Jennifer found her duffel bag and retreated to the bathroom, while Davis shucked his jeans and sneakers in front of the couch, throwing on stiff, starched khakis over his boxers. He pulled his golf shirt over his head, and, as he did so, Bobby Jack turned the corner and greeted him.

"Long time no see," he said to Davis's back. Bobby Jack held a crystal highball, dark bourbon melting over ice. He observed the gold and navy Celtic cross between Davis's shoulder blades, the Greek symbols at its center.

Davis froze at the sound of his father's voice, and then he continued to dress. He searched through his bag for a white undershirt. Not looking up, he said, "Hello."

"That badge you wear on your back requires more of you than the world requires of other men," Bobby Jack observed.

Davis pulled his clean shirt over his head and turned to look briefly at his father before he reached to the back of the couch to retrieve a pressed, white dress shirt.

"You know, you don't have to spout Sigma Chi dogma at me," he said, slipping one arm, and then the other into the shirt. "But, I guess if you needed an ice-breaker, that was as good as any." Davis shrugged his shoulders to adjust his clothes, then began buttoning.

"Danny Robert and I have been talking," Bobby Jack said. "We've decided that I get the furniture, he gets the house, and we're cutting the trees now and splitting the proceeds. He's having the NRA come in and appraise the guns, and we'll be selling those, too."

Davis considered his father's words. "Is that what the will says?" he asked.

"There is no will, not that we can find, anyway."

"Have you looked for one?" Davis asked, unbuttoning his pants to tuck in his shirt. He pinned him to the wall with his eyes, saying, "I figured you'd be the executor."

"Well, we assume it's in one of the safes in the vault," Bobby Jack hedged. "We've put a call in to Liberty Safe, but we have to send them a certified copy of both death certificates and the serial numbers of the safes in order to get them to release the combinations."

"That shouldn't be too hard."

"It's just time-consuming."

"I suppose we all have plenty of that," Davis countered. "We got to go through probate, assuming there's no will."

"Look, Annie said she didn't have a problem with working things out that way. And being *intestate* beats the hell out of whatever strings your grandfather attached to this monstrosity." Bobby Jack waved his arm, indicating the house around them, and sloshed his drink as he spoke.

"So, are you *asking* me what I think about it, or are you just telling me, for my information?" Davis asked. He sat down on the edge of the coffee table to pull on dress socks.

"I don't have to have your approval for anything," Bobby Jack said, reaching into his shirt pocket for a cigarette.

"Annie doesn't want you smoking in the house," Davis said, looking up when he heard the lighter flare.

"This isn't Annie's house," Bobby Jack said, inhaling deeply, then exhaling through his nose.

"It isn't?" Davis asked.

"No, she and Marcus have a house down the way. She lives there. Danny Robert lives here."

"Marcus doesn't have anything around here anymore, and his name doesn't even deserve to be mentioned," Davis said, lacing up his wingtips.

"Look, I didn't come down here to debate you. I came down here to say that Artiss should be here for visitation, and knowing her, she'll be asking about the will. There's nobody left here who wants to run a deer camp. We just want the money, and we want out. My advice to you is to just keep your mouth shut when she gets here. We don't need you or that nigger-woman sheriff screwing up our finances."

"First, I didn't ask for your advice," Davis said, sliding his belt through the loops of his khakis. "Second, you're the wrong generation to get away with that kind of bullshit slur. I put up with listening to it from Pawpaw and Mom. I just tried to pretend they didn't know any better." He walked to the bathroom door and rapped on it. "Ready in there?"

Jennifer opened the door and smiled weakly at him. With one look Davis knew she'd heard the whole conversation. In her mounting anger, her neck and chest had turned splotchy and red; her v-neck black silk dress did not hide her emotions well.

"Ready," she said. She reached behind the bathroom door and grabbed his navy sport coat.

"Well speaking of generations, your generation wasn't going to get anything out of them anyway," Bobby Jack said as they walked past him, toward the stairs. "You'll have to wait till I'm dead before you see any of this come your way." He paused, then added, "If I don't spend it first."

Davis adjusted the cuffs of his shirt and then turned to look at his father. "I already got more out of you and Pawpaw than I ever asked for."

"And what's that?" Bobby Jack chided him.

"This—this *generational curse*," Davis said, grasping for words, and pointing at his father's half-empty glass. "I don't know how much longer my family has to endure it, but maybe our kids will be luckier." Davis took Jennifer's arm and turned from his father to leave.

Jennifer's heart leapt at Davis's Freudian slip, and a broad smile spread across her face. When they began to mount the stairs she whispered to him, "I'm not sure what you meant back there, but my family's nothing but a bunch of Irish Presbyterians with a few firewater-swilling Choctaws thrown in the mix. I'm not sure whose genes are worse."

"Just shut up and keep walking," Davis whispered, and he goosed her from behind as they arrived in the living room. Annie met them at the entrance to the stairwell.

"Is your daddy smoking down there?" she asked him.

"Of course," Davis said. Annie pushed Davis aside, stood at the top of the stairs and yelled: "Hey! I'm pregnant, and I told you not to smoke in the house. Respect me for just four more months, okay?"

Bobby Jack did not reply; so, Annie turned to Davis and said, "I got to pee. Go beat the crap out of your daddy for me."

"I'm through with him, Annie," Davis said, and he and Jennifer made their formal entrance to the wake.

Great Aunt Vera Wadsworth was the first to descend upon the couple. Pawpaw's oldest living sister, Aunt Vera was approaching eighty. She'd had quadruple bypass surgery twenty years earlier, and, at her doctor's recommendation, she began consuming large quantities of garlic to help her heart. Aunt Vera's scent preceded her everywhere she went, to the point that even her own grandchildren called her Granny Garlic behind her back.

Also in attendance was Aunt Vera's younger son, Ricky. He had never left home, except to ride his bicycle through town. Occasionally, he played cops and robbers by dressing in a police uniform and walking the streets of Mercy, passing out traffic tickets to all who would take them. Mom and Pawpaw had spent their entire married life denying any relationship to Ricky Wadsworth.

Aunt Vera pulled Davis aside to speak to him privately, and Ricky homed in on Jennifer. Cousin Ricky walked straight up to the defenseless girl who stood alone in the center of the family room and introduced himself. "Hi, I'm Ricky Wadsworth, PFC," he said in a quick and high-pitched tone.

Jennifer unwittingly welcomed the introduction and took his hand to shake it. "Jennifer Martin," she replied. "Very nice to meet you."

"I'm Davis and Annie's cousin," Ricky continued.

"That's nice," Jennifer countered.

"Where you from?"

"Bedford."

"Oh, I know Bedford! I drove a gravel truck outta Bedford to Como every day for ten years, from 1962 to 1972, if I recall it correctly." Jennifer could see Ricky calculating in his head. "Yeah, those were the days," he said with a reminiscent sigh.

"Really?" Jennifer said. "That's a long way to haul gravel," she said. "What were they doing with it?"

"You know, I don't rightly reconnoiter," Ricky said.

Jennifer found that to be an odd response, but tried to continue the conversation. "Was that before you joined the military?" she asked, still confused by his inability to carry on a conversation even though he sported a seemingly well-groomed façade.

"You know, I don't rightly reconnoiter," Ricky repeated. He stared at Jennifer, sizing up her petite and well-balanced form for a moment, and then he leaned to say in her ear, "So, are you and Davis gonna get married?" His voice at the end of the question became so high pitched that

Lovey looked up from her spot on the couch and cocked her head to one side.

Jennifer intended to end their conversation, smiled at him, and said coyly, "You know, I don't rightly reconnoiter." Then she scanned the room, looking for Davis or Annie or anyone else in the family whom she recognized. Finding no one in plain sight, Jennifer excused herself under the pretense of finding the powder room and hastily ducked into the kitchen as an escape. Lovey, who had been watching the exchange, jumped down from the couch with a graceless, heavy thud and followed her.

Davis and Aunt Vera stood in the kitchen, Davis with a plate of tuna casserole in his hands, a side of green congealed salad perched on one side. He ate obediently as he listened to what senseless gossip Aunt Vera conveyed to him in hushed tones. He took a big bite and then reached for a tall glass of sweet tea as a chaser before realizing that Jennifer had joined them. So happy to see her, and to have a diversion from his dinner and garlic-laced conversation, he quickly gulped the bite down and set the plate on the countertop, reaching his hands out to her.

"Aunt Vera," he said, struggling with the remaining tuna casserole in his mouth, "this is my friend, Jennifer Martin."

"Nice to meet you, Mrs.—"

"Wadsworth," Vera finished Jennifer's sentence.

"Where have I heard that name?" Jennifer asked.

"Aunt Vera is my double great aunt," Davis said.

"You mean great-great aunt?" Jennifer asked, confused.

"No, she's my great aunt on both sides of the family."

"Oh," Jennifer said. "When did we cross over into West Virginia?"

All three laughed, and Davis explained that Aunt Vera was a Sanford who'd married a Wadsworth, which was what Mom had been before she'd married a Sanford.

"Double dates with brothers and sisters," Aunt Vera said, "lead to double first cousins, they always say."

"Right. Cletus and Ricky are my father and Danny Robert's double first cousins," Davis said.

"So, Ricky Wadsworth, PFC, is your son?" Jennifer asked. "I just met him in the living room."

"You know what PFC stands for don't you?" Davis asked, winking at her.

"Private First Class?" she asked, haltingly.

"No. In this case it stands for 'Plum Full of Crap.'"

"Oh dear," Aunt Vera said. "He didn't say anything inappropriate, did he?"

"Oh, no, ma'am," Jennifer said. She looked down at the floor as Lovey sat on her foot.

Aunt Vera looked dismayed at the sight of the old dog. "I don't know why Danny Robert keeps that ugly thing around," she said. "It's nothing more than a wingless bat, I tell you."

Lovey sniffed, then sneezed twice at Aunt Vera, but did not move from her spot on Jennifer's foot.

"She acts like she knows what I'm saying!" Aunt Vera exclaimed.

Davis pushed his plate toward Jennifer, who politely refused. Aunt Vera saw the interplay and said, "Well Davis, you should get her a plate of her own, especially with that walking stick and all. She doesn't need to be doing anything for herself."

"Oh, that's okay," Jennifer said. "It looks great, but I don't eat tuna—you know, the mercury content and all." She pulled her foot out from under Lovey and moved back two steps.

"Oh, right," Aunt Vera said. "I think I read about that, but since I'm long past having children, I figure I can eat two or three cans a week."

"That's great. If only I were so lucky," Jennifer said.

"Oh, you'll get there one day," Aunt Vera said, and she looked down at the dog that had backed up to Jennifer's leg and sat down again.

"She likes you," Davis said.

"She's tormenting me," Jennifer countered.

The doorbell rang in the front room, and Aunt Vera said, "Let me go out there and greet whoever that is. It is so good to meet you, Jennifer. I hope you'll come back soon, when the circumstances are better." She nodded and patted Jennifer's hand before bustling out the door to see who had come to call.

Davis took one look at Jennifer and said, "I got to get out of here before I get sick." He made his escape down the hall and through Danny Robert's kitchen, Jennifer hard on his heels. Danny Robert stood at the waffle iron, stamping out sausage-flavored snacks for the dogs, and called out to them, "Where you headed?"

Davis did not answer. Jennifer shrugged her shoulders at Danny Robert and followed Davis out the kitchen door, across the screened porch, and out to the carport to her car.

THIRTY

Within ten minutes the pair was off Sanford property and onto federal land at the Noxubee Wildlife Refuge. They turned off Yellow Creek Road and onto Mt. Sinai Church Road, merely a dirt path perpendicular to a gravel trail.

The sun had set at a little past six, and with the myriad of trees surrounding them, it was quite dark. Their headlights told them that they were still on federal ground so long as they continued to see white spray paint markers on the tree trunks every few hundred yards.

Occasionally they would come across a creek or a stream that had been forded by a steel-grate bridge just wide enough for one vehicle at a time to cross. The bridges came up off the road at a sharp, almost forty-five-degree angle, then spanned the gap, and came down again symmetrically on the other side.

Davis had seen this sort of bridge since he was a child, but Jennifer had not. She was not happy with the prospect of Davis driving her car across them. Each time they crossed one, the roar of tires on steel cauterized her ears and she winced outwardly.

Upon the approach to the third bridge, Davis stopped short and said, "You want to get out and walk?"

Jennifer was in low heels and a silk dress, but she rapidly agreed, shedding her shoes to walk barefoot on the cool, almost-muddy road. Davis killed the engine and the headlights, and he got out and walked up to the bridge. He looked behind to wait for Jennifer, who hobbled up behind him and looked down at the overpass. A dark, cool stream rushed along below it, cypress knees bordering its banks.

"This is barely a trickle in the summertime," Davis commented, and he stepped up onto the grate. Jennifer tried to follow him, but her feet would not allow it. Davis started to back down, but instead went to the center of the bridge and spread out his jacket. He then returned to her, picked her up in a honeymoon cradle, and carried her to the middle, gingerly placing her down on her feet.

The bridge had no railing, and Davis sat down on the edge and dangled his feet over the side. Jennifer did the same. She looked over at him, grasped his hand, and smiled. "Rough day," she said.

Davis sighed through his nose, raised his hand in frustration, and then rubbed his forehead. "Yeah," he said, turning to her to return the smile. A half-moon sky was becoming brighter as their eyes adjusted to the night without headlights.

"Tell me about this place," she said.

"Oh, not much to tell," Davis said. "You can pretty much figure that any place I know that's off the beaten path is just a place I used to come to smoke dope."

Jennifer stared down at her bare feet and swung them back and forth. She did not let go of his hand.

"Not too many good memories here," he said. "It was just the place I'd go to get out of the house."

"Yeah?"

"Yeah. But I was thinkin'," and he turned Jennifer's chin to his with the tip of his forefinger, "maybe we could make a good memory for this place." They leaned together, and he kissed her for the first time since their arrival in Mercy. Jennifer drank in his kiss, savored his smell, and relished the moment and the night around them. She pulled away and whispered to him softly, "Davis, this metal grate is killing my butt."

He laughed aloud, stood up, and heaved her up over his shoulder and carried her, fireman style, to the other side of the bridge. He stood her up, ran back for his sport coat, and joined her.

"Where are we going?" she asked.

"Just up the road a little ways."

The two strolled, hand-in-hand, down the winding cow path, enjoying the night air and the solitude. At the end of the lane Jennifer spied a small, one-room, white church, up on cinderblocks, backed up to a stand of loblollies. A light shone within. To the right and behind the church a creek flowed; to the left a cemetery stood.

As they drew closer, Jennifer could just make out above the door three block letters, painted free-hand: *AME.*

"What's *AME?*" she asked Davis.

"Well, I didn't know it until a while back, but it's African Methodist Episcopal."

This was the only signage on the premises, and the two continued their leisurely walk around to the left, toward the graveyard. The side yard of the church was peppered with grave markers, all of which were small and made crudely from concrete. None more than knee-high, each was curved at the top to form a traditional tombstone shape.

Jennifer knelt beside the first one for a closer inspection and was awed by the beauty. Someone had carefully imbedded the name in the stone using chips of broken, colored glass, in an almost mosaic pattern. She stood and walked to the next one. Each one was similar. Some were cobalt; some were bright green. Others incorporated multiple colors. There were no epitaphs, and some did not have the years of birth or death, but of the fifty or more stones, each one had been lovingly handcrafted into a remarkable work of art.

"These are amazing," Jennifer said, looking up at Davis. He stood beside her, hands shoved deep in his pockets. When she was ready to stand, he gave her a hand up, and they moved reverently through the yard, admiring the work of artisans from many decades.

Toward the rear, and closer to the creek that meandered around back, several of the stones lay atop the graves, broken into two or three pieces, but placed back together as pieces of a puzzle. "These must be really old," Jennifer said, and she bent down to inspect one further. She ran her hand across the uneven surface and considered the survivor who could not afford to replace the stone. She looked back over her shoulder to voice her thoughts to Davis and found he was not there.

"Davis?" she said hesitantly. Using her cane, she carefully steadied herself and stood, turning to search for him. He was half-standing, half-crouching, twenty feet away. His hands were on his knees, and Jennifer could hear him choking back tears.

"Hey," she said, coming up from behind. "Are you okay?"

Davis stood upright and wiped his face, but he would not look at her.

"What's the matter?" she asked.

Davis attempted to regain his composure; he smoothed his hair back as he was apt to do when feeling self-conscious. "I'm okay," he said. Then he added, "It's been a long day."

Jennifer bear-hugged him and buried her face in his chest. In the lonely darkness, with both of them still, they heard something. A voice emanated from within the church; a chant, with a rhythmic sway to the words, began to make itself heard.

The couple stood still and listened attentively but could not make sense of what was being said. Intrigued, Davis took her by the hand and pulled her through the yard and toward the front door of the church.

She whispered, "What are we doing?"

"Going inside," Davis said.

Jennifer did not argue but followed his instructions. As they turned the corner to the front of the church, Jennifer saw for the first time a 1970's model Buick parked to the right of the building. The front fender was green; the rest of the car was an oxidized navy blue.

Davis tried the front door, and it opened readily and admitted them inside. The walls were painted white, and beneath their feet lay worn heart-of-pine. The pews were simple and strong, with just the right angle for long hours of back support. Davis slipped into the back row and Jennifer sat beside him.

In the pulpit stood a fifty-something African American pastor. His hair was stark white, and his body was short, sturdy, and pear-shaped. He was in the closing minutes of his Saturday-night dry-run before Sunday morning worship. Jennifer and Davis were the only parishioners. The preacher's voice rose and fell in a melodic cadence as he lectured:

"I took my grandkids to the zoo up in Memphis, and we saw all the animals there. And Diondra say to me when we was there, 'Dandad,' she say, 'where do they get the monkeys?'

"And I say, 'Well, they ketch 'em, out in the jungle.' And they's swingin' through them cages, way up high, and Diondra say to me—you know she only four—she say to me, 'How, Dandad? How?'

"Now don't that beat all? If you ain't blessed with a four-year-old, then you cain't understand that this querstion was about the millionth querstion I been axed that day. So, I say to her, 'I don't know, Diondra.' And then she say, 'Why?'

"So, because I was *tired,* and because I didn't think I could *bear* to hear that chil' axe me again, I say to her, 'Let's axe the keeper.'

"And you know what that keeper say? He say they don't need no cages to trap monkeys. Naw suh. All they need is a shiny coin and a long-neck bottle. They tie the bottle to a tree, and then they put the coin inside the bottle.

"And these monkeys, they so attracted to this shiny penny or nickel or dime, that they stop, an' they stick they hand in that jar, and they get the coin. But, then they cain't get they hand out the jar while they holdin' to the object. And then the trappers come, and they take 'em away. Now, all the monkey have to do is let go the object, and they free.

"Now I axe you, Christian, ain't we nothin' but the monkey at the zoo?

"An' now, you be sayin' 'But Brother, I'm *blessed.'*

"An' I be sayin' to you, 'If you can't get up out of your California king-sized bed in your California king-sized house because you have no *joy,* then your *stuff* ain't your *blessin'.'*

"Everything I have, it come from the *Lord.*

"My house, it come from the Lord. And I got *joy* in my house.

"My car, it come from the Lord. And I got *joy* in my car.

"My job, it come from the Lord. And I got *joy* in my job.

"This church, it come from the Lord. And I got *joy* in this church.

"You see, Christians, you can have the *stuff*, but if there is no *joy*, then there's no blessin' in it.

"You see the funny thing is you can have joy even if you ain't got stuff. But your stuff may never bring you *joy*, because *joy* comes from the blessin' of the *Lord.*

"Is your house your *cage*? Do you serve your *house*? Or do you serve the *Lord*?

"Is your job your *cage*? Do you serve your *job*? Or do you serve the *Lord*?

"Is your brand-new Cadillac, your brand-new BMW, your brand-new Humvee your cage? Do you serve *Detroit*, or do you serve the *Lord*?

"Is your family your *cage*? Do you serve your *family*? Or do you serve the *Lord*?

"Brothers and sisters, the Bible say in Ephesians 6:1, 'Obey your parents *in the Lord.*' Sometime we forget that *'in the Lord.'* Maybe your parents *ain't* in the Lord! Maybe your *brother* ain't in the Lord.

"The Bible say in Luke 16:13, 'You cannot serve God and mammon.'

"What's your mammon? Is it your car? Is it your house? Is it your job? Is it your family who not in the Lord?

"The Bible say in Matthew 6:13, 'Seek ye *first* the kingdom of *God*, and his *righteousness*; and *aaaall* these things shall be added *unto* you.'

"Seek ye *first*, brothers and sisters. Seek ye *first.*

"Christians, you can have the stuff and not *be righteous.*

"You can have the stuff and have no *joy.*

"You can have the stuff, and not have a *blessin'.*

"But until you know that it is *from* God—

"Until you know that it is *through* God that all blessin's flow—

"And until you know and accept the mercy that is from everlasting to everlasting through the fellowship of the Holy Spirit and the graciousness and righteousness of Jesus the Son of God, you can have the *stuff* but not have the *joy.*

"Brothers and sisters, it's all God's stuff. You just the keepers of it. Whether or not you get a blessin' with it depend on your relationship with the Lord.

"Who you servin' today? Are you servin' God? Or are you servin' mammon?"

The preacher railed, "Who you servin' today? Are you servin' God? Or are you servin' mammon?"

His fever-pitch subsided and he stepped down from the pulpit he'd been clenching. "Who you servin' today? Are you servin' God? Or are you servin' mammon?" This time he looked straight at Davis and Jennifer, asking the question directly.

Davis stood and met him halfway down the center aisle. "I'm servin' the Lord today, brother," Davis said. He pulled his hand from his pocket and shook the preacher's hand, sliding him the remains of the stack of large bills with which Danny Robert had funded him the day prior.

The preacher wrapped his arm around Davis and walked with him to the altar railing, and the two men knelt together, talking in muffled tones. When they arose, the money lay on the altar, the two men shook hands, and Davis returned to Jennifer. He helped her to stand; his hands were shaking, and his nose was red.

She looked first to Davis, then to the preacher, who nodded and gave a small wave. The couple headed for the door, and Jennifer paused to speak.

"Thank you, sir," she began.

He nodded an acknowledgment.

"Not much of a crowd here on Saturday night, but we appreciate the words."

"I'm not usually here on Saturdays, but the Lord made my house a little unbearable this evening, with a herd of grandchildren and a broken air conditioner. I had to work out what the Lord wanted me to say, and he sent me here tonight. The Lord knows who needs his words. I'm not the author; I'm just the vehicle. The Holy Spirit's been movin' tonight."

The two nodded, then left the church and returned to the Mississippi darkness. Making a direct path for the car, three hundred yards away, Davis said nothing but kept his arm around Jennifer's shoulder.

He lifted her up as they approached the bridge and carried her across to her car. Helping her inside, he closed the door behind her when she was settled, then walked around the front of the car to the driver's side. He started the engine, performed a three-point-turn, and pointed the car back home.

Both were quiet for five minutes, until, unprompted, Davis began, "The summer I turned fifteen I used to come out here a lot—every Friday night, nearly. Me and a couple of thugs from Mercy. We'd smoke some weed and drink some beer. Hell, we'd drink a lot of beer.

"Anyway, one night we come up here, and me and the boys went back to that church back there. One of the fellas said that it wasn't a real church. He'd heard it was a place for witches. And anyway, he pointed to all the tombstones back there. And he explained that he'd been told that the colored glass on the tombstone was some sorta voodoo stuff." The pitch of Davis's voice began to rise, and Jennifer reached to put her hand on his shoulder.

"Not that I ever needed an excuse to break stuff, but I listened to him, and I let him convince me that trashin' the place would be some sorta upright, fine, and Christian thing to do. And I was drunk, and that's no excuse, but I was. And I did it. Me and them boys broke a half-dozen or more of those tombstones out there. Probably woulda done more, but we were too drunk or stoned or—" Davis's voice became softer and softer until he trailed off into silence.

"God forgive me," he said, and he turned the car onto Sanford property.

It was a quarter until nine o'clock when Jennifer's Mercedes rolled across the gravel drive and into its appointed parking spot at the Sanford home. The dogs were kenneled, and all the visiting cars were gone except Bobby Jack's. Both Davis and Jennifer saw the car, but neither made a remark.

Exhausted from the day's events, Davis escorted her up the steps to the back deck as the pair tried to make their way quietly through Danny Robert's darkened kitchen and into the main part of the house. Annie and Danny Robert had retired to their respective quarters, their doors pulled closed. Jennifer and Davis, his sport coat slung over one shoulder, passed their rooms and emerged, holding hands, in the trophy room, where the two caskets remained, albeit closed, due to the hour.

Bobby Jack sat in his mother's chair, his feet propped on the ottoman, with a dark glass of Booker's resting on his stomach. This room, too, was darkened except for the stained glass dragonfly lamp at Davis's father's side.

"Where've you been?" he asked Davis.

Davis bristled at the intrusion, but answered, "Church."

"I see."

Neither man spoke, and several seconds passed before Bobby Jack conceded: "I guess that tough love thing has some merits after all." His speech was slightly slurred.

Davis gripped Jennifer's hand and turned to look at her. "Can you give us a few minutes?" he asked.

Jennifer quietly excused herself and went to the basement. Lovey watched her go, then hopped down from her post on the couch to follow her as she turned the corner to the stairs.

Davis draped his jacket on the back of the couch and sat down across the room from his father. He propped one foot on the coffee table and began unlacing his shoes. "Tough love?" Davis queried. "Is that what you call that?"

"I didn't know what else to do with you, boy. You were out of control."

Davis considered his drunken father's words and then agreed. "Yes, I was."

"But, you don't seem to be hurtin' now," Bobby Jack said, taking a sip of the strong bourbon.

"I'd say I've gotten a lot of things together," Davis said, slipping off his shoe and starting on the second one.

"Yeah, well, you look good anyway. And she seems like a nice young kid."

"Jennifer is nice."

"Nice car. She come from money?"

"Not like we do."

Bobby Jack thought about that statement and then took another drink. "Ever thought about going back to school, boy?"

Davis said nothing, but instead took off his second shoe and placed it next to its mate on top of the coffee table. His sock feet in a wide stance, Davis leaned his elbows on his knees and allowed his hands to hang between them. He looked up at his father.

"Have you ever wondered how I was doing?" he asked, changing the subject.

Bobby Jack stared uncomprehendingly at his son.

Davis continued, "I mean, these last seven, eight years. Did you ever wonder?"

Bobby Jack stiffened, but Davis continued, switching his glance back and forth from the rug beneath his feet to the eyes of his father. "I mean, did you ever *really* wonder? Sure, you knew I was *alive*, especially my freshman year—hell, you saw me near every day. But did you ever wonder *how* I was *doing*? Was I happy? Was I miserable? Was I lonely? Was I in love? Did you ever wonder that?" Davis rattled off his list of questions.

"I mean, 'cause if you did, then that sure was some *tough* love you were giving me there. *Tough* love. Teachin' me a lesson, for sure.

"But, then again, the way I figure it, if you didn't ever really wonder about me enough to speak to me, or to call me, or to write me, or to maybe even ask my mama about me, then all I can really call that is just plain-old *tough*. Not much love to it, really." And Davis rose from his seat. He picked up his shoes in his left hand and reached for his jacket with his right, draping it over his back. He waited for a rebuttal.

"I'd be happy to pay for your school if you wanted to go back and finish. And law school, too. That's what you were majoring in, wasn't it?"

"I never wanted your money, Dad," Davis said, shaking his head, crossing the room for the basement stairs. "I never wanted your money."

The Regulator announced from his grandfather's room that it was nine o'clock.

THIRTY-ONE

He nodded and walked, trance-like, toward Pawpaw's bedroom. Annie grabbed his hand and pulled him down the darkened hall. "Snap out of it, Davy. I already got one patient and a couple of basket cases back here. Don't need another," she said.

When they got to the master suite, he could see in the lamp-lit room the empty bed, tussled sheets, and a bright light in the adjacent bathroom. Annie continued to drag him toward the lavatory. They could hear a commotion from within.

"Good God!" Frank Sanford did his best to bellow, but a hoarse whisper was all he could manage. He had been unceremoniously positioned on the toilet, his pastel blue cotton pajama trousers wrapped around his elephantine ankles. Danny Robert held him steady by kneeling in the floor, one hand at his father's elbow, the other on his knee. Cora stood beside the pair, hands clenched together at her mouth.

"Get this God-forsaken tube out of my nose," Frank ordered. All four individuals made motions to assist, but Annie stepped up and pulled the oxygen supply from his red and bulbous nose, unfastening the ear straps and pulling it over his head. She began to roll up the clear tubing from her thumb to elbow, thumb to elbow, working her way back toward the oxygen tank on wheels.

"Don't go lighting no cigarettes, none of ya," she said, turning off the supply.

"I've a mind to light two of 'em," Frank replied.

"Stop it, Pawpaw," she said sternly. "Can we try to make this as pleasant an experience as possible?"

"It's my death, I'll do it like I see fit," he replied.

"Have it your way. Always have," she said, wheeling the tank out of the bath and into the bedroom.

There was silence. Davis leaned on the doorjamb to the bathroom, saying nothing, but watching the melee unfold.

"It ain't right that it should happen this way," Frank continued his hoarse, whisper of a rant. "I'm supposed to die peaceful—in my sleep."

"Oh, Frank," Cora said, and she kneeled beside him. A fecal odor began to permeate the room. "You can't leave yet. You got to stay with me a little while longer."

Frank's face softened as he looked into the eyes of his wife. "Baby," he said, "I can't stay much longer. This old body of mine's give out."

"No, you have to stay a little while longer," Cora said. "Our anniversary is coming up. Stay for that, won't you?"

Frank looked away. He stared intently at the wall. Mumbling at first, and then finally aloud, he said, "Just a second. I need more time." He returned his gaze to Cora and gave her a weak smile.

Davis watched from the doorway, arms crossed, lips pursed into a hard line across his tanned face. His eyes welled up, and he quickly wiped a tear away with the back of his hand.

Frank reached to stroke Cora's short, white locks. "You used to have the prettiest red hair, Cora. Too bad the boys got mine instead of yours."

"Don't go Frank," Cora said. "I still need you here. Who's gonna take care of me?"

"Danny Robert will take care of the dogs. Annie can cook." He held her hand with one of his and pressed against the wall with the other. His face turned ashen, and he looked frantically about the room.

"You need a trash can, Pawpaw?" Annie asked. She produced one from beside the clothes hamper, helped Mom up with one hand, and positioned it in front of his legs with the other. "Help him, Daddy," she instructed Danny Robert, and pulled Cora away and back into the bedroom. The prodigal backed up as Annie dragged her past where he had been standing.

Danny Robert stood up from his kneeling position and reached for a tri-fold bath cloth from a large stack next to the bathroom sink. He ran hot water over it and wrung it out. Kneeling back beside his father, he wiped his face and then sat down, knees up beside his chin, forearms resting atop them, hands hung down in defeat.

"Well, Dad, this is it," he said.

Frank said nothing. He gathered the remains of vomit in his mouth and spit it into the garbage can in a slow, long string. His breathing was shallow.

"I reckon we've been comin' up to this for years now," Danny Robert continued.

"Diabetes is a bitch, ain't it?" Frank whispered.

"You know, it's ironic that you ever started believing that yourself," his son said.

Frank became still, though his breathing was still ragged.

"Tell a lie long enough, and I guess that can happen to you. Worked out well enough for me. You know, when I first thought you was hurtin' my Annie, I thought about killin' you then. But, I lied to myself about it for long enough, and I started to believe it. And then when I found out for sure you were, I decided I was gonna. It just took me a while to figure it out. I ain't never been the go-getter in the family, and I guess Annie's suffered for it. But, I reckon it all works out. You suffered way more'n she did."

"What in God's name are you talkin' about, son?" Frank managed a hoarse whisper, his eyes lasered in on Danny Robert's.

"I'm talkin' about the heartworm medicine I've been shootin' you up with for the last five years. Started off real slow. Didn't know how much would kill you. Didn't matter really. At first I just wanted to make sure you couldn't hurt her anymore. And then I wanted you to suffer like me and her have." Danny Robert took the bath cloth to the sink and rinsed it out, giving his words time to sink in. He wrung it out and dropped it into the clothes hamper.

He returned to his father's side, knelt, and said, "Gives off all the same symptoms as diabetes. Dang, you even started to believe it. To tell the truth, I'd come to think you'd found me out there a while back, but I reckon you hadn't. Don't matter. That last round of cortisone shots I drew up for Annie to give

you was nothin' but anti-parasite meds. Least ways you can die knowin' that
the worms ain't gonna bother you in Hell."

From the bedroom the three family members heard Danny Robert call,
"Mom, Daddy needs you."

All three returned to the bathroom, and Danny Robert, on his knees, deftly
set the garbage can in Annie's path. She picked it up and carried it into the
bedroom to deal with later.

Cora hesitated, not wanting to come closer. Annie returned, took a wash-
cloth from a stack on the vanity, wet it in the sink, and came to mop the patriarch's face. Frank nodded appreciation and looked up at the spectators. He saw
Davis for the first time.

"Glad you could make it for the show," he whispered.

"Didn't know you were bad off 'til this morning," Davis said, moving
closer, arms still crossed.

"Damn way to go, ain't it?" His grandfather's hands were shaking, black
and blue from the IV's that had been removed just hours earlier. He stared
again at a spot on the wall, whispered, "I'm not ready. Just a few more minutes."

At that, Davis knelt beside him, taking Danny Robert's place. "How about
a courtesy flush?" Pawpaw said in Davis's ear. Davis did as his grandfather
instructed.

"I hear you got religion, boy," Frank said.

"Yeah, I suppose you could call it that. Who told ya?"

"Oh, you hear things, you know," Frank looked disoriented and lost. "He's
calling me, Davy. He's calling me home."

"Well, what say you?" Davis said.

"What about Mom?" Frank asked.

Cora cried outwardly now, clutching a tired, old tissue in her fist. Bent at
the waist and knees, she gasped for air between sobs.

"Now, Pawpaw, she's gonna be fine."

"She's not ready for me to go yet. Tell her," even his whisper was beginning
to fail. "Tell her I got her some stuff to look at in the gun room. It's in the
vault, in a manila envelope with her name on it: a gift, a letter."

"Okay, Pawpaw, she's right here; she heard you. And she's ready." Davis maneuvered in his crouch in order to extend a hand to his grandmother. "Mom, come here," he commanded.

She shakily moved toward the pair, kneeling beside them.

"Okay Pawpaw, now Mom's got something she wants to tell you," Davis said and nodded toward her, giving her a firm look.

Without anyone noticing, Bobby Jack appeared in the doorway of the bathroom, Jennifer hanging behind.

Cora snubbed and gurgled a bit, wiping her nose, her tears wetting her wrinkled face.

"Frank?" she said, hesitantly.

Frank was staring at the spot on the wall. He spoke indiscernibly, his wheezing much more pronounced.

"Frank," she said again. "Annie and Davis tell me I got to tell you this. I don't want to, but they say I got to."

Frank looked at her, his dark eyes failing.

"Frank. It's okay. It's okay for you to go now. I will be all right. You hear? Frank? I say it is okay for you to go," she said a little louder. "I will be all right without you for a little while."

Frank's eyes focused on hers, and there was clarity for an instant. "Thank you, baby," he said. "I will see you soon." And with that, Frank Sanford slumped over and was gone.

The wind-up Regulator clock in their bedroom struck eight o'clock.

THIRTY-TWO

Jennifer awaited Davis at the bottom of the steps. She had not wanted to eavesdrop, and she could not really hear the exchange between the men. But in light of the day's events, she wanted to be close by at all times.

"Hey," he said, as he realized she was sitting on the bottom step, the glow of the Wurlitzer the only light in the room.

"Hey," she said, rising.

"Need to check email?"

"Need to check on you," she said, holding out her hand.

He took it and they walked past the pool table and into the sitting area. Davis dropped his shoes and jacket on the couch. He crossed the room, moved the Masonic Bible from its home and popped the hidden latch to the vault's secret door. Jennifer followed him past the display of guns and into the office where her laptop was sitting.

"I've been thinking," Jennifer began.

"We need to print that letter," they said in unison. They made eye contact and smiled. Davis began the start up process on both Jennifer's work machine and on his grandfather's computer. When the operating system chimes indicated that her computer was running, Jennifer quickly seized the phone line and dialed in for email.

Both stood as they operated their respective systems, mousing and clicking their way through tasks. Davis found the path where she'd previously restored the document and opened the letter. He scanned it quickly before executing the print command. The printer initialized, printing on one page, then feeding a second one through itself with only a scant mark on the leading edge of the paper.

Jennifer pulled in her email, briefly studying what she needed to do for work. She hacked out a short note to Charlotte informing her that she would be home sometime Monday, queued the message for delivery, and then looked up at Davis.

"So? Are we done in here?"

"I am. Are you?" he asked, reaching for the printed letter. He picked up both sheets, gave a cursory glance to the second page, and tossed it in the garbage can under the desk.

"I am," she said and looked after the paper in the garbage. "What's this?" she asked, retrieving it.

"Garbage," Davis said, pausing to look over the top of the letter he was re-reading.

Dangling from the bottom of the page, a cellophane wrapper hung for a second, then drifted to the floor. Jennifer reached to pick it up.

"A wrapper from a pack of cigarettes," she said.

"Yeah, that was in there Friday when I was looking for this letter."

"Really?" Jennifer asked.

"Yeah."

"Does Honey take the trash out in here?"

"I'm not sure if Honey knows this room exists," Davis said.

Jennifer thought aloud. "So, who took out the trash? Annie?"

"I don't know," Davis said. "Why do we care who takes out the trash?"

"Well, maybe whoever took the letter was the same whoever who left their cigarette wrapper in here. And whoever that was didn't consider that no one was going to clean up after them in here.

"Of course, that doesn't really narrow it down. Dang, whole family smokes," she said.

Davis took the wrapper with the gold foil pull-tab and read it. "But not everybody smokes Marlboro," he said.

"Who does?" she asked.

"My father smokes Salems. Pawpaw smoked Camel Filters. I saw a stash of 'em in his nightstand."

"So, that leaves Danny Robert?" Jennifer said.

"Yep, but if that's him, what's to say that he just wasn't down here writing a check or doing some work for the club?"

"I don't know, but it seems to me that there'd be some other garbage in that can if any work had been done. You know, bill envelopes or something."

"I guess. So, you think Danny Robert found the letter after Cletus left with Mom? And he got rid of the paper copy, found it on the computer and deleted it, but left a cigarette wrapper behind," Davis hypothesized.

"Maybe."

"So, he's protecting Annie, right?" Davis asked.

"Or he's hiding the fact that there's a will that says something he and your dad don't want to deal with."

"But he'd be protecting Annie first," Davis said.

"Unless he knows Annie wasn't the one doing it, and he was protecting himself," Jennifer said.

Davis frowned. "Either way, if he got rid of the letter, it'd serve at least one purpose."

From the other room, Jennifer heard a ring tone that alerted her to a voice mail on her cell phone. Surprised, she got up and went to find her purse on the couch.

"You know, there's not very good cell phone coverage in a basement in the suburbs of Mercy," Davis said.

"You just can't buy good service anymore, can you?" she joked, pressing buttons to retrieve the message. She put the phone to her ear and walked back toward the vault, stopping short when the service began to disrupt. She put her free hand over her ear and walked back toward the sofa where she'd first dialed. "It's a message from the sheriff," she said and extended the phone toward Davis.

Davis crossed the room and took the phone, placing it at his ear. "Wait," he said. "How do you rewind?" He pulled the phone back down to stare at the keypad.

Jennifer took the phone from him, pressed two buttons and then handed it back. He listened intently and Jennifer waited.

"They took the sample to Oktibbeha General and used their personnel to test it."

"And?"

"Pawpaw was right about part of it at least."

"So the test was positive?"

"Yep. He'd positively been poisoned."

"Great."

Davis handed her the phone and collapsed on the couch. Jennifer rewound the message and listened to it herself. "*High* levels of arsenic," Jennifer said, closing the flip phone and returning it to her purse.

"Yep."

Jennifer sat beside him. "So, now what?"

"Well, if you're on with the Hank Jacobs theory, you stop drinkin' the tap water. But since we're *not* crazy, we call Artiss back and beg her to wait to arrest anybody until after the funeral tomorrow."

"She won't be able to do that, will she?"

"Legally? No."

"Maybe she can come out here now and figure it out. I mean, without causing a public scene."

"I'm sure she's sittin' in her car right now, waitin' for the call back."

"Well?"

"Well, let's get it over with," he said, holding out his hand for Jennifer's phone.

She acquiesced, handing it over, having already dialed the last incoming number.

"Hey, it's Davis Sanford," he spoke into the phone.

"Yeah, we just printed it," he said of the letter.

He paused to hear the sheriff speak, and Jennifer leaned in to hear.

"Any chance we can save face until after the funeral tomorrow?"

He paused.

"I didn't figure. So, you coming out now?"

He stood as he listened.

"Okay, don't forget to shut the gate."

Davis hung up and looked at Jennifer. "I was wrong," he said.

"About what?"

"She wasn't waiting. She's at the gate now."

After retrieving the printout from the vault, Davis and Jennifer ascended the stairs, still in their wake attire, to find Bobby Jack half dozing in the living room.

"You're still here?" Davis said, astonished.

"Sittin' up with the dead," his father responded, pushing up from his slouch and clearing his throat.

"Well, sit up with the living. Artiss is here."

Bobby Jack sat erect, spilling his drink on the front of his shirt in the process. He stood, retrieved a handkerchief from his pocket, and dabbed at the miscalculation. Dissatisfaction on his countenance, he mumbled *intestate* before looking up at his son. He returned his handkerchief to his pocket and said, "Work with me on this, son," and he smoothed his hair back with his palms.

"I don't think she's coming to express her sympathies," Davis began. "And, I'm not much on giving advice, but I'd suggest you tell her the truth about everything you know."

Bobby Jack looked quizzically at Davis, but before he could speak, a knock came at the front door. Jennifer moved to open it as the two men stood frozen, squared off, one facing the other.

Sheriff Artiss Yarbrough stood in the doorway, all six feet and one hundred eighty pounds of her former Semper Fi self. Jennifer nodded and silently stood aside to welcome the justice officer. Artiss was casually dressed in blue jeans and a Mississippi State golf shirt, but her sheriff's jacket and hat gave away her business motives. "Evening, Jennifer," she said, stepping inside.

Davis walked to greet her, extending his hand. Artiss shunned it, offering instead to bear hug the man she'd formerly known only as a juvenile delinquent. "I'm so sorry for you, Dave," she said, and then tried to resume her professional appearance.

"Mr. Sanford," she said, extending her hand to Bobby Jack. "I'm sorry for your loss."

"Thank you Sheriff. It's been somewhat of a trial."

"I'm sure that it has."

"I mean, we knew Dad was going, most likely sooner than later, but Mom was an out-and-out surprise."

"Yes, to all of us," Artiss said.

Everyone stood awkwardly for a moment until Davis interrupted the silence.

"Won't you sit down?" he asked.

Each jockeyed for position in the trophy room, Bobby Jack opting for the ottoman in front of his mother's chair, Jennifer and Davis waiting until Artiss positioned herself on the edge of the sofa cushion, her hat held between her knees.

Always the hostess, Jennifer went to the kitchen to find drinks for those without them. Davis hovered between the two, awaiting Artiss's next move.

"Annie here?" Artiss began, gazing at first one trophy and then the next.

"As a matter of fact, she is. But she's already turned in for the evening. I think the pregnancy is getting the best of her," Bobby Jack said.

"Hmmm," Artiss mused. "And Danny Robert?"

"Him, too, though he doesn't have pregnancy as an excuse."

They all chuckled nervously.

"Well, Bobby Jack, I can't lie and say I'm here just because of that there," she said, nodding toward the two caskets that monopolized the room. She then retracted, saying "Well, maybe it wouldn't be a lie."

"What's on your mind, Sheriff?" Bobby Jack played well at sobriety.

"I had a concern brought to my attention regarding the death of your father. So, I ran over to Cletus's office and picked up his post mortem sample."

"What in the world for? To confirm he died of diabetes?" Bobby Jack said defensively.

"Well, just acting within my legal purview, and acting as a responsible law enforcement officer, I was obligated to verify or put to rest this concern. So, a deputy and I took the sample to Starkville for a toxicology screen—"

"Toxicology?" Bobby Jack asked.

"Yes," she continued, exuding a strong, calm demeanor. "For a toxicology screening. And the results came to me about a half-hour ago, showing high concentrations of organic arsenic in Frank Sanford's blood."

Bobby Jack sat still, the sheriff's words hanging in the room among the three of them. Jennifer returned with four bottles of water, offering one to each.

Bobby Jack accepted his, placing the bottle on the floor next to him. He broke the silence. "I don't suppose that could be incidental."

"Not unless everyone else in the house has the same levels," Artiss said, placing her hat next to her on the sofa. She opened her bottle and took a drink. "Which, based on everyone's overall health, I'd think is unlikely."

"So, how did this happen?" Bobby Jack asked, lowering his defenses somewhat.

"Given how Cora passed, I'd say it happened intentionally through repeated injections of an arsenic compound. That's what the folks at Oktibbeha General are sayin'."

"So, are you sayin' that Dad poisoned himself over and over again until it took?" he asked incredulously.

"No, I'm sayin' somebody poisoned him, intentionally, over probably a long period of time. Signs of arsenic poisoning are pretty easy to spot, unless you've been misdiagnosed with diabetes: lesions, jaundice, kidney failure."

"How do you know all this? They teach it to you in the Marines?"

"No, I'm just repeatin' what I've been told," she said. Artiss replaced the cap on her bottle and stood. She continued, "Now I understand that y'all found a letter Frank wrote to Cora."

"No," Bobby Jack said. "I don't know about any—"

"Yes, we did," Davis said, and he pulled the incriminating document from his pant pocket, surrendering it to the sheriff.

Bobby Jack looked at Davis, in shock.

"I'm the one that called her out here, after I found this. Pawpaw told me about the letter. It just took me a couple of days to find it." He shrugged, then shoved both his hands in his pockets.

"What does it say?" Bobby Jack asked, standing and crossing to read over Artiss's shoulder. She finished reading the document, then yielded her grasp, allowing Bobby Jack to peruse it alone.

After giving him a moment to read to the end, Artiss said apologetically, "So, she is here, isn't she?"

From behind them, Danny Robert spoke as he leaned on the doorjamb to the hallway. "She's here," he said, "But she's not the one."

Surprised, the congregation turned to see Annie's father, dressed only in sleeping pants, standing in the room.

"You're wrong about Annie. She hasn't hurt anybody. Don't think she knows how. I done it. I used my stash of Immiticide I got from Doc Purvis. I drew up the needles every six weeks. Annie didn't know. She'd come in, tired from work, and I had 'em ready for her. She thought she was givin' him cortisone."

"Come in here, Danny Robert," Artiss said, a stern, disdainful look spread across her face. "No, wait. Put a shirt on, and *then* come in here."

Danny Robert retreated and returned, pulling a plain white shirt over his head as he crossed the living room floor.

"Now talk to me, Danny Robert," Artiss said. She sat him down next to her on the couch and looked at him as though he were a misbehaving toddler. Bobby Jack gave his chair to Jennifer, and he and Davis stood next to each other, watching the Sheriff work.

Danny Robert began, "I don't know when it occurred to me. About a year after Annie moved out, I guess. I'd known how he'd been hurtin' Annie for a long time. I mean, I knew it in my head, but my heart couldn't make sense of it."

"Hurtin' her?" Artiss asked.

Davis and Bobby Jack exchanged glances, and Jennifer rose to escape the confession.

"No, now you sit down, Jennifer Gee. 'Cause one day you might have a baby girl, too, and then you'll understand." Jennifer sat down obediently and crossed her hands in her lap. It was excruciating to hear.

Danny Robert continued, "Yeah, Sheriff, against her will, for some time. Davis's mom tried to make me believe it a long time ago, but I just couldn't. And Annie wouldn't confess it, though she cried enough that I had to disbelieve her."

"I shoulda just shot him," he continued to ramble. "But, he'd long since gotten too fat and drunk to hurt her, and she'd married off to that Coon-ass, and then *he* started to rough her up.

"I guess that's what made me believe what Brenda had said all them years ago. 'Cause she never once cried over anything Marcus ever done, but she cried like a baby about Dad. I knew he had to have hurt her more, and there's not too many other ways to do it, without leavin' signs, you know?"

Artiss nodded and patted Danny Robert's hand.

"But anyway, I didn't shoot him. I just made him suffer a real long time like he'd done to my baby. And I guess his body got full up of it." Danny Robert hung his head. "I shoulda just shot him the first night I knew."

Artiss sat erect and still, her hands around Danny Robert's. She squeezed them and gave them a pat, then stood.

"You know, I got a baby girl, too. Goes to State. Majorin' in elementary education." She sighed, retrieved her hat, and then crossed the room to the front door. "Danny Robert, you get your mom and Frank buried, and if you feel like it tomorrow afternoon, come on by my office. Tell Annie I'm sorry I missed her." She opened the front door and pushed open the screen. "Lord, we been busy," she said. "Sure could use a vacation. I hear it's real nice in Cancun this time of year."

And with that she pulled the door closed and allowed the screen to slam behind her with a creak of the hinges and a bang in the doorjamb.

THIRTY-THREE

Twelve men of Mercy took turns, six at a time, moving first one casket and then the other from the living room where the memorial service had been held to the front lawn where the graveside service would be. The family had declined to have a funeral *per se*, opting instead for a small gathering of family in the morning, and then a public graveside service at one o'clock on Sunday afternoon.

Danny Robert led the procession of family, followed by Bobby Jack and Mary, and then by Annie, and Davis and Jennifer. As the family assembled underneath the mortician's green tent at the graveside, five men in suits, fezzes, and small white aprons aligned themselves around the caskets, one draped in red roses, one in yellow daffodils. They stood as the five points of a star, each bowing his head as their leader began. A fine mist of rain began to fall as he spoke.

"Let us unite with our Chaplain in prayer."

The chaplain on his cue, and from memory, said: "Unto Thee, O God, Father of all men, do we come in our hour of grief and bereavement. Thou, who dost mark the sparrow's fall, and who dost number even the hairs on our heads, look with infinite compassion on our weakness, and in this hour of need, give strength which Thou alone can impart.

"As we commit the body of our Brother, Francis Carrothers Sanford, to its resting place, may we realize how weak is every human arm, and may we trust in Thy might alone. Grant Thy mercy to these dear ones this day and may Thy comfort be theirs as they await that day when death shall be swallowed up in victory. Amen."

At the end of the prayer the remaining four points of the star, along with an untold number of mourners spoke in unison, "So mote it be."

Jennifer was startled and looked up as the words were spoken. She realized that the five men in fezzes were not the only Masons present. Throughout the assembled crowd she started to count men in white aprons. She stopped when she reached twenty, realizing that the bobbing of her head was distracting those around her. The rites continued; again, the words were spoken from memory.

"Loved ones, friends and Brethren: We assemble today to perform the last duty the living can render the dead. We pay our tribute of love and esteem to our departed friend and Brother, who was a beloved member of The Merciful Father Lodge, Number 1226, Ancient Free and Accepted Masons. We mourn the loss of our Brother, whose spirit has been summoned into the presence of the Lord and Father of all men. While we are assured that the storms of life can no longer disturb him, we should consider the certainty of death, and the vanity of all earthly ambitions."

Jennifer scanned the group of mourners as the elder's words registered in the background of her mind. At the edge of the lawn, she saw Hank Jacobs, leaning against the trunk of an old oak, keeping his distance, but present, nonetheless.

"From time immemorial, it has been the custom among the Fraternity of Free and Accepted Masons, at the request of a Brother or of his family, to perform the last rites with the usual ceremonies of the Craft. In conformity to this usage, we are assembled in the character of Masons to offer to the memory of Francis Carrothers Sanford, this tribute of our affection.

"The passing of our Brother from the cares and troubles of this transitory existence has removed another link from the fraternal chain by which we are united, man to man. May we who survive him be more strongly bound in the ties of friendship and union. Unto the earth we consign the body of our deceased Brother. We trustingly leave his spirit in the hands of Him who doeth all things well. With those of his immediate family we sincerely and deeply and most affectionately sympathize, and we place you in the arms of our Heavenly Father who grants his love and protection to those who put their trust in him.

"When we look about us, we see the marks of change and decay written upon every living thing. The cradle and the coffin stand side by side—and it is the truth that as soon as we begin to live, that very moment we begin to die. Yet how seldom do we seriously consider our own approaching end? We go on from design to design, add hope to hope, and lay out the plans for the employment of many years. Then the messenger of death comes when we least expect him. What are all the externals of majesty, the pride of wealth, or charms of beauty when nature has paid her last just debt? In the grave all fallacies are detected, all ranks leveled, all distinctions are done away. Here the scepter of the prince and the staff of the beggar lie side by side.

"Let us see to it, and so regulate our lives by the plumb line of justice, ever squaring our actions by the square of virtue, that when the Grand Warden of Heaven shall call us from our labors we may be found ready. Let us cultivate the noble tenets of our profession—Brotherly Love, Relief, and Truth. Then, when our summons draws nigh, let us with joy obey and go forth from our labors on earth to eternal refreshment in the presence of an All-Wise Governor, where because of an unshaken faith in the merits of the Lion of the Tribe of Judah, we shall gain admission into the celestial Lodge above, where the Supreme Architect of the Universe presides."

Then, holding out yet another white apron for all to see, he continued:

"The lambskin or white apron—the first gift of Freemasonry to our departed Brother, Frank, is an emblem of innocence and the badge of a Mason. This I now deposit in the grave of our Brother." He carefully draped the apron over the top of the casket, and then stepped back to his position in the star.

"We are reminded by this of the universal dominion of death. The arm of friendship cannot interpose to prevent his coming; the wealth of the world cannot purchase exemption; nor will the innocence of youth or the charms of beauty or the serenity of age change his purpose."

The speaker then produced a small branch of a Loblolly, and continued, "This evergreen is an emblem of enduring faith in the immortality of the soul. By it we are reminded that we have a life within us that shall survive the grave, and which shall never die. By it we are reminded that we, too, like Frank, shall soon be clothed in the robes of death, yet through our belief in the mercy of God, we may confidently hope that our souls will bloom in eternal spring."

Joined by two, thus far silent, Masons, each held a tip of the branch and carefully placed the pine branch atop the drape of roses. In unison they said, "We consign the body of our Brother to the earth."

Then, the elder of the previously silent ones spoke the words, "We cherish his memory here."

And the younger said, "We commend his spirit to the God who gave it."

Their leader spoke again, unpinning the rose boutonnière from his lapel and crushing it in his palm, "The dust shall return to the earth as it was, and the spirit shall return to God who gave it." And with that, he scattered the petals over the top of the casket.

The chaplain then spoke. "Let us unite in prayer. Almighty God, we now turn from this solemn service to the duties of life. As we go, we pray, O God, that Thy hand will lead us in all the paths our feet will be called upon to tread, and when the journey of this life is ended, may light from our immortal home illuminate the dark valley and voices of loved ones, gone before, welcome us home to that house made with hands eternal in the heavens. Amen."

And again, the congregated brothers in Masonry said in unison, "So mote it be."

The chaplain continued, "May the blessings of Heaven rest upon us. May brotherly love prevail and every moral and social virtue cement us. Amen." He then removed his boutonnière, tossed it onto the casket, turned from the grave, and, joining the Mason who spoke the longest, led the procession away from the burial site. The three remaining Masons followed him gravely, forming a column of mourners. Next, the twelve pallbearers walked to the caskets and deposited their boutonnières, following the brethren's cue.

Danny Robert stood next and approached the grave. He paused only briefly, then turned and walked toward the middle of the lawn. Bobby Jack and Mary Nguyen paid their final respects, and Davis was the last to approach. He paused over the grave of his grandfather and carefully placed his rose on the coffin. He continued to stand for a second more. He pulled his left hand from his pocket, removed his Masonic ring from his finger, and tossed it into the grave, the clattering of metal making a jolting noise in the otherwise misty silence.

He recited quietly, but aloud, the inscription from their joint tombstone: "What God hath joined together, let not man put asunder." He then turned to Jennifer and Annie and extended his hands. The two ladies arose, and he escorted them, one on each arm, as they picked their way across the muddy yard, through the daffodils, and into the house.

THIRTY-FOUR

The last of the mourners gone, Annie reposed on the couch in the trophy room, her feet slightly elevated on a throw pillow. Honey bustled between the kitchen and the front room, gathering plates and glasses and finishing up the last of the cleaning from the late family luncheon. After Cletus and his crew had lowered the coffins and filled in the holes, he'd taken down the awning, pulled up the indoor-outdoor turf from the muddy lawn, and loaded it all in the back of the hearse.

Davis wrote him a check out of Pawpaw's checkbook, forging his uncle's signature. Danny Robert had not returned to the house after the services. Davis did note that several checks were missing from the checkbook, and he hoped that Cancun, or wherever his uncle landed, would be free from ghosts.

Davis gathered all of Jennifer's work equipment from his grandfather's desk, wrapping cords and meticulously packing peripherals into their proper place in her bag, as he knew she would have done. He scanned the room once more before he departed, then turned out the light to the vault. Once inside the sitting area, he pulled the steel door shut, and returned the shelving unit back over the entrance, again masking the room from view. He started to push the Masonic Bible back over the latch, but instead took it from the shelf and sat down on the couch, dropping Jennifer's bag beside him.

The ancient tome was old and worn, its navy leather binding cracked from the years. Inside, in his grandmother's hand, the names of several family members from generations back had been painstakingly recorded: their births, marriages, and deaths. Some even had the name of the cemetery where they'd been interred. He continued to page through, looking at full-color pictures of Masonic icons as well as more traditional Christian visages.

Scanning the pages, Davis allowed himself to mourn for a moment the loss of his grandparents, who despite their shortcomings had offered him much upon which to build his life. He could not reconcile his memories with his current knowledge, and his cognitive dissonance prevented him from focusing on anything.

He sighed and closed the Bible heavily and clumsily, so that it fell to the floor, face down and sprawling, the golden-edged tissue pages folded and creased under their own weight. Reaching to retrieve the Book, he noticed that some papers had fallen from the volume and landed just under the edge of the coffee table. He knelt to pick up the loose items.

Yellowed and weathered, one was printed on heavy stock, not more than three inches tall and about the width of a standard piece of copy paper. Printed at the top and centered on the left-hand side were the words *Selective Service System*, and below that was inscribed *Status Card*. Davis read the document carefully, seeing that it bore the name Francis Carrothers Sanford. In the upper left-hand corner, the class status of 4-F was duly recorded.

Davis turned the card over in his hand, then looked at the second scrap of paper, which had been torn from an ancient receipt book. Wadsworth Clinic was stamped on the left-hand side, and the receipt had been written for a charge of fifty exorbitant dollars for a physical examination.

He folded the card in half and carefully placed the receipt between. He turned to the third chapter in Ecclesiastes and wedged the papers into the crease of the spine, covering the sixth verse.

He shut the Bible and returned it to its resting place. Turning from the bookshelf, he gathered their belongings and, with heavy burden, mounted the stairs for the last time. He stopped for a moment to turn off the lights, leaving only the glow of the Wurlitzer in the otherwise darkened room.

THIRTY-FIVE

Danny Robert approached the skinning shed in disbelief. It was only fifteen minutes past six o'clock; the sun was shooting beams of light, low and through the trees on its ascent. Marcus manned the tractor, loader on one end, backhoe on the other, lifting a black and wooly wild boar in order to hang it from an exposed rafter on the outdoor shelter.

"Good God, Marcus," Danny Robert said, flicking his cigarette to the ground. He stepped through the flock of yellow butterflies that congregated at the sandy spot where gamy blood was regularly spilled. "What've you done? It ain't hog season; hell, it ain't any season right now."

Marcus did not look up to acknowledge his father-in-law properly, but dismounted the heavy machinery and stoically quoted the Mississippi hunting regulations in a thick Cajun accent, 'Designated agents of landholders may take predatory animals year-round on lands owned or leased by them.' And this monster has been ruttin' up my yard the last three nights after I ran the split seeder over it Friday."

"So you shot it?"

"This morning, right before Annie got in the shower. She saw it out the front window while she was making coffee. She come and got me out of bed, and I shot it from the front porch." He climbed into the lowered bucket of the tractor, using it as a step stool to reach the gambrel between the hog's hind legs.

He continued working with the animal, pulling a belly spreader from his back pocket and inserting it into the carcass.

"I thought I heard shots this morning. So, what's he weigh in at?" Danny Robert asked, inspecting the three-inch tusks that protruded from its mouth.

"I didn't weigh him, but seein' as how I couldn't drag him, I figure he's got to be four-fifty." Marcus jumped down and wiped his hands on the seat of his jeans. "I can't decide if I should just butcher him here, or take him into town."

Danny Robert's pack of dogs had started to drift across the yard toward the shed where the activity was. "Well, you're gonna get this head mounted, ain't ya?"

"I already live with one wild hog. Can't see a reason to pay for a second," Marcus commented.

"What's that supposed to mean?" Danny Robert asked, bristling at Marcus's reference to Annie.

"Have you seen her lately?" Marcus posed, finally making eye contact. "I can just say that pregnancy don't become her." He kept moving, jumping back into the driver's seat, and restarting the engine to return the tractor to its garage area at the western end of the shed.

Danny Robert stood and reflected over his son-in-law's comments while he waited for him to jog back to the day's kill. He did so, continuing glibly, "To be honest, I'm a little vexed with Miss Annie right now."

"What for?"

"Well, she'd promised that she wouldn't tell anybody about the baby until we decided whether or not we wanted to have it."

"I see," Danny Robert said, soaking in the words.

"But then yesterday I was up at the Rexall, and Fred Bowdrie goes and congratulates me on being the 'proud father of a baby girl.'" He wagged his head akin to Mr. Bowdrie's affectation. "So I came home and really lit her up."

"Yeah?" Danny Robert asked. He watched as Marcus moved to set up the commercial-sized meat grinder and pull out bone saws and skinning knives.

"So much for keeping it on the q.t. Help me roll this over there, would ya?" he asked Danny Robert, totally engrossed in the meat preparations. Danny Robert stoically moved from the edge of the concrete pad to help him move the cart over to the hog.

"There's a cooler settin' in the freezer. Haul it out here, would you?" he asked off-handedly.

Danny Robert mechanically moved to the walk-in freezer and pulled down one of the coolers that were stacked three-high around the inside. He dragged it behind himself with his left hand, searching in his shirt pocket with his right for another cigarette.

"So, y'all were thinking about not having the baby?"

"Well, I thought we were, but I guess we weren't on the same wavelength."

Danny Robert lit his cigarette and took a drag. "I see."

"I don't know why she'd be so opposed to it. It's not like we were plannin' it."

Danny Robert said nothing, but let Marcus continue to ramble as he lay open the flesh of the hog and started filling the cooler. "Give me a hand here," he said to Danny Robert, his arms covered in blood up to the elbows.

"Hey, you're screwin' this cat. I'm just holdin' the legs." Danny Robert stuck his free hand into his pocket and took another puff from his Marlboro.

Marcus looked at him in disgust. "Vous ne dites pas?" He looked down at his hands and shrugged. He wiped them on the seat of his pants and reached for a bone saw. His hands were sticky, so he removed his class ring and set it on top of the cart, next to the meat grinder.

"I can't stand it when you speak Coon-Ass."

"You don't say?" Marcus replied. "I just figured she knew that I don't need a baby right now."

"Mmm."

"If Frank was still in his prime, I reckon I could blame it on him," he mused, then scoffed.

"What do you mean by that?" Danny Robert asked, dropping the cigarette butt to the concrete and crushing it with his heel.

"What do I mean? 'Bout Frank likin' to keep it in the family, so to speak?"

Danny Robert walked toward the workbench and inventoried the tools hanging on the pegboard, saying nothing.

"Well, Annie Mae hadn't ever been one to keep a secret. I reckon I should have known the whole town'd find out." He continued to labor at the remains of the hog, working quickly, steadily filling the cooler.

Danny Robert opened the middle drawer of the workbench and surveyed its contents. He reached in and selected a torque wrench. He felt the weight of it in his hands, assessing its fortitude and his own. "So, you gonna grind it up here or take it into town?" he asked, as he approached Marcus from behind.

"I've got an envie for some andouille, and that processor up there in town don't know andouille," he trailed off. "Oh, mais ouais, I'd like some andouille," he intentionally spoke in a thick Cajun drawl.

"Fermer votre bouche, you son-of-a-bitch," Danny Robert muttered under his breath, and before Marcus could turn or reply, he felt his father-in-law's wrath come down on the back of his head.

"Tonnerre mes chiens," he exclaimed, raising his hands in a futile attempt to ward off two more blows from behind. Marcus staggered into the hanging hog, which did not relinquish its place, but instead forced him into the utility cart, sending him careening and its contents cascading to the concrete floor. Two more blows, and Marcus did not move again.

Danny Robert stood over him, trembling, torque wrench frozen above his head. Marlboro still between his lips, he relaxed a little, and removed it, eyeing the end, from which the fire had been knocked off in the scuffle. Danny Robert stared up at the house. All was quiet. Pinky, who was never far from her master, reared up onto the hog and licked its chest cavity.

Danny Robert looked at his watch. It was only twenty-five past six o'clock. He stared down at the hired man and cringed. He knelt and took the pulse of the corpse. A puddle of blood was forming around the nose, causing Pinky to take interest in the subject. "Go on," Danny Robert commanded the dog. She sat back on her haunches, but did not move away.

He looked toward the house, at the meat grinder, and back at the body of Marcus Broussard. He hoisted the grinder onto the cart and set the brake, then plugged it into an electrical outlet and flipped the switch. It began to hum. Danny Robert sighed, and then he squatted down again. He rolled Marcus over and began to unbutton his shirt. "I guess I'm screwin' this cat now," he said to Pinky.

THIRTY-SIX

The morning air was cool and still as the sun crept past the treetops and finally reached the Sanford lawn. The rain had stopped, and the weatherman predicted a continued respite for several days running.

Annie had released the dogs at six, started the morning coffee, and let Davis and Jennifer sleep. She'd emerged from the log estate at nine o'clock, rusty trowel and bucket in hand. Crossing the yard, she stopped every few feet to dig and separate a clump of daffodils and drop a section of each selection into her pail. Occasionally, the mother-to-be stretched her aching back, bracing it with one hand or the other as she waddled to the next variety.

Filling the bucket with ten different hybrids, she made her way to the fresh graves and dumped the foliage there. Again she made the rounds, selecting other colors and species, returning to the same location to deposit her harvest. Annie knelt between the grand matriarch and patriarch and began planting the daffodils in clumps atop the gravesites.

At a quarter past ten, she stood, stretched, and looked at her watch. There was still no stirring within the house, and she decided to check on her guests. Turning on her heel, she sensed movement out of the corner of her eye and noticed Davis standing in the carport, loading bags into the trunk of Jennifer's car.

"Hey, you," she called out. "'Bout time you got out of bed!"

Davis turned as he closed the trunk, acknowledging his approaching cousin with a smile and a wave. She trudged across the lawn, carrying her trowel, her garden gloves and knees muddy from her pursuits. Davis began to sprint toward her, met her more than halfway, and lifted her up and spun her around.

"I love you, Annie," he said in her ear, as she squealed.

"I love you, too, you big doof." He put her back down on the ground and they started to walk back toward the house together.

"You sure you're stayin' on?"

"I'm sure, for now anyway."

"If ever there was a time to fly south," he began.

"This goose will let you know," Annie replied.

Just then, Jennifer opened the back door from Danny Robert's kitchen, walked out of the house, and crossed the screened-in porch to meet the two under the carport.

"Did you get my makeup bag?" she asked Davis.

"I think I got everything," he said.

"Not quite," she said, pointing to the empty dog crate that sat between the two cars.

"Oh, yeah," he said, leaving the two girls alone for a moment. Trudging back inside, he went through Danny Robert's kitchen and turned left into Annie's old room. There lay Lovey at the foot of Annie's old bed. She raised her head and tilted it to the left, questioning Davis's motives.

Davis scratched the old dog between the ears and scooped her up in both arms. She did not resist, but enjoyed the attention as he carried her outside. Before she could catch on or complain, Annie and he quickly crated her and then carefully set the crate on the backseat of Jennifer's car.

"You're sure?" Davis asked again.

"I'm sure. I'll call you."

"You'd better," he said, hugging her one more time. "When's that baby coming?"

"July fourth, so they say."

"Well, that'll be some fireworks for you."

She smiled and said, "For you, too. 'Cause y'all are gonna be here."

"We'll come as soon as we're called. You just have to hold out for us to get here," Jennifer said.

"I'll do my best," Annie said.

With one last round of hugs, Davis climbed into the driver's seat and lowered the windows before shutting his door. Jennifer took shotgun.

"Watch out for dogs," Annie threw out to them as Davis started the engine.

"Will do," he said, and Annie stepped away so that they could start their ride home.

"And call me when you get there," she called after them.

Davis waved out the window as they pulled around to the front of the house, past the daffodils and the family cemetery. He slowed down and looked one last time at the old tree he'd played under as a boy. He wondered if the tree would still be standing when he returned that summer.

As he pulled farther down the drive, Pinky ambled across the yard and stood atop the grave of Frank Sanford. She turned three times in a circle, a long thin bone clenched between her jaws, before she settled down on Annie's fresh plantings for a mid-morning snack.

Pinky positioned the bone between her front paws and began to gnaw on one round and bulbous end. A small metal pin slid back and forth on the top, holding the plateau of the tibia together.

If you or a woman you know is a victim of sexual or physical abuse, please contact your local law enforcement officials, the National Domestic Violence Hotline at 1-800-799-SAFE, or the National Sexual Violence Resource Center at 1-877-739-3895.

²¹'Then Peter came to Jesus and said, 'Lord, how many times may my brother sin against me and I forgive him, up to seven times?' ²²Jesus said to him, 'I tell you, not seven times but seventy times seven!

²³'The holy nation of heaven is like a king who wanted to find out how much money his servants owed him. ²⁴As he began, one of the servants was brought to him who owed him very much money. ²⁵He could pay nothing that he owed. So the king spoke the word that he and his wife and his children and all that he had should be sold to pay what he owed. ²⁶The servant got down on his face in front of the king. He said, 'Give me time, and I will pay you all the money.' ²⁷Then the king took pity on his servant and let him go. He told him he did not have to pay the money back.

²⁸'But that servant went out and found one of the other servants who owed him very little money. He took hold of his neck and said, 'Pay me the money you owe me!' ²⁹The other servant got down at his feet and said, 'Give me time, and I will pay you all the money.' ³⁰But he would not. He had him put in prison until he could pay the money.

³¹'When his other servants saw what had happened, they were very sorry. They came and told the king all that was done. ³²Then the king called for the first one. He said, 'You bad servant! I forgave you. I said that you would not have to pay back any of the money you owed me because you asked me. ³³Should you not have had pity on the other servant, even as I had pity on you?' ³⁴The king was very angry. He handed him over to men who would beat and hurt him until he paid all the money he owed. ³⁵So will My Father in heaven do to you, if each one of you does not forgive his brother from his heart.'

—Matthew 18:21-35, NLV

The quality of mercy is not strain'd,
It droppeth as the gentle rain from heaven
Upon the place beneath: it is twice bless'd,
It blesseth him that gives and him that takes:
'Tis mightiest in the mightiest; it becomes
The thronèd monarch better than his crown:
His sceptre shows the force of temporal power,
The attribute to awe and majesty,
Wherein doth sit the dread and fear of kings;
But mercy is above this sceptred sway,
It is enthronèd in the hearts of kings;
It is an attribute to God himself;
And earthly power doth then show likest God's,
When mercy seasons justice. Therefore, Jew,
Though justice be thy plea, consider this,
That in the course of justice none of us
Should see salvation: we do pray for mercy;
And that same prayer doth teach us all to render
The deeds of mercy.

—Portia, in William Shakespeare's *The Merchant of Venice*, Act IV, Scene 1

In loving memory of our own walking ottoman,
Gilligan "Little Buddy" Moody.

978-0-595-67615-6
0-595-67615-4

Printed in the United States
45379LVS00004B/133-156